THE GABINIAN AFFAIR

Also by Ray Gleason:

A Grunt Speaks: A Devil's Dictionary of Vietnam
Infantry Terms (2009)
The Violent Season (2013)

Available from Amazon and Unlimited Publishing

THE GAIUS MARIUS CHRONICLE

THE
GABINIAN
AFFAIR

De Re Gabiniana

RAY GLEASON

New York

THE GAIUS MARIUS CHRONICLE
THE GABINIAN AFFAIR
De Re Gabiniana

Published in New York, New York, by Morgan James Publishing. Morgan James and The Entrepreneurial Publisher are trademarks of Morgan James, LLC.
www.MorganJamesPublishing.com

The Morgan James Speakers Group can bring authors to your live event. For more information or to book an event visit The Morgan James Speakers Group at www.TheMorganJamesSpeakersGroup.com.

A **free** eBook edition is available with the purchase of this print book.

CLEARLY PRINT YOUR NAME ABOVE IN UPPER CASE
Instructions to claim your free eBook edition:
1. Download the BitLit app for Android or iOS
2. Write your name in **UPPER CASE** on the line
3. Use the BitLit app to submit a photo
4. Download your eBook to any device

ISBN 978-1-63047-479-9 paperback
ISBN 978-1-63047-556-7 eBook
Library of Congress Control Number:
2015901025

Cover Design by:
Rachel Lopez
www.r2cdesign.com

Interior Design by:
Bonnie Bushman
bonnie@caboodlegraphics.com

In an effort to support local communities and raise awareness and funds, Morgan James Publishing donates a percentage of all book sales for the life of each book to Habitat for Humanity Peninsula and Greater Williamsburg.

Get involved today, visit
www.MorganJamesBuilds.com

Habitat
for Humanity®
Peninsula and
Greater Williamsburg
Building Partner

To my babies . . .
Jaqueline,
Michael,
Diana,
KC,
and
Mallory

Special thanks to my text editor Cathy Tulungen,
who now knows why she didn't take Latin in school.

TABLE OF CONTENTS

DRAMATIS PERSONAE

Gaius Marius Insubrecus Tertius, our hero, known variously as follows:
- Arth Bek: "Little Bear," by his grandpa
- Pagane: "The Hick," by his Roman army mates
- Gai: by his family, close friends, and his few girlfriends
- Insubrecus: by his army colleagues and casual associates
- *Prime*: "Top," but that's much later in his military career

Familia Sua, **Gai's Family:**

Gaius Marius Insubrecus Primus, our hero's gran'pa, also known by these titles:
- Cunorud mab Cunomaro: "Red Hound," his Gallic name
- *Cura*: "Trouble," his army name

Helvetia Minor, "Valeria," our hero's mama; *mulier Romana ferox*, a formidable woman of Rome and a redhead

Secundus Marius Insubrecus, his father, a henpecked farmer (kind of a pun)

Lucius Marius Insubrecus, his older brother, who wants to be a farmer like their dad

Ceri, his grandmother, whom he calls "Nanna"

Lucius Helvetius Naso Iunior, or Avus Lucius, his maternal grandfather, also known around the taverns of town as *Naso*, "The Nose"

Gaius Marius Insubrecus Iunior, his *patruus*, a paternal uncle, who doesn't live long enough to make it into the plot

Maria and Maria Minor, his *amitae*, paternal aunts

Marcia, his *avia*, maternal grandmother, another redhead

Lucius Helvetius Naso Tertius, his *avunculus*, maternal uncle

Helvetia Maior, his *matertera*, maternal aunt

Amici Sui, **Gai's Friends:**

Quintus Macro, his mentor; the *vilicus* of Aulus Gabinius' villa in the Padus Valley; a minor army officer invalided out of the legions; only Rufia gets to call him Quintus

Rufia, the madame of the best little brothel in Mediolanum; more to this lady than what she lets on; also a redhead

Athvoowin, daughter of Gwili, of the Glas Sect of the Insubreci; Cynthia is her professional name, an employee of Rufia and Gai's "first wife"

Cossus Lollius Strabo, "Squinty," an Eighth Legion *optio*

Lucius Bantus, a veteran rejoining the legions

Tullius Norbanus, "Tulli," another veteran legionary

Dramatis Personae Aliae, **Other Players:**

Gabinia, or Gabi, the daughter of Aulus Gabinius; has romantic fantasies about poets and handsome, Gallic brigands who ride by the light of the moon

Aulus Gabinius, Senior, a senatorial mid-bencher, who does well and is elected consul

Aulus Gabinius, Iunior, Gabinius' oldest son and political heir, who takes his reputation and that of his family very seriously

Marcus Gabinius, Gabinius' younger son, not a scholar

Stephanos, the *magister*, a faux-Greek from Neapolis, tutor of the little Gabinii, known to our hero as "The Stick"

Dion, Stephanos' slave and a real Greek

Gaius Marius, Infamous Roman consul, *imperator* and *dictator*

Quintus Antonius, Commander of Marius' praetorian cohort

Gaius Iulius Caesar Senior, senatorial associate of Gaius Marius

Aiofe & Gwin, brother and sister who work on the "Insubrecus estate"; Valeria romanizes Aiofe as Amanda

Wulfgar, Rufia's *maior domus* and bouncer; a German who doesn't think much of Romans, if he thinks about them much at all … only Rufia gets to call him "Wolfie"

Galenus, a member of the urban cohort of Mediolanum and a mate of Macro's from their campaigning days in Asia; he and his wife Dora, are expecting any day now

Maariam, Macro's lost love

Dalmatius, the Roman army recruiter in Mediolanum; another chum of Macro's

Sevso, Dalmatius' assistant… not to be trusted

Metella, Mrs. Aulus Gabinius

Math, "The Bear"; a tavern owner in Medhlán; no fan of *Romanitas*

Rhun, Math's foster son

Melonius, or "Mollis" to his mates; a legionary recruit with flat feet

Arth Mawr, or Arth Uthr, legendary *Brennus*, High King of the Gah'el

Goualc'mei, nephew of Arth Mawr

De Qua Causa Scribo Praefatio
A PREFACE ON WHY I WRITE

My formal Roman name is Gaius Marius Insubrecus Tertius, the third of that name after my grandfather and an uncle, whom I never met. My oldest son is Gaius Marius Insubrecus Quartus, the fourth of that name. We have been *Quirites*, Roman citizens, since my grandfather was granted the franchise by the Roman *Imperator* and *Dictator*, Gaius Marius, whom he served as a soldier and a *Praetorian*.

Throughout my life, I have been known by other names.

My mates in the Tenth Legion called me *Pagane*, "The Hick," because I was such a farm boy when I joined up; they swore a dung cart dumped me at the camp gates with the rest of its load.

I was the Senior Centurion, the *Primus Pilus*, First Spear, of the Tenth. When my legs couldn't hold up to the thirty thousand *passus*, forced marches, *impeditus*, with full kit, I was promoted to *Praefectus Castrorum*, the Prefect of the Camps. Then, the other officers, even the legates and the broad-stripe tribunes, called me *Prime*, Top.

Most importantly, Caesar himself, and now his son down in Rome, *Princeps noster*, our First Citizen, called me *amice*, friend.

My dear wife has been badgering me to write my memoirs. I suspect that her interest has nothing to do with an appreciation for Roman history or fine literature. Retirement has not been easy for me, and she just wants to keep me occupied and out of her hair.

I served over twenty-five years in the army, most of it with the Tenth Legion. I served from the time *Divus Iulius*, Julius the God, launched himself into the boondocks of *Gallia Comata*, long-haired Gaul. I remained with the legions during the civil wars. I was there when Octavianus, *Filius Divi Iuli*, Son of Julius the God, who now calls himself *Augustus*, the Exalted One, defeated Marcus Antonius and his Egyptian tart.

I am hard-pressed to remember two years in a row that we weren't up to our asses in barbarians, Greek hirelings, Egyptians, a Parthian or two, and Romans who were fighting for some other way of running things down in Rome.

Now, I can't get through a single day without the memories of some dead mate, his throat torn out, staring up at me from the bloodstained grass; or the terror of being locked shield-to-shield with some son-of-a-bitch trying to gut me with a sword or split my skull open with an axe; or the smell of burning huts and human flesh; or the screams of women begging for mercy, when there's none to be had.

Now my flesh is cured the color of a leather hide, except for the jagged white lines of old scars, bearing witness to when I didn't get my shield up in time or some bastard snuck one in through my open side.

But, the dream is the worst.

I see myself in a shadowy squad bay with my *contubernales*—my squaddies, my tent-mates—guys I know are long dead. They're saddling up their kit for an inspection, telling me to hurry or I'll be missed.

But I know they're all dead—long dead.

"Move it, *Pagane*!" they shout. "The centurion will have your balls if you're late for roll call!"

I'm not supposed to be here, I think. *I'm done with this!*

"Get your ass in gear! Move it!" they shout.

Then, in a cold sweat, I wake up screaming, "No! I'm alive! I'm alive!"

I wake the wife up, who nearly pisses herself thinking that mad barbarians from across the Rhenus or some rebel army's breached the walls and are slaughtering us in our beds. All the next day, she complains about my waking her up and how she couldn't get back to sleep.

It's the soldier's lot, I guess; no one survives unwounded in some way.

I have the scars and aches of old wounds, but for reasons I can't even begin to imagine, the dream is the worst.

So, I don't really blame my dear wife. I need a hobby to occupy my time other than wine, beer, dice, and remembering.

Perhaps if I write this, tell the stories of my mates, lost and long dead—so someone will remember their names, make offerings to their memories—then their *lemures*, their restless spirits, will stop haunting the darkness of my dreams.

I.

Quomodo Civitem Romanam Familia Mea Acquisit
HOW MY FAMILY BECAME ROMANS

My life can be divided into three stages: youth, maturity, and old age. Youth is the time before I joined the legions; maturity, while I served in the legions; and now that I have retired from the legions, old age.

When I was a kid, my grandfather called me *Arth Bek*, which means "Little Bear" in the language of our people, the Gah'el, whom the Romans call *Galli* and the Greeks, *hoi Keltoi*. Grandfather said when I was an infant and wanted attention, I screamed like a little warrior, so he named me after a mythical hero-king of our people, *Arth Mawr*, the "Great Bear." I suspect the name had more to do with my being somewhat swarthy—thick-built, short-legged, and barrel-chested, like a little bear—than any noises I made as a squeaker.

My grandfather was the first Roman citizen in our family. When he was a youth, the Krauts came storming down from the North and rampaged by the thousands through the Roman *Provincia* up in *Gallia Transalpina*, Gaul-Over-The-Alps. They slaughtered more Romans than Hannibal, plus a couple of consuls for good measure—not that our people cared much about dead Romans.

A new Roman consul, Gaius Marius, was raising troops in our lands in the Padus Valley to fight those piss-headed *cunni*. My grandfather, who fancied himself a warrior-hero of the *fianna*, the ancient Gallic war bands, joined the Roman army. Since he wasn't a Roman citizen, he enlisted in one of the local auxiliary units, the *Cohors Prima Gallica*, the First Gallic Cohort. Like most auxiliary units, the First Gallic was a mix of infantry and cavalry.

My grandfather's Gallic name was Cunorud, which he explained meant either "Red Dog" or "The King's Hound," depending on how much beer he had in him. His Latin-speaking mates, who couldn't pronounce that "tongue-twisting Gallic shit," called him *Cura*, Trouble. My grandfather hated the name, but tended to prove it accurate.

He got himself assigned to one of the cavalry wings, *alae* the Romans call them. Gran'pa claimed he cut quite a dashing figure with his mustachios reaching down past his chin; his *spatha*, a long Gallic cavalry sword, hanging at his side; and a jaunty brass helmet, polished like a mirror and sporting a crimson plume, on his head. He rode a huge, snorting black stallion. As he put it, riding was always better than slogging in the mud with the *muli*, the infantry grunts. Besides, if things got really bad, he could make a quick exit, and once he did, he always knew exactly where his next meal was.

The First Gallic marched over the Alps with Marius and wrecked the Germans at a place the Romans call *Aquae Sextiae*. But, a bunch of Krauts got around the flank of the Roman army, through the Alps and down into our lands, which the Romans call *Gallia Cisalpina*, Gaul-This-Side-Of-The-Alps. Marius caught up with them near a town called Vercellae and didn't leave enough of those *mentulae*, those pricks, alive—man, woman or child—to stage a gladiator show in an outhouse.

What happened near Vercellae is family legend.

As best I remember the story—only having heard it a few dozen times before I assumed my *toga virilis*—my gran'pa, after a few bowls of beer with his cronies, told it like this:

Before the Battle of Vercellae, me and me mates are sent out to reconnoiter the Kraut positions. Marius, the chief, likes to see things for himself, so he goes along for the ride. We're strung out in a file below a wooded ridgeline. We're trying to keep high ground between us and where we think them piss-headed *mentulae* are at. We're moving through a narrow place, between the edge of the woods and some marshes, when them hairy-faced *cunni* bust out of the trees right on top of us.

We're thinkin' we're *perfututi* as the Roman boys say, absolutely screwed. We have them marshes at our backs and them Krauts chargin' down the ridge at us from them woods. We freeze, but one of me mates yells out, "What you waitin' for, boys? We got those sheep-shaggin', piss-headed *podices*, those arses, right where we wants 'em! Let's go chop them bastards!"

So we pull out our swords and charge up the ridge right into 'em.

The chief's pretty ballsy for a toga-boy, and he goes right in with us. We hit them Krauts like a battering ram and pretty much knock 'em back into the woods. I'm feelin' now's the time to make our break. Then I sees the chief all tangled up with a bunch of them bastards, but he's waving around one of them little Roman infantry swords, *gladius* they calls 'em. The only way he's goin' to kill a Kraut from a horse with one of them little Roman pig-stickers is if the Kraut laughs himself to death. He can't even reach 'em with the thing.

I thinks, *Just like a Roman to bring a knife to a sword fight.* But, he's our chief, even if he scrapes his face so's it looks like a girl's ass. So I turns me horse and charges into the bastards and gets between them and the chief.

"Get your ass outta here, Chief!" I yells over to him. "Leave the Kraut-choppin' to us guys with grown-up swords."

Next thing I know, one of them German *verpae*, pricks, grabs me belt and pulls me down off me horse. Now there's nothin' that'll piss a cavalryman off more than to have some ground-poundin', sheep-shaggin' *podex* pull him off his horse, and them shits never dealt with a pissed-off Gah'el before. I hits the ground and rolls to me feet and starts choppin' and stabbin' in every direction. Pretty soon I gets three or four of the bastards on the ground, and the rest of them piss-haired *cunni* don't want to get anywhere near me. I looks up, and there's the chief with me horse.

"Mount up, Trooper!" says he. "Time to get our arses outta here."

Well, I jumps up on me horse, and me and the chief tear ass down that ridge before them Krauts can figure out what hit 'em. When we catch up with the rest of the boys, the chief says to me, "A Roman doesn't forget his obligations, Trooper Cura, and I will not forget mine to you."

While I'm still reelin' at his calling me "Cura," he grabs me right arm in one of them Roman handshakes. Then he rides up our column to the head of our troop.

Well, I don't think too much of it, what with the battle and all, but a couple days later, after we have pretty much cleaned up all the shit, one of the chief's fancy-boy tribunes, a broad-striper no less, comes down to where we're set up. I watches him dance through the mud and horse shit around our horse lines so's he won't ruin the shine on his fancy boots. He grabs hold of one of our Decurions, who points me out.

"Twooper Cuwa?" he asks in that thin-lipped, upper-class Roman lisp all them toga-boys from *Roma* use.

I comes to attention, like I should, and says, "That's what I'm called, sir!"

"Twooper Cuwa, Gaius Mawius, Consul of the Woman People, Impewator, Savior of the Nation"—them Romans lay it on thick, makes 'em feel good about themselves—"Commands you to weport to the Pwefect, Quintus Antonius, Commander of the Pwaetorian Cohort, at the Pwincipia immediately."

With that, the purple-striped fuzz-face turns about, dances back through the piles of horseshit, and heads off in the direction of the Roman camps.

Well, I'm all covered in shit from horse stables, and I smells so good that some of the stallions are starting to give me the eye, but the little gob-shite said immediately. So, I throws me *lorica* and helmet on, throws me sword belt over me shoulders, washes most of the big clods of shit off me boots with a bucket of water, and heads over to where the legions are set up.

Now them legion boys is somethin' in the field. There's an old joke about this *mulus*, a legionary grunt, who's marching across a field—sixty paces a minute, three feet a pace—when he runs into this beautiful shepherdess. Well, she invites him for a go and takes off her clothes. The Roman halts, pulls out his entrenching tool, digs a trench and a parapet around her, pops her, fills in the trench, and continues the march. The camps them boys build are better than most towns I've seen: ditches, parapets, and streets laid out in straight lines; tents all in neat rows; a place for everything, and everything in its place.

I goes through the main gate of the camp like I owns the place. I knows the sergeant of the guard's thinkin' about busting me balls a bit, but after he gets a whiff of me, he just waves me through after I gives him the password. I walks down the street to the *Principia*, the headquarters. It's in a big tent where the two main streets of the camp cross, like it always is. I asks the sentry where the boss of the Praetorians is, *il' capu'*, "the boss," they calls him. The grunt points to a smaller tent next to the *Principia*. I walks into the tent and sees this Roman officer chewing on some poor snuffy.

"And, if you ever show up for one of my goddamn inspections with your kit looking like shit again, I'll slice off your balls with a rusty knife and hang them around your goddamned neck! Do you understand me, Soldier?"

"Yes, sir!"

"What was that, Soldier?"

"YES! SIR!"

"Two weeks latrine duty! Now get your sorry ass out of my sight!"

The legionary shoots out of the tent like he's launched from a *ballista*.

Then the officer notices me. "What in the stinking latrines of Hades do you want, Trooper?"

I snap to.

"Sir! Trooper Cura reporting as ordered, sir!"

"Cura? Cura? Let's see here . . ." The officer shuffles through some *tabulae*, wax slates, on his desk. "Oh, right! You're the Gaul the old man wants . . . By Hercules' balls, Cura! What in the name of Hecate did you do? Crawl through a stable on your way here?"

"Sir! The tribune said report immediately, sir!"

"*Cacat!* Shit! Next time, take some time to at least throw yourself in a stream. You a Gaul, Cura?"

"Yes, sir!"

"What's your real name?"

"My real name, sir?"

"Come on, Cura. No Gallic father's going to name his kid *Trouble!* What's your real name?"

"Uh, back home, I'm called Cunorud, sir!"

"Cunorud, eh? Red Dog . . . *Canis Ruber* . . . I like that. A red dog that smells like a mare in heat! You live long enough, you see everything in this army. *Bene*, Trooper Red Dog, effective immediately, you are assigned to the old man's praetorian cohort. What is it, Trooper?"

"Sir! I'm not a Roman citizen."

"Really? You want to march over to the *Praetorium* and tell the old man his mind is *defututa* . . . totally clapped out?"

"Uh, no, sir!"

"Me neither. Now—with your permission, of course—let me get through this: You are assigned to the third cavalry wing of the praetorian cohort with the rank of trooper. You will turn in your kit to your old unit . . . let's see . . . the First Gallic, and you will draw a new kit with us. Bring your mount with you. By the way you smell, I think you already did. While in the praetorian cohort, you will have immune status from all fatigues and work details. Your rate of pay is six hundred seventy-five *denarii* a year—that's triple the standard legionary rate. Get your pay records from your standardbearer and turn them into the standardbearer of the praetorian *ala*. Any questions, Trooper Red Dog?"

"No, sir!"

"*Bene!*" He shoves one of them slates toward me. "You have to be enlisted into the Roman army. Can you write, Trooper?"

"Write, sir? No, sir!"

"It bloody-well figures. *Scriba*!"

A Roman soldier armed with a slate and stylus comes from the back of the tent.

"Sir!"

"Witness this, Soldier! Trooper, you have a clan mark?"

"Yes, sir!"

"Mark the slate there! Now stand at attention, raise your right hand. That's the one your sword goes in, not your prick. Raise your palm toward the sky, and repeat after me."

I assumes the position.

"I . . . state your real name."

"I, Cunorud mab Cunomaro, of the Glasso clan, of the Anderica band, of the Insubreci tribe, do solemnly swear by Father Iove, greatest and all-powerful, whose eagle I now follow, and by all the gods, that I will defend and serve the Roman nation. I will obey the will of the senate, the people of Rome, and the officers empowered by the senate over me and my general, Gaius Marius. I swear that I am a free man, able to take this oath, and obligated by bond or debt to no Roman. I will remain faithful to the senate and the Roman nation, to the officers empowered over me, and to the army of Rome until I am legally discharged by my time of service, by the will of the senate and People of Rome, or by my death. I offer my life as the surety of my oath."

"*Bene*, Trooper! First, the good news! You are now privileged to be a Roman soldier for the next three years. Now the other news: I am Prefect Quintus Antonius, commander of Gaius Marius' praetorian cohort, and until the crows come to chew on your rotting carcass or the army sees fit to discharge you, your sorry ass belongs to me. If I ever see you in this horse-shit condition again, I will personally skin you down to the bone and feed your fat to the camp dogs! Do you understand me, Trooper?"

"Sir! Yes, sir!"

"Not only are you now a Roman soldier, the sight of which alone makes Parthians drop their perfume bottles and long-haired Gauls soil their plaid trousers, you are a praetorian. On the battlefield, you will be the baddest *pedicor* who ever sucked his mother's teat and swung a sword. In garrison, you will shine so bright that when you show up, everyone will think the heavens have opened and Mars himself has come down to pay some nymph a visit! I want your shit so tight that I couldn't drive a greased dagger up your ass with a sledge hammer. Am I clear to you, soldier?"

"Sir! Yes, sir!"

"The first thing you're going to do is get your sorry ass over to the bathhouse and scrape the dirt and horse shit off your sorry carcass. Then find the barber and get that bush on top of your head cut down to regulation. And make sure he gets rid of those Gallic horse tails growing under your nose. You following me, Trooper?"

"Sir! Yes, sir!"

"*Miss' est!*"

I just stands there.

"I said, '*miss' est*,' Trooper, post! That's army talk for 'get your horse-shit-smelling ass out of my sight'!"

I shoots out of the tent like I'm launched out of a *ballista*.

So begins my grand and glorious career in the Roman army.

In wartime, the army tries to kill you with steel. In peacetime, it tries to kill you with chicken shit. When the fighting's done, the army spends most of its time at war with its own equipment.

Now, as far as fighting goes, the Roman kit is a lot better than the shit they stick us with in the auxiliary units. The Roman *lorica* is made of chainmail with extra armor over the shoulders, instead of the boiled leather crap I wore in the First Gallic. The stuff's great when you get slashed at, but won't do much for you when some *podex* tries to put the point to you. The Roman helmets are steel, not bronze, so they turn a slashing blow, instead of adding shards of bronze to the iron sword that splits your skull open.

But, that Roman iron crap rusts if you as much as look at it.

In peacetime, the primary job of the praetorian cavalry is prancing around a parade field, looking fierce and shiny when the chief wants to be entertained. So our horses' rigs are covered with shiny bronze and iron gewgaws that catch the sun when we ride. All of that shit—all of it—loves to rust and mold.

So, my main job is to scrub and scrape the rust off Roman steel. Me hands are as red and raw as a housewife's. And *il' capu'*, our prefect, may the Furies drag his boney ass off to Tartarus, can find a speck of rust in a steel forest. So, when I'm not scraping and shining, I'm double-timing around the outside of the camp ditch, holding me kit over me head, apologizing to it for not taking care of it proper—much to the amusement of the *muli* on guard duty.

The guys in me *ala* turn out to be okay. I'm a little nervous at first, being a Gah'el, but most of the guys in the unit aren't real Romans either. We have guys from both Gauls, even a few who grew up among the long-haired Gah'ela north of the *Rodonu,* the river the Romans call *Rhodanus.*

I'm surprised to find out the guys from *Hispania* are Gah'el too, but I can hardly understand what they're saying, especially when they get excited about something and start flappin' their hands around.

Even the Italian and Roman boys are okay. The Italians are mostly hicks, *pagani*, farm boys. But, they're good riders and know a lot about takin' care of the horses. The guys from Rome are funny. Most of them grew up in the slums, the *subura* they calls it. Most of them never even seen a horse except on a dinner plate or had their own boots until they joined the army. They got into the cavalry because they hated all the humping and digging the infantry did, but they still gets a bit nervous around the horses. We Gah'el and the *Spani*—that's what we calls the guys from *Hispania*—take bets on which of them Roman guttersnipes is going to screw up and fall off his horse during parade first.

We all get along pretty good, probably because we all hate *il' capu'* and his surprise inspections worse than we can ever hate each other.

The guys from Rome don't speak Latin like the officers do. When an officer talks, it's all this "Oh-twooper-faw-bawbawian-weally-vell-you-wide" sounding shit. They like to mix the words around when they talk, so half the time you got no idea what they're talking about—and you got to wonder if *they* do. Our Roman slum boys' Latin comes out pretty straight.

Among us, we have our own way of talking—mostly gutter Latin with some Gallic, and even a few Kraut words mixed in. Like, *mentul* is a prick, and *bas me' cul* is kiss me arse! And, of course, there's always the universal and well-used *cunne*!

One day, the chief moves the army down into Italy to Rome for his big victory parade. The Romans call it a *triumphus*, but I got no idea why. The Roman boys say it has something to do with the time Rome had kings, and they were the only ones who could lead the armies and thank the gods for victory.

Once we cross into Italy, every place we march, people are cheering us and givin' us stuff. Village babes run up to us to throw flowers, give us a drink from skins full of wine, a little kiss or two, and from up on me horse, I get a great view of their talents. I don't see what these Italians see in wine—it's sweetish, watery shit. Give me a mugful of good, brown Gallic beer anytime. But, every night, I goes into camp half in the bag and with a hard-on for some village babe who stroked my horse.

When we get down to Rome, we set up in a big field outside the town called *Campus Martis*, The Field of Mars. One of our Roman guys tells me this is where the toga-boys come out to play soldier, when things are safe. Seems the chief can't go into the city while he's in charge of the army—another one of them Roman rules. So, we have to set up out in the field.

Just like the Roman army! We're in the middle of Italy, close enough to Rome to piss on the walls—which we do regularly—everybody just lovin' us, but out come the picks and shovels and the *muli* build a complete fortified camp for every legion. It's a great show for the city Romans who're fascinated by work. They come out every day and watch us. On a good day, they bring us bread, cheese, and something to drink. On a really good day, the local talent takes us down to the river and *perfututi*, screws our brains out, for a few copper *asses*.

On the day of the chief's big parade, they roll us out at the end of the third watch to get ready, while even the birds are still snorin'. *Il' capu'* goes through our stuff like he owns it hisself. My helmet's so shiny I can stand ten feet away and still use it to shave.

They get us all formed up when I sees some staff officer raising hell with *il' capu'*, pointing back to where we're formed up. Then *il' capu'* tells us we got to go back to camp and dump the armor we spent all night shinin' and form up in clean tunics, belts, and swords. The Roman boys tell me this is because a Roman army can't cross the *pomerium*, the sacred boundary of the city, under arms. It's accursed—*malefactum* the Roman boys call it.

So, back we go to camp, dump the kit we spent all night shining, find clean tunics, and re-assemble. It's a classic, Roman army goat rope.

Finally, the whole army's formed up on the field. Since we're the praetorian cohort, the cavalry is supposed to stick to the chief's chariot like dried shit to a horse's tail. The *muli* are guarding the prisoners and the trophies.

When I sees the chief, I almost falls off me horse—which the Roman boys would really get a kick out of. The chief is dressed up in a purple outfit, and his face is painted red. The Roman boys tell me the chief gets to dress like a king today. His face is painted red so when he gets to Iove's big temple on Capitol Hill, the god will know who he is.

The chief runs up and down the column a couple of times, waving to the army, and the *muli* are going nuts shouting back at him. I thinks most of them are already half in the bag. When he passes us at the head of the column, he pulls up and shouts over, "Trooper Cura!"

"Yes, sir!" I says.

"Trooper! When this dog-and-pony show is over, before you go off with your mates and get shit-faced, come and report to me in the big temple on the hill!"

"Yes, sir," I says, wondering what kind of shit I've gotten myself into this time.

The chief takes up his position at the head of the column, and the army settles down. Then we just stand there staring at the city walls and a closed gate. This is still the Roman army, so we hurry up to wait.

The city Romans start to gather along the walls above us. Most of them are ogling the army, screaming insults at the rows of Kraut prisoners, and pointing at the trophies and painted battle scenes on the carts waiting to go through the gate. A few of the city babes lean way over the parapets to get a good look. We troopers get a good look too and show our appreciation with whistles, cat calls, and invitations. This, of course, encourages them fair Roman maidens to lean farther over the parapets and give 'em a good shake. We're cheerin' 'em on when *il' capu'* decides he's had enough and tells us to shut our shaggin' gobs.

Some dumb-shit civilians start flinging rocks, clods of mud, and horse apples at the prisoners. Of course, being civilians, they more than not miss the prisoners and hit us and the horses. If this goes on much longer, we'll lose more men and horses to the Roman mob than we did to the Krauts.

Then, the crowd quiets down, and they seem to be looking at something going on over on their side of the wall. The closed city gate slowly groans open, and a large group of old men in white togas with broad purple stripes come out. The dog-and-pony show is about to get going.

The chief gets down out of his chariot, marches up to them and salutes. "Conscript Fathers, Gaius Marius, Senior Consul of the Roman Nation and *Imperator* of the army, surrenders his authority of command to you from whom all authority derives."

The chief is wearing platformed, red boots! If the Krauts saw him made up like this at Vercellae, they'd of laughed themselves to death and saved us a lot of work.

A tall, thin toga with white eyebrows as bushy as the tail of a mare in heat steps out from the crowd of togas.

"Imperator! The senate and the Roman people welcome you! We congratulate you on your victory! We accept back the *imperium*, the power given you to command our armies. For your victory, we decree you *Vir Triumphalis—*"

At that, some drunken wit behind me sniggers, "'Guy with three pricks.' The chief's going to need every one of 'em today!"

Il' capu' hisses, "Shut ya shaggin' gob!"

"—and invite you to enter the city and to process with us along the route laid out and made sacred by our founder, Romulus, to give thanks to Father Iove, fount of all victory."

"*Princeps*! Leader of the senate! Conscript fathers! Gaius Marius, Consul and *Vir Triumphalis*—"

"Three pricks."

Sniggering.

"Shut ya shaggin' gobs!"

"—accepts!"

The chief inclines his head, and Eyebrows places a crown of golden leaves on it.

The chief hops back up on his chariot without breaking a leg in his sissy-boots. The togas turn around and walk back into the city, and the grand goat rope begins.

The buglers from the grunt units follow the togas through the gate, making a racket loud enough to wake up the gods, and over the noise of the horns we can hear the roar of the city mob. Next go the carts, guarded by a couple of centuries of our *muli* so the mob don't help itself to a few torques, some gilded helmets, or the other crap we took off the battlefield after *Aquae Sextiae* and Vercellae. The Romans in our wing say that all the captured junk is to be dumped in the Temple of Mars.

Next, two huge, white oxen draped with flowers are driven through the gates by a couple of *muli*.

"Io! Quint!" one of our boys yells. "Don't let that big cow shit all over your boots!" Our prefect has pretty well given up trying to keep any semblance of military order by this point.

The grunt named Quint responds with the "Roman finger." To the delight of our boys, one of them oxen drops a load right on Quint's boots.

Next, our infantry boys march through the gates with the captured Kraut standards and flags. Behind them the prisoners are herded forward. The piss-headed Krauts are loaded down with tiny, silver chains, not big enough to hold them but obvious enough to get the point across. At the head of the herd is the biggest Kraut I ever saw. He's bare-headed, bare-footed, and covered with tiny, golden chains.

"That's their king," one of our boys says. "He's for it when they get to the pit." I got no idea what that means, but I'm too busy gaping at the show to ask.

Next, twelve thugs in togas, real knuckle-draggers, carrying bundles of sticks bound in leather, march through the gates.

"Get ready!" hisses *il'capu'*. "Sit tall! Look smart!"

One of the tribunes standing behind the chief's chariot gives our prefect the nod.

"Sections one and two," he shouts, "double file . . . at the walk . . . forward . . . move!"

The head of our wing jerks forward toward the gate.

"Stand fast," me section leader hisses.

As soon as our boys clear the gate, the chief's chariot lurches forward, followed by a gaggle of tribunes and legates in their military tunics and a bunch of togas I never saw before.

When they clear the head of our column, our section leader gives the command, "*Ala* . . . double file . . . at the walk . . . forward . . . move!"

As we approach the gate, the section leader yells over his shoulder, "Hold your mounts tight, boys! Here it comes!"

Good advice! When we clear the gate, the noise hits us like a wave of screaming Krauts. Me poor horse tries to rear up, and I leans forward on his neck to calm him and to keep from falling off on me ass in front of a bunch of *irrumptores*, worthless civilians.

Rome is a madhouse: tall buildings, narrow streets, and thousands of screaming Romans dressed in every color of the rainbow. They throw flowers, coins, clods of shit, stale bread. They're screaming stuff like, "*Avete!*"; "*Se fut'uete!*"; "*Io, Triumphe!*"; "*Io, Irrumt'res!*"; "*Salvete!*"; "*Io, Culi!*" The Roman boys say when Romans really like you, they insult you—so they must love the shit out of us.

We're no more than ten paces through the gate when something strange—pleasant, but a bit strange—happens. One of the local talent runs up to my horse, grabs my tool, and then runs back into the crowd. I have no objection to this, but, if it's an invitation, how am I going to find her again in this crowd?

Then it happens again!

After the third time, I turns to one of the Roman boys ridin' next to me. "You see that?" I says.

He laughs!

"What in the name of Venus' *landica* is that all about?" I asks him.

"The ladies of Rome want to know if it's true what they say about you barbarians."

"What're you talkin' about?"

"You see, Cura, when the gods created men, they decided to give each man one special gift. The Greeks, they gave brains; the Romans, dignity. When they got to you Gauls, all the good stuff was gone. So, the gods asked the Gaul what he wanted. The Gaul thought about it for a few minutes. He knew he couldn't be as smart as the Greek or as dignified as the Roman, so he told the gods, 'I want every woman to love me.' And, wham! The gods granted his wish."

"I don't get it," I says.

The Roman laughs, points to my crotch, then held his hands a foot apart.

"And these Roman babes believe that shit?"

"Obviously!" he laughs.

I decides right then that before this day is over, I'm going to give as many of the Roman ladies I can the chance to test the myth.

After a bit, the parade grinds to a jerky halt, and the crowds become even more frenzied. I sees up ahead that a couple of our infantry boys are draggin' the German king out of the line. As the chief looks on from his chariot, they lower the Kraut into a pit, golden chains and all. The hole must be pretty deep because they need ropes to do it. When the Kraut goes down, the crowd quiets. We all sit there waiting. Then this guy in a black robe and a high-pointed cap, who's looking down into the hole, looks up, raises his hands, and shouts, "The gods of the underworld accept the sacrifice offered them by the Roman people!" The chief raises a salute in the general direction of the hole, the crowd begins screaming again, and the whole shaggin' dog-and-pony show moves out.

By the time we get to Jove's big temple on the top of the hill, me ears are ringing and me prick is rubbed raw by the Roman babes who want to know what the gods gave me instead of smarts. A crowd of togas with purple stripes are standing on the temple steps. The chief pulls his chariot to a halt in front of the temple, hops down, and slowly climbs to the top of the stairs. He halts and turns to face the crowd, which again goes silent. The chief raises his hands slowly and removes the golden wreath from his head. He presents the wreath to the togas and the Roman mob. Then he turns slowly and lays the wreath on the top of the temple stairs. Again he turns towards the crowd and lifts his now empty hands for them all to see. The place goes absolutely wild, screaming, "*Io, Triumphe . . . Io, Triumphe*!" And chanting, "Mari . . . Mari . . . Mari."

"What's that all about?" I hisses over to me Roman buddy.

"The chief's refused to be the king," the Roman says.

"Why, in the name of Mars' *culus,* would he do that?" I asks.

"We Romans don't want no shaggin' king. We threw all those bastards out centuries ago! And, since then, we won't allow a king to rule us. This is the difference between us and the barbarians . . . no offense, Cura. This is why Jove favors us."

"No offense taken. So who's in charge now?"

"The chief has given Jove's authority to rule Rome back to the people and the senate."

"Seems messy to me."

"Usually, but we like it that way."

The chief goes up the stairs into the temple. The thugs with the bundles of sticks follow and so do the purple-stripers. The crowd starts to dissolve, heading for the tables of food and booze that are set up all around us. We get a little antsy to get at the party, but we're soldiers and stay in formation. Our prefect rides in front of us and halts.

"Cohort! Attennn . . . SHUN!"

We snap to.

"Fourth Century! Return to camp for *principia* security! Second Century! You'll relieve the Fourth for the night watches. The rest of you men are on leave until the sixth hour tomorrow! Show up on time! Show up sober! Cavalry, make sure you take care of horse stables before you get yourselves lost in the crowd! Disss . . . MISSED!"

Me Roman buddy slaps me on the arm, "Let's go, Big Dog! There's wine to drink and babes to do."

"You go ahead, Gai! The chief told me to report to him when this goat rope ends!"

"Too bad! Sometimes it just sucks being you. Catch you later!"

I gets off me horse and hands the rein off to one of the temple slaves, who's standing at the foot of the stairs. I slips him a couple of pennies. "They'll be a few more for you when I gets back."

"Yes, *Domine!*" he says, looking down.

"I'm not no shaggin' lord. I'm still working for a living."

"Yes, *Domine!*" He's still looking down, but I catch a glimmer of a grin.

I climbs the temple stairs and goes in. Before my eyes can adjust to the shadows, one of the bundle-goons stops me short by poking a finger into me chest.

"No one gets in unless he's a senator or a city magistrate, Soldier," he says in me face.

Now, normally, any civilian who puts his hand on a soldier and mouths off like that is about to be minus his balls. But, this guy's so big, I really got to think twice about it. So, I decides on discretion.

"I'm reporting to the chief . . . I mean, the *imperator* . . . as ordered," I says into his face.

"Wait here!" he says.

The thug walks over to one of the purple-stripers, who looks over at me and flares his nose like it was a hot day in a fish market. He shrugs and walks over to where the chief is sitting on a dais before the statue of the god. He's planted on one of them little, Roman stools with low arms and no back—a thing like that can't be comfortable, so I don't know why the Romans want to use 'em. He's still in his painted toga, but he's sweated through most of the red paint on his face. He's having an intense conversation with old Eyebrows, so the other toga waits for him to be done. When there's a break in the action, Purple-Stripe talks to the chief, who looks over to where I'm standing with the bundle thug.

"Trooper Cura! Come forward!" says he.

The thug steps aside, and I steps up to the dais and assumes the position.

"Sir! Trooper Cura reports as ordered, sir!"

"Yes! Trooper Cura! You have caused me a bit of a problem!" He looks over to the left. "Caesar! Bring me that report!"

One of the purple-stripers comes up to him and hands him a rolled scroll.

"Cura!" the chief says. "This is my brother-in-law, Gaius Julius Caesar. He's got three names like a real Roman nob. The rest of us have to make do with two."

The chief's brother-in-law doesn't react at all to the ribbing. He slightly inclines his head toward me. This is the first time I gets a good look at the posh gob-shite. He looks a few years older than the chief, and he's tall and thin as only a nob who doesn't have to work for a living can afford to be. He has thin, sandy hair, already receding. But, it's his eyes that get me. They're pale blue. I can see intelligence there, but no feeling. This is a guy who can stick you in the belly with a *pugio*, watch for hours while you writhe in agony, then go play with his kids like nothing happened. I makes a note never to turn me back on the guy.

"Trooper Cura!" My attention snaps back to the chief. He's slapping that damned scroll on the palm of his hand. "It has been reported to me that you have enlisted into the Roman army fraudulently, that you have offended the gods and the Roman people by raising your hand to the *sacramentum* while not being a Roman citizen. Is this true, Cura?"

Where's this going? I thinks. "Yes, Sir!"

"*Cacat*! Shit! The barbarian admits his guilt! What are the precedents for such a crime? Caesar?"

By now, there is absolute silence in the temple. I catches the looks of offended dignity on the faces of the togas standing around the dais.

"Well, sir," Caesar responds, "if the man proves to be a run-away slave, he will be branded on the face for escaping his master and then crucified for the sacrilege of swearing fraudulently to the gods. If, however, he is a free man, then his sacrilege has endangered Rome and all his comrades by angering the gods. The *mos maiorem*, the custom of our ancestors, demands he be turned over to his prefect who will order the men of his section to beat him to death with clubs."

"*Mille gratias*, Caesar!" says the chief. "Roman justice should be swift! Since I am the ruling consul this month and I sit in the chair of state, is there any reason why I shouldn't pass judgment on this barbarian bastard immediately?"

All the shaggin' togas are nodding, encouraging the chief to cut me balls off.

"Well, sir," answers Three-Names, "there is the issue of his having saved the life of the consul commanding troops in the field. If he were a citizen, he'd be awarded the Civic Crown and the senate would have to stand in ovation for him."

"Damn!" says the chief. "Why can't these things be simple for once?"

The chief stands and the other togas don't know what to do.

"Cunorud mab Cunomaro, of the Glasso clan, of the Anderica band, of the Insubreci tribe, by your gallantry and quick action, you not only saved the life of a Roman citizen in battle and stood your ground alone against an armed hostile force, you saved *my* ass! You are a credit to your unit, to the Roman army, and to the senate and people of Rome. Had you been a Roman citizen, you would have been awarded the Civic Crown and all these senators you see here would have to kiss your arse. But, such awards cannot be given to a *peregrinus*, a foreigner, no matter how brave and devoted to the Roman nation he may be. So, I cannot crown you, but I, as the ruling consul of the Roman people, can fix this little problem with your enlistment."

The chief raises that damn scroll so everyone in the room can see it.

"By this diploma, you are granted Roman citizenship as a plebian and enrolled in the voting tribe, *Sergia*. This bestowal is effective from the day of your enlistment in my praetorian cohort, so you were and are a legitimately enlisted soldier of Rome. Finally, since Cunorud mab Cunomaro is not an appropriate name for a Roman, from this day hence you will be known as Gaius Marius Insubrecus. See that, Caesar, even a plebian can have three names."

All the togas in the room, who a few seconds earlier were panting for me blood, are now smiling and applauding. Even Caesar is smiling, but it doesn't suit his face at all.

The general steps forward, hands me the diploma, and squeezes me shoulder.

"I owe you my life, Gai, and a Roman never forgets his obligations. Congratulations and thank you!"

I don't know what the proper protocol is for this, so I acts the soldier, takes the scroll, assumes the position, gives the chief a smart nod, and gets me ass out of there before someone changes the chief's mind about having me clubbed to death.

By this time in the story, my gran'pa would be well into his cups. I secretly suspect the whole story was engineered to empty a keg at somebody else's expense.

My gran'pa stuck with Marius, even when Sulla eventually forced him to flee down to the African province. When Marius died, gran'pa figured that his obligation to the Roman army had expired too. Besides, he didn't have much tolerance for Sulla and his pompous, patrician bullshit, and it wasn't really safe in Rome for anyone connected to, or worse, named Marius. So, he took his discharge.

Before he left Rome, Caesar summoned him to a tenement—*insula*, island, the Romans call them—where Caesar lived with his wife and son. Although Caesar was a patrician and claimed to be descended from the goddess Venus through Aeneas' son, Iules, he normally didn't have two *denarii* to rub together, so he lived in the *subura*, the Roman slums. Caesar told my gran'pa that in his will Marius had bequeathed him a small farm up in the Padus Valley, west of the city the Romans call Mediolanum, Medhlán to us Gah'el. Caesar told him the gift was free of *debitum*, obligation. Due to his service to Marius, my gran'pa's family and Caesar's were connected by bonds of honor and patronage.

Gran'pa had no idea what Caesar meant, but thanked him for the gift and, never being comfortable around Caesar, left.

The last thing gran'pa did before leaving Rome was to hike out to Marius's grave—Sulla hadn't dug him out and pitched his ashes into the Tiber yet—and pour a skin of wine onto the tomb. He said he would have brought some beer, but Marius' *manis*, his spirit, being Roman, probably preferred that Roman swill.

When my grandfather got back to Gaul, he was landed Roman gentry and acted the part. He kept his hair short, his face shaven, and spoke Latin. After a few beers, his mates would tease him, saying he sure didn't look like any damn Roman they had ever seen. Then, they would ask him where he hid his plaid trousers, because no noble Roman would be caught dead wearing a sturdy pair of Gallic *bracae*, even in *Ianuarius*. Or, they'd ask him what a Roman really wears under his toga.

Gran'pa would go all red in the face, pop out his chest, and declare for all to hear, "*Quiris sum!*"—the legal formula for stating Roman citizenship. His cronies would respond, "Oh, *Domine*! Forgive us poor, long-haired, ignorant, beer-swilling barbarians! We are not worthy to be in your trouserless presence!" At which point the whole bunch of them would be laughing so hard that beer ran out of their noses.

Gran'pa was never cut out to be a farmer. Fortunately, before he ran the farm into the ground, he married my grandmother, who was Gah'el. There's a huge difference between Gallic and Roman women. The Romans expect their women to be invisible, subservient, and fertile. Gallic women would never put up with that shit. Gran'pa told me that in the ancient times, the women of the Gah'el were expected to pick up a shield and spear and fight shoulder-to-shoulder with the men. Roman women are dangerous because if you piss them off, they'll put a few extra spices in your hash, and you won't live to see another sunrise. But, Gallic women are dangerous because if you piss them off, they'll cut your balls off—or make your life so miserable with their nagging and scolding that you beg for death.

That pretty much described my grandmother, except most of her fighting spirit was directed toward gran'pa. She took one look at the damned mess he had made of the farm and straightened it out—in spite of anything gran'pa thought. Within a couple of years, the farm was making a small profit, and my gran'pa's son and heir, my uncle, Gaius Marius Insubrecus Iunior, was born.

But the gods have no regard for the hopes of men. One winter when my father, imaginatively named Secundus Marius Insubrecus, was two years old, my uncle Gaius caught the coughing sickness and died. After that, there were only daughters, my aunts, Maria and Maria Minor, who were married off to city folk. So, it was my father, Secundus, who was married to a proper Roman girl from Mediolanum and who eventually inherited the family "estate," as my Roman mother liked to call our farm.

But, more about my parents later.

II.

De Avo Meo ac Terra Juventis

GRAN'PA AND THE
LAND OF YOUTH

J have many fond memories of my grandfather, who journeyed to the "Land of Youth" before I became of age and took my *toga virilis*.

My favorite memories were of the winter months, when there wasn't much to do on the farm but try to stay warm and not starve. In those days, we were still living in the original round, Gallic, mud-plaster farmhouse with waddle walls and a thatch roof. That was before my Roman mother, deciding that living like a Gallic peasant didn't befit her station as a landed Roman matron, had the square stone house built.

In our round house, the fire stood in the middle of the main room, most of the smoke rising up to the ceiling and escaping up through the open eves and the thatch. We spent the long winter nights as close to the warmth as we could. My mama and grandmother used the scant light to see their sewing and

23

mending. My father and older brother, Lucius, spent the hours working on farm equipment that needed repairing or sharpening.

Gran'pa would sit in his chair with his feet toward the fire, a cup of beer in his fist, his old brown military *sagum* over his shoulders, and a pair of faded, woolen Gallic trousers stuffed into a pair of woolen socks knitted by my grandmother—his Roman affectations never got in the way of his staying warm in the winter. It was on such evenings that Gran'pa would tell me stories of our people in the old days, before the Romans came.

I remember during the winter, the birds used to fly in through the eaves in the rafters. They would puff out their feathers and, once warm, sing to us before flying back out into the cold. My Roman mother hated the birds because they made a mess in the rafters. But, once, when she picked up a broom to chase them, my grandmother ordered her to leave the birds alone.

When I asked Gran'pa why Nanna protected the birds like that, he told me the "old people" believe that the winter birds are the spirits of those who have died coming back to visit us, and if we offer them the heat of our fire and a few crumbs of food, they will bring us good fortune. If they sing for us, it is a sign that they are pleased. He said we have to show them respect because from the *Samhain*, the time after the harvest, to the time of Belli's fire in the spring, the middle world is theirs, not ours. If we make offerings to them, they will return the favor, and we'll have a good harvest.

One winter night, after hearing this tale, I asked him, "Gran'pa, what happens to us when we die?"

He was silent for a few seconds and took a deep draught of his beer. "That's some question, Little Bear. No one really knows what happens. Some of the Romans think nothing happens. We are just snuffed out like the flame of a candle. Others believe what the Greeks told them, that ghosts go to a prison cave deep under the earth where we're held in the cold and dark. Why the gods would do this, no one knows. Others think our ghosts wander the earth, scaring people, and playing tricks on the living."

"That's dumb, Gran'pa. If the ghosts of all the dead people were just wandering around, there'd be so many of them, we'd be bumping into them all the time . . . and I've never seen one . . . what do you really think happens?"

"Our people believe that the spirits of the worthy go to the Land of Youth."

"What happens there, Gran'pa? What's it like?"

"Oh, it's a grand place. It's never cold, and there's always plenty to eat and drink. There's neither sickness nor pain. You don't age; you're young forever."

"But, I want to get older, Gran'pa!"

"You do now, Little Bear, but there'll come a time when you will want time to slow down. But, if the gods are kind, you'll have many years before you need to worry about that!"

"Does everybody get to go there, Gran'pa, to the Land of Youth?"

"No, not really. If you're brave and honest, if you treat people right, don't cheat, and keep your word, Dána will welcome you to the Land of Youth."

"Who's Dána?"

"He's the god who rules the 'other' world, like the god Lugh rules the land of the living, the 'middle world.'"

"Mama says Lugh's real name is Apollo."

"That's what the Romans call him. And they call Dána 'Pluto,' but they are the same."

"Gran'pa! Where's the Land of Youth?"

"No one really knows. The old ones say it's an island in the west, where the sun goes down, an island in the great salt sea the Romans call '*oceanus,*' beyond the lands of the middle world."

"Can we go there?"

"We can't. It's hidden and Dána will not reveal it to a living man. Although the old ones do tell the tale of Arth Mawr, the Great Bear, who found it, but then lost his son there."

"Then how do we know the story?"

"When Arth returned with seven of his warriors, one of them was Gwion, a storyteller. So, Gwion told the story for the people to remember."

"Will you tell me the story, Gran'pa?"

Gran'pa reached over, refilled his cup with beer from his barrel, took a long drink, and as was his way, said, "Storytelling's dry work."

Then, as was her way, Nanna said, "For you, breathing's 'dry work.'"

Gran'pa grunted at her comment and began:

Arth Mawr was the greatest hero of the first age of our people, a great warrior who commanded other heroes, like the sons of Lír-Manawen, who swam in the ocean and commanded the fishes and monsters of the deep; or like Brán, the Raven, who flew above the earth and saw all. Gwion the Wise was his drui, his advisor, and made sure Arth's deeds would live as long as the people exist.

Arth was born of the god, Lugh, and a mortal woman, Igerna, daughter of Gorlois of the Western Isles. When Igerna was still a maid, Lugh saw her from his chariot, which was the sun, and fell in love with her instantly.

Lugh went to Gorlois and asked for Igerna as his wife, but Gorlois was a foolish and greedy man. He told Lugh that he wanted his chariot as Igerna's dower.

"What's a 'dower,' Gran'pa?" I interrupted.

"It's the fortune a woman brings to her husband when they're married," he answered.

"What was Nanna's fortune?"

"Her beauty and her wit, Little Bear . . . her beauty and her wit."

"Oh, for the sake of all the gods! You're still a golden-tongued devil, you are!" Nanna sighed.

"And that's why you love me, Mother," Gran'pa said. "Now, let me get back to my story.

Lugh knew that no mortal could drive the horses of the sun without destroying the middle lands, so he begged Gorlois to ask for something else. But, Gorlois was a foolish man and said that if Lugh was unwilling to give him the chariot, he was equally unwilling to give him his daughter. And, as an insult, Gorlois gave Igerna as wife to a warrior called Uthr, the cruelest warrior in the Western Isles.

On the night of Igerna's wedding, Lugh disguised himself as a *fili*, a singer of songs, and went to Gorlois' *dun*, Tintagelo, a great fortress on the Western Ocean. It is a great misfortune to turn a singer of songs away from your door, and since a wedding is a great celebration, Lugh was welcomed into the *dun*. But, when Lugh began to sing, he performed an enchantment that put Gorlois, Uthr, and all the wedding guests into a deep slumber. Lugh then placed a dream into Uthr's mind so that he would think that he was lying with Igerna.

***

"Gran'pa!" I interrupted again. "What does that mean, 'He was lying with his Igerna'?"

"Get yourself out of that one, oh, wise 'teller-of-tales'!" Nanna chuckled.

Gran'pa drained his cup and poured himself another. "Well, Little Bear, remember in the spring, when we were watching the sheep . . . how the male climbed on the back of the female?"

"Yes, Gran'pa."

"And remember I told you this is how the little lambs are made?"

"Uh-huh."

"Well, uh . . . people do something like that, uh . . . to make babies, and we sometimes call it, uh . . . 'lying together.'"

"Oh! You mean to make me, Papa and Mama—"

"I think you get it, Little Bear! Let's get back to the story."

Nanna was shaking and making funny sounds through her nose. Mama had her Roman *putet*, this-smells-bad, look on her face.

***

So, while the wedding guests slept, Lugh went to Igerna as a husband would on the wedding night, and fathered Arth on her. Because of Lugh's dream, Uthr always thought that Arth was his own son, but he was to become Lugh's revenge on Uthr and Gorlois.

Uthr was a cruel husband to Igerna. He worked her hard and beat her when she didn't please him—and no one could ever please Uthr. One day, when Arth was a youth, just about your age, Little Bear, he and his mother were walking through the forests that surround Tintagelo when they witnessed a wonder. A glowing sword, as bright as the sun, hovered above the forest path in front of them. Next to the sword sat a woman, who was so loathsome, so disgusting, that it was difficult to look at her without shuddering.

When Igerna and Arth approached her, in a squeaky voice, she croaked, "Behold *Durn Gwin*, the bright sword of Lugh! This is the sword of wonders. Each time it is swung, it will taste the blood of its enemies! No warrior who bears this sword can be defeated by mortal hands. Only the worthy one, the son of Lugh, may wield it. All others will be destroyed."

Igerna turned to Arth, "Take the sword, my son! It is a gift from your father!"

Arth hesitated.

"Take it, my son, for you are not Arth mab Uthr, you are Arth mab Lugh, child of the sun god! This sword is your destiny."

Arth reached for the sword and grasped it! When he did, the loathsome hag transformed into a beautiful maiden with the glowing red hair, a princess of the sun god's kingdom.

"Arth mab Lugh," she said, "where you rule, the land will prosper, for I will always be a willing and fertile wife to you." This maid was indeed the goddess Eriu, who chooses the king of the land, who is to be her husband. Then, Eriu vanished.

When Arth and Igerna returned to the *dun*, they went to Uthr, who was already deep in his cups, as was his habit, and when he saw them, he screamed at Igerna, "Where have you been, woman? The fire's out, and my meat is not boiled."

"You have servants enough to boil your meat!" Igerna answered him.

"Ah! It's a princess we are now! The high and mighty one!"

He got up from his bench to strike Igerna, but before he could lower his fist on her, Arth, with the strength of the sun god, grasped his arm and held it.

Uthr, as drunk as he was, was amazed by the boy's strength. "Take your hand off me, boy! A son should never raise his hand against his father. I'll settle with you after I'm done with this lazy slut you call a mother!"

Arth answered him, "I am no son of yours, Uthr! And now I bring you my father's vengeance!"

Arth turned Uthr's arm, forcing him to his knees. As Uthr kneeled before Igerna, Arth drew *Durn Gwin*, which flashed like the sun as it leapt from its scabbard, and he struck off Uthr's head. Even though the head, which rolled to a stop at Igerna's feet, had been cut cleanly from Uthr's body, there was no blood. With the heat of its anger, the sword of Lugh had sealed the wounds it had inflicted.

Arth sheathed *Durn Gwin* and picked up Uthr's head by its hair. Then, with his right hand, he reached for his mother's hand and led her to Gorlois' hall.

When he stood before the king, he said, "Grandfather, I bring you a gift!" He offered him the head of Uther and presented Igerna to her father as a free woman.

"What have you done, boy?" Gorlois croaked in shock. For to the old ones, as it is today, there was no greater crime than the killing of a parent, and Arth was offering to the king the head of the man everyone knew to be Arth's father.

Ever since Gorlois had refused Lugh Igerna as his bride, his lands had been living under a great enchantment, which had brought blight and suffering to the people. Gorlois' lands were covered by a black mist, which the sun's rays would not penetrate. The lambs would not foal in the spring; the crops would not grow; the women were barren; and when danger threatened, the warriors of the land lost the strength to lift their weapons. Gorlois feared that a patricide would only worsen the curse on the land.

"This man was no father of mine. He was an affront to my true father, Lugh, the god who gives life to the land! My gift to you, Grandfather, is the head of the one who angered the god. And, I restore your daughter, Igerna, the beloved of Lugh, to your house."

Arth then turned to the Council of Three Generations, who were gathered around Gorlois' chair—

"Gran'pa! What is the 'Council of Three Generations'?"

"You're going to give the boy bad dreams with all this Gallic nonsense about heads and curses!" Mama interrupted. "If you insist on telling him stories, you should tell him worthwhile stories about the great men of Rome, like the noble Cincinnatus, who conquered Italy, or the great Africanus, who destroyed Hannibal."

"No, Gran'pa," I insisted, "I want to hear about Arth! Why would he bring Uthr's head to Gorlois?"

"The old ones believed that a warrior's courage, his spirit, resides in his head. When you defeat a great warrior and take his head, you capture his spirit. That way, when you enter the Land of Youth, he will have to serve you."

"Really, Gran'pa?" I questioned. "Did you take heads when you fought the Germans? Where did you put the heads? Can I see them?"

"No, Little Bear. Romans don't fight that way. They believe the spirit leaves the body with the *spiritus*, the last breath. When a man is dead, there's nothing left in the body."

"So what is the 'Council of Generations,' Gran'pa?"

"The old ones believed that the king, the *brenna*, was selected from among the members of the warrior families by three generations of the people— grandfather, father, and son."

"Who's our *brenna*, Gran'pa?"

"We're Romans, Little Bear, and don't have kings—"

"At least you got that right!" my Roman mother snorted.

"We don't have kings *now*," Gran'pa continued, ignoring Mama's interruption. "Before the Romans came, the people were ruled by the *brenna*, the leader of the war bands; the *bre'ons*, the keepers of the law; the *fili*, the keepers of the past; and the *drui*, the speakers of the gods. They say that in the North, beyond the Roman lands, the Gah'el still have kings, but I've never journeyed there."

"Barbarians!" Mama snorted. This time Nanna shushed her.

"Can I go there, Gran'pa?"

"Maybe when you are older, Little Bear. Now do you want to hear the rest of the tale?"

"I want to hear the story of how Arth Mawr conquered the Romans!" I demanded.

"Your 'Art Mor' never conquered Rome," Mama corrected me. "The Gaul, Brennus, besieged the capitol, but the great Roman general, Marcus Furius Camillus, annihilated him and his horde of drunken barbarians."

"*Filia*!" my grandfather responded as if to a somewhat dim, but stubborn, child. Mama hated it when he spoke to her like that, calling her "daughter." She was a "city-Roman." Her father in Medhlán was a rich and successful man, a member of the Roman order of *Equites*, knights. She had never really accepted being subordinate to a "round-hut Roman," as the city folk referred to us. But, Gran'pa was the *pater familias*, the head of the household; it was his right to call her *filia* and to expect her acquiescence.

"The boy is right," Gran'pa corrected her. "*Brennus* was not his name, like you Romans think! It was his title! He was the *Brenna Uk'el*, the High King of the Peoples—*Rex Optimus* to you Romans. We of the Gah'el call him *Arth Mawr*, the Great Bear, sometimes *Arth Uthr*, the Terrible Bear, because he was frightful in his wrath and ruthless to his enemies."

<hr>

The Romans betrayed Arth Mawr's trust. They came to him under the pretense of a truce and pretended to be diplomats, *lisgen'adonu*, sacrosanct under the laws of the Bre'ons. They claimed that they wanted to negotiate a dispute between one of Arth's tribes, the Senones, who were seeking land, and a city-people called the Etruscans. Then, the Romans broke the law sacred to the gods and all nations, taking up arms during a sworn truce and killing the *Pen Lwoth*, the tribal chief of the Senones, who was unarmed.

Arth Mawr was enraged. He destroyed the Roman army and then their city. The last wretched Roman survivors huddled in the temple of their chief god, Iove, on the only one of their revered seven hills not destroyed by Arth Mawr's wrath, the Capital itself.

As Arth Mawr was leading his army up the hill to exterminate the last remnant of that impious race, some geese that the Romans considered sacred stood before him, as if they were the Romans' last feeble line of resistance. Then, Arth Mawr remembered that geese are also sacred to our god Lír.

Some say they are his children, transformed by some dark magic. He took it to be a sign that Lír wanted the slaughter to end.

Arth Mawr was a pious king. The rage fell away from him. Despite being on the very threshold of destroying his enemies, he obeyed the sacred *ges*, the command of the god. He halted his army on the very slopes of the undefended Roman Capital.

He sent his nephew, the great warrior, Goualc'mei, to demand that the Romans ransom their lives with the weight of Arth's sword in pure gold. These Romans, still greedy despite their terror, thought that to buy their lives and their wretched city back with gold equal to the weight of a mere sword was a bargain indeed. So, that wretched race of farmers, sheepherders, and shopkeepers readily agreed.

What they did not know was that at his side, Arth Mawr carried the great *Durn Gwin,* the bright sword of Lugh, an invincible sword of fire and light forged by the gods and presented to Arth Mawr by the *Bren'ine o dan u door*, the Queen under the Waters, Eriu herself, in her disguise as a loathsome hag. When a thousand Roman pounds of the purest gold did not tip the scales against Arth Mawr's sword, the Romans protested, saying he had tricked them.

To them, Arth Mawr declared, *"U' goresgin unr'iou deouwis*! The conquered have no choices!"

The Gah'el filled a hundred carts with the purest Roman gold and returned to their lands in the north, leaving Rome a pile of smoldering ruins. To our people, the Insubres, Arth Mawr granted the lands of this fertile valley, where we have lived since the great king passed over the mountains.

If you look to the north, in the sky over the mountains, you will see that the gods have shaped the stars into the image of a bear. For the Gah'el, this is an eternal reminder that Arth Mawr still lives, slumbering deep within a great mountain. Woe to the Roman, the Greek, or the German who awakens him, for he will ride forth from under the mountain to champion the Gah'el and destroy their enemies.

"But, Gran'pa," I protested, "I already know this story. Tell me about Arth Mawr and the Land of Youth!"

"I think it's time for bed," Mama interrupted.

"I agree," Nanna chipped in.

When the Gah'el and the Roman agreed, there was no appeal, so I was packed off to my bed up in the loft without learning the connection between Arth Mawr and the Land of Youth.

III.

De Mama Mea, Qua Muliere Romana Feroce

MY MAMA, A FORMIDABLE
WOMAN OF ROME

When I think about my parents, I think mostly of my mother. Helvetia Minor was her formal Roman name, and she was as *formal* a Roman as one could be. Not that my father, Secundus, was insignificant to me. It was just that, well, he was a farmer, with little ambition beyond working the land. That was the way my Nanna brought him up, and that's the way he brought up my older brother, Lucius, his heir, who was named for my maternal grandfather in Mediolanum. But, Papa was the man who, through his hard work on the farm, made my life possible. He just didn't contribute as much as my mother to the man I eventually became.

My mother's father, Lucius Helvetius Naso Iunior—who used to say, "Just call me Naso . . . like 'nose'! It was good enough for my father, and it's good enough for me!"— was, by our dirt-farmer standards, a rich man.

34

He lived in the city, and he made his money as a military contractor. He didn't bother with any of the "fancy stuff," as he called it, that the military needed, like the basic Roman infantry sword, *gladius hispanensis*, or the standard infantry javelin, *pilum*, or the long cavalry sword, *spatha*, or the infantry chainmail, *lorica*, or even the basic infantry shield, *scutum*. Such "fancy stuff" later became the basic tools of my trade, when I joined the legion.

No, the way Avus Lucius, "Grandfather Lucius" as Mama insisted he be addressed, saw it, most of the fancy stuff required skilled craftsmen, and that meant expensive labor, long production times, and a cash-flow problem. Instead, Avus Lucius made all the other metal bits—horseshoes, belt decorations, fasteners, bridle attachments, mess kits, maybe a helmet or two—that the army bought often and in great quantities. Cheap labor, even slaves, quick turnover, and high margins were Avus Lucius' business plan.

And it worked! Avus Lucius was rich enough to qualify for the Equestrian order, easily meeting the minimum property requirement of 50,000 *denarii*.

Not that Avus Lucius was pretentious. He rarely wore the gold ring that indicated his Equestrian status. He was a "hands-on" business man. When we visited him in the city, we usually found him covered in soot from nosing about his foundries making sure no one was stealing from him or lying down on the job.

He kept an especially careful eye on his accountant, a Sicilian slave he simply called *scriba*, "clerk." Scriba and Avus Lucius shared the same desk in the back of one of the forges down near the south gate in the city. Scriba would make accounting entries onto a wax tablet and pass them across to Avus Lucius, who would scrutinize the numbers. Then, Avus Lucius would either grunt, "*Bene!*" and file the tablet in a cabinet behind his desk, or pass it back to Scriba, berate him as "an incompetent turd" who was robbing him blind, and tell him what needed correction.

Whether Scriba had had any name previously, no one really knew. When he was freed in accordance with Avus Lucius' will, he became Lucius Helvetius Scriba and made a nice living running a foundry that Avus Lucius had bequeathed to him.

Avus Lucius had three children who survived to adulthood: his son and heir, Lucius Helvetius Naso Tertius, and two daughters, Helvetia Maior and Helvetia Minor, my mother being the youngest.

My aunt, Helvetia Maior, was married off to a mid-level functionary in city government. According to Avus Lucius, government jobs are steady and dependable. You'll never get rich, even with collecting the *stipes*, the gratuities that are expected from petitioners who want their requests moved through the bureaucracy quickly. But, you'll always have an income—that is, unless you become too greedy and attract the attention of the wrong people. In that case, you are likely to end up as part of the foundations of some new public building.

No one is sure why Avus Lucius married off his younger daughter, Helvetia Minor, to my father, the oldest son of a subsistence, round-hut farmer out in the boonies. Gran'pa claimed it was due to our connection, albeit tenuous, with the patrician *gens Iulia* down in Rome, the Roman clan of Gaius Iulius Caesar. But, the more credible explanation is that Helvetia Minor was a hellion, and Avus Lucius was willing to fob her off on the first credible prospect he could find. That was my Papa.

It made sense in several ways. First, Mama and her mother, Avia Marcia, were redheads, and Avus Lucius had enough on his hands with his foundries. He didn't need the trouble of having two redheads under one roof. The second is evident in the pet name he gave Mama, "Valeria." Mama said it meant "fierce." Gran'pa said it meant "good riddance."

Despite all that, Avus Lucius had given Mama a first-class Roman education. She could read and write Latin. She knew her Roman history and literature. She could work up the household accounts on a hand abacus. She even used to help Avus Lucius and Scriba with the business accounts, even though she considered it slave work.

Avus Lucius gave Mama a fine dowry worth over 25,000 denarii, which brought Papa halfway up to qualifying for the Equestrian class. But, of course, being Avus Lucius, he tied the money up so tightly that Papa couldn't get a brass *as* of it between his fingers while Avus Lucius was alive, and after he went off to wherever dead Roman businessmen go, Mama did the same. Mama used to refer to her dowry as her *divitiae*, her fortune, especially when she was arguing with

Gran'pa, and after Gran'pa went off to the Land of Youth, arguing with my Papa, and after Papa went off to wherever dead Roman farmers go, arguing with my brother, Lucius, and after Lucius joined Papa in that paradise of farmers—surely, a place where they didn't have constantly to hear the clacking of Mama's sharp tongue—arguing with her grandson, Lucius Iunior.

It is said that redheads thrive on conflict. My Mama was certainly proof of that. Mama and Nanna were at war from the time Mama first entered the house. The initial battle occurred when Nanna tried to assign Mama her household chores. Roman matrons do not sweep out the hearth, collect the eggs in the morning, or air out the bedding. Nor do they perform the various tasks that farm women need to do to keep a household functioning. Nanna quickly established that in *her* house the *merc' u ti*, the woman of the house, outranked the *Matrona Romana,* and Mama had to knuckle under if she expected to get fed.

The unrelenting battle between Roman and Gah'el, though, was fought over the house itself. For Mama, living out in the sticks in a Gallic round-house held together by wooden posts, wattle-and-daub panels, and a thatched roof, was worse than living in the poorest, most sordid tenement in the city. Mama said that a family who claimed to be the clients of the patrician *gens Iulia* should have a proper Roman masonry house with a tile roof, a proper furnace, hot water, and a working bath. Gran'pa told her that if she were willing to build it with her "fortune," the family would be happy to live in it, but until that happened, she should shut her gob and go about her chores.

When Gran'pa went to the Land of Youth, and Papa became the *pater familias*, the battle was over. Papa could never stand up to Mama. I think she scared the shit out of him, and after years of constant combat, I don't blame him a bit. Mama never did have to use her "fortune" to build her "estate." She just marched Papa into the city to some bankers that Avus Lucius knew. They provided the money for Mama's palace, and Papa assumed the mortgage on the farm.

The thought of all that debt on a farm that, at best, made only a modest profit slowly killed Nanna. In fact, less than a year after Papa borrowed the money, Nanna followed Gran'pa to the Land of Youth.

The best thing Mama did for me, though, was to ensure that I was educated as a proper "Roman gentleman." She clearly understood that I had no prospects within the family. My older brother, Lucius, would get the farm, and my uncle, Lucius "the Younger Nose," would get the businesses—or at least what was left after Scriba robbed them blind. So, Mama was determined to groom me to find my fortune outside the family in the Roman world. To do that, I had to shake off my Gallic stink and assimilate.

That my skin was as pale as a maiden from the other world and burned whenever the sun shined didn't help, but, fortunately, I had none of the Gallic height that seemed to intimidate Romans. I was five Roman *pedes* and a wide palm in height—although I have lost a bit of that over the years. I was somewhat short-legged and, from the farm work, broad in the shoulders and chest. The dark-blond hair of my childhood had turned to dark brown. My eyes were brown and hazel, but looked brown from a distance. So, I could easily pass for an Italian, even a Roman. But, Mama knew I had to learn to read and write Latin elegantly, speak with polished rhetoric, and most importantly, lose that damned Gallic brogue.

In short, I needed a Roman tutor.

Being in debt up to our ears, however, we couldn't afford a tutor. So, Mama devised a plan.

About five Roman miles to the east was the country estate of a real nob, an actual senator from Rome, Aulus Gabinius. Gabinius was a rich, plebian mid-bencher in the senate, but he was connected, an ally of a real up-and-comer, the "Great One," Gnaeus Pompeius Magnus, who was himself the son of a "new man"—as the Roman nobility sneeringly called those who rose up out of the Equestrian order. Furthermore, Gabinius seemed to be on friendly terms with the political leader of *gens Iulia*, the patrician, Gaius Iulius Caesar, the younger—not the one Gran'pa knew.

Gabinius' place wasn't a working farm. It was a huge house surrounded by dozens of *iugera* of good fertile farmland that, although fussed over by dozens of slaves, produced nothing but a few fruit trees, some flowers, and a bit of grass. Gabinius kept the place as an escape from the summer heat of Rome—and from its politically and otherwise unhealthy environment.

The closest members of his *familia* resided there year-round to stay out of harm's way. There were children, my mother thought, so there must be a tutor.

One morning, only few days before the Calends of *Iunius*, when the planting was done and it was already hot as blazes, Mama had me scrub all the farm dirt from my ears, face, and hands—especially from under my fingernails—and dress in my cleanest, best-mended tunic with a broad leather belt and my best leather sandals. I thanked the gods that I hadn't yet assumed my *toga virilis,* or she would have had me throw that on, too!

Mama dressed herself in a bright yellow *stola* and draped her best pale-green *palla* over her shoulders. She rouged her cheeks a bit, checked to make sure that her hair was in place and that the day was *fastus*, propitious for business, and off we went to Gabinius' place, which was five thousand *passus* down a country road. We took the farm cart to within about a hundred *passus* of Gabinius' driveway, concealed it in a grove of trees, and then walked the rest of the way to the house.

Unfortunately, Mama had not anticipated Gabinius' *maior domus*, a pumped-up door-slave, who believed his duty was to shield the *gens Gabinia* from all the country riffraff that lived about. That was probably what the senator wanted also, but neither he nor his slave had anticipated Mama.

When the *maior domus* tried to turn us away, Mama rose to her full height and then some, unfolding like some primal force from the netherworld. She struck an orator's pose, as if she were about to deliver an address to the *comitia* of plebs from the *rostra* in the Roman Forum, and delivered an oration to that poor slave, intimating that we were somehow descended from the great Roman Dictator, Gaius Marius, whose reputation had been greatly rehabilitated since the death of Sulla, and that we were on the most intimate terms with the *gens Iulia*. Caesar himself—I thought I heard her say—would want to hear from Gabinius why his door-lackey, a mere slave, had turned away Caesar's most cherished clients!

Of course, the *maior domus* crumbled. Chastened, he led us from the vestibule through the atrium, which was really quite simple for a rich-man's house. Besides wall paintings, there was a marble of a seminaked nymph seeming to rise from the *impluvium*, a cistern to capture rain. From the atrium, we were led back past the closed doors of various *cellae*, small rooms, whose purposes I could not begin to imagine.

Finally, just as my eyes were adjusting to the dimness of the house, we arrived at the *peristylium*, a garden open to the sky but within the house itself. It was like emerging from a dim cave into a jungle paradise of colors. The opaque, black eyes of second-story windows in towering stucco walls of another wing of the mansion glowered down at us. I felt as if I were standing at the bottom of a shallow well. The feeling was intensified by a fountain bubbling up from the ground and the large pool spreading out from it. The *piscina,* or fishpond, filled most of the *peristylium* under the open ceiling. In the *piscina,* among the green lily pads and colorful aquatic flowers, I saw flashes of gold and white, as carp darted to the surface to feast on any insect foolish enough to linger too close to the water's surface.

I must have stood gawking for some time. Mama was already seated in a comfortable chair under the shady cloister formed around the *piscina* by the overhanging roof. She had dropped her *palla* off her shoulders, onto the back of the chair, and was draping her *stola* about her—all the while looking in my direction and repeatedly inclining her head toward the empty chair beside, as if to signal for me to sit down before causing her any further embarrassment in front of the slave. I finally broke from my trance, took Mama's not-too-subtle hint, and sat. The *maior domus* asked if we desired any refreshment after our journey, some water, perhaps. When Mama declined, the slave announced that he would inform the *dominus,* the master, that he had callers. He then retreated back into the shadowy depths of the house.

I was about to say something to Mama, probably something about the size of the house, or about the marble floors in the atrium, or about the fishpond and garden in the middle of a house, or about the towering stucco walls around us, when she hushed me and gestured back toward the shadowy cloisters. When I turned and peered back into the shadows, I realized we weren't alone. There was a man, a slave, I imagined, standing motionless near a closed door in the back of the *peristylium*. He wore a somber-colored tunic, which allowed him to fade into the shadows.

"That's the *culina*, the kitchen," Mama hissed so the slave could not hear. "His job is to serve the senator and his guests. He is supposed to be invisible until he's summoned."

Before I could ask some inane question about actually having a kitchen inside the house, I glimpsed movement, a flash of white, within the house. As I turned to look, I saw a balding and somewhat overweight man approaching from across the *peristylium*. Then I spotted the broad, purple bands on the sleeves and hem of his tunic. He sported a strange, empty smile, one without any genuine warmth—the same smile I have since become so familiar with on the faces of politicians of every stripe.

Without thinking, I leapt to my feet.

Mama, if anything, just seemed to relax further into the depths of her chair. She languidly extended her hand in the direction of the fat purple-striper, whom I correctly assumed to be the senator himself, Aulus Gabinius.

I was about to get my first lesson in what I later called *Certamen Romanum*, the "Roman Game."

"Sit down, sit down!" he said to me, taking Mama's offered hand in both of his. "To what do I owe the pleasure of your visit, Helvetia Minor? Or, may I call you Valeria?"

Mama blinked twice, a bit surprised.

"Ah!" continued the senator. "Perhaps you didn't know, then? Your father, Naso, is one of my oldest and most noted clients here in *Insubria*. We go way back! How is he, by the way? Still poking his *nose* in every nook and cranny of his wide-flung enterprises?" the senator chuckled at his own pun.

Mama recovered quickly, "My father is well. Thank you for asking, Senator. He sends his warmest greetings to you and your *familia*."

"Please, Valeria. Call me Aulus," the senator responded. I noticed that he had yet to release Mama's hand.

Two more blinks from Mama. The game continued.

"Ah! Where are my manners?" Gabinius said. "You must be exhausted from your journey on such a warm day. Isn't that your estate five miles from here?"

Estate? I wondered.

"Yes, Aulus," Mama answered. "We like to live modestly here in the country."
Who is this woman? I wondered.

The senator clapped his hands and called over, "*Serve*, Slave!"

"*Ti' adsum, Domine*," the invisible slave responded from the shadows, "At your service, Lord!"

"Some refreshment for my guests," Gabinius ordered. "Some cool lemon water for the lady, I think. And, some wine, well-watered, for us men," he flattered, as the game continued.

"I have some *rhaeticum*. I have it brought up from the city . . . a modest wine, good quality," he said to me. "Would that suffice, young man?"

"Yes, sir," I responded. I didn't know the difference between *rhaeticum* and mare piss, but I was quickly learning how the game was played.

"The *rhaeticum, Serve*," Gabinius called over into the shadows, "well watered, and the lemon water for the lady."

"*Stat', Domine*, immediately," I heard from the shadows.

I heard a door open and close, caught a whiff of cooking pork, and swore I saw a puff of grey smoke waft into the sunlight of the *peristylium*. It was as if the slave had gone to the underworld to fetch our drinks.

Gabinius finally released Mama's hand, but not without a gentle stroke. Mama . . . two blinks.

He sat down in a chair next to hers.

"So, tell me, Valeria, to what do I owe this great pleasure?" His voice said *pleasure*, and I would have sworn his eyes also said *voluptas*.

"How is your dear wife, the Lady Metella?" Mama countered. "I do hope she enjoys our temperate climate here in *Insubria*, after the heat of Rome."

Now it was Gabinius' turn to blink.

"The Lady Metella thrives, thank you," Gabinius recovered. "We should have you and your husband for dinner some evening.

"But, who is this?" he said turning his attention to me. "Is this Naso's grandson? Lucius, is it not?"

"Lucius is with his father learning to manage our estates," Mama said—there was that word again. "This is our younger son, Gaius Marius. It's about him I have come to ask your advice."

Just then, two slaves arrived with our drinks. While one balanced a tray with cups and pitchers, the other arranged a low table before us. He placed a drinking cup of high-quality, blue Italian earthenware before each of us. He poured some liquid into the cup before Gabinius, stepped back, and waited.

Gabinius took the cup, sipped its contents, and finally nodded his approval. The slave topped off Gabinius' cup, then filled mine. He put the pitcher down on a side table, out of the sun. Then he took the second pitcher from the tray and filled Mama's cup. The slave did not wait for her approval. He placed the second pitcher on the side table, dismissed the other slave, and then took up his station behind us, again invisible in the shadows.

"Refreshment first," Gabinius announced, holding up his cup. He took a long drink. His Adam's apple, oddly prominent on such a fat man, bobbed up and down like a pump draining the liquid from his cup. Mama lifted hers and barely wet her lips, but even that slight moisture seemed to redden her lips a shade or two. I picked mine up and sniffed it carefully. Mama kicked my ankle, and I took a small sip. *So, if this is rhaeticum, I might actually prefer mare's piss*, I thought. I set my cup down.

"So, Gaius Marius, is it?" said the senator addressing me. "That's quite a name to bear. He was one of our greatest soldiers—despite what that bunch of snobs hanging about Sulla thought. Perhaps in your future is a career in the legions? With your connection to the *gens Iulia*, you could go places."

I wasn't sure whether the fat man was patronizing me, but Mama was: "That's so *kind* of you to suggest, Sena . . . I mean, Aulus . . . but, there is one matter concerning Gaius here that I would like to discuss with you."

"Certainly, Valeria," Gabinius responded, turning his complete attention back to Mama—*voluptas*, again.

"We have brought Gaius up in the country," Mama continued her fable. "It's so much healthier than the city."

Gabinius nodded at Mama—a simulated grin on his lips, *voluptas* in the eyes—the Roman Game continued.

"There just isn't that great an opportunity for a boy to be educated as a proper Roman gentleman up here," Mama went on. "I'm sure you understand." Nod, nod, nod, grin, grin, grin. "So, I've come to ask a great favor of you—"

"Oh, Valeria," the fat man interrupted, "you know there are no *favors* that need to be asked between a *patronus* and the daughter of one of his longest and most valued clients. Just ask me, and I'm sure we can work something out." Gabinius' hand reached across the table and covered Mama's—blink, blink.

"Oh!" Mama said, recovering her hand and placing it flat below her throat in a well-staged gesture of relief. "I'm so glad to hear you say that, Aulus. I am! I knew you were a man to whom an honest and virtuous Roman matron could come to solve her petty, little domestic problems." Nod, grin. "I was so hoping that you might allow my Gaius to share the tutors that I'm sure you have brought up from Rome to educate your own children."

"Share my children's tutors?" Gabinius repeated. Blink, blink. "Valeria, that's the very least I could do to help launch this fine, young lad on his career."

"*Serve!*" the senator called over to the invisible slave.

"*Domine,*" a voice out of the shadows.

"Fetch Stephanos for me!" Gabinius ordered.

"*Stat', Domine!*" Footsteps retreated back toward the atrium.

"Lad," the senator addressed me, holding up his cup, "would you mind reaching over and refilling me?"

I reached over to the serving table, luckily remembering that the server had tied a small, white napkin to the handle of the pitcher holding Mama's lemon water. I grabbed the pitcher of watered wine and filled Gabinius' cup.

"*Gratias,*" he mumbled as I finished. I pretended to refill my own still-full beaker, not wanting the fat man to think I wasn't mature enough to handle my late-morning wine. I placed the pitcher back on the serving table without upsetting anything.

As I did, a man burst into the *peristylium* from within the house. He was tall, almost six Roman *pedes*, I would say, and thin as a sapling. His hair was blond, shot through with grey. He had blue eyes that seemed to burn into anything they beheld and a nose that would have done the *rostrum* of a warship proud. His mouth formed a knife-cut across his face; he seemed to have no lips. The skin of his face seemed to stretch so tightly, I imagined that if he tried to smile, his entire face would tear.

"You summoned me, Senator," he announced.

"Ah . . . yes . . . Stephanos," the senator seemed to stammer as if he too was slightly intimidated by the man. "Allow me to introduce a neighbor, Helvetia Maria Matrona." There was barely a nod in Mama's direction from the Stick. "And this is her younger son, Gaius Marius Insubrecus." No response at all from the Stick.

The senator continued, "I have agreed with the lady that you and your staff will provide for the education of young Gaius, here." Two blinks from the Stick. "Why don't you take him back to your office and get acquainted . . . while the lady and I work out some details?" Nod and grin in Mama's direction. Mama just gazed up at the Stick, who was benignly blank.

"*Veni, puer,*" the Stick ordered. "Come, boy!" He turned on his heels and headed back into the house.

I jumped out of my chair, narrowly avoiding tripping over the table where our drinks rested, and chased into the house after Stephanos.

I took a last look at Mama and the senator as I left the *peristylium*. He again had his hand over hers. Blink, blink.

I hurried after the Stick into the darkness of the house back toward the atrium. After the brightness of the open-air *peristylium*, I could barely see through the murk to follow him. The fluttering, white entity that seemed to beckon me further into the shadows made me feel as if I were following one of the *di inferi*, the underworld spirits, who lead the souls of the recently dead down into Hades.

Finally, as I found my way into one of the *cellae* that we had passed earlier on our way through the house, the aroma of dry papyrus was overwhelming. The walls were lined with overstuffed scroll cubicles. There was enough reed paper in the room to corner the Egyptian market! The Stick took a seat behind a large desk covered with mounds of scrolls, individual sheets of paper, and *tabulae*, wax tablets. There was nowhere for me to sit, so I stood before his desk.

"First," he began, "you will address me as *magister*, master. Do you understand?"

"Yes," I answered.

Seemingly out of nowhere, a real stick whistled through the still air and smacked into my upper arm.

"'Yes, *Magister*,'" Stephanos hissed. "Try it again, boy!"

"Yes, *Magister*," I repeated, rubbing the welt on my arm.

"That was an easy lesson, boy . . . your first," the Stick said. "You will speak only when spoken to. Your answers will always be short and to the point. Until you have something marginally intelligent to say, I suggest you restrict answers to, 'Yes, *Magister*' and 'No, *Magister*.' Do you understand?"

"Yes . . . yes, *Magister*," I recovered.

"*Bene*! If you have a question, raise your hand, and wait to be recognized. Understand, boy?"

"Yes, *Magister*!"

"*Bene*," the Stick continued, "have you had any lessons in reading or writing?"

"No, *Magister*!"

"Do you know your letters?" he asked.

"My letters—?" I began.

Thwack! The stick bit into my upper arm.

"No, *Magister*," I recovered

"Then you're not ready to join the other students . . . Dion!" he shouted. "Dion! Get in here!"

Behind me, I heard a door open somewhere out in the *atrium*, then footsteps crossing the hall. I didn't look around. I didn't know whether looking around was permitted, and I wasn't going to give the *magister* another excuse to work on me with his stick.

A dark-haired man around my height came into the room wearing the unbleached, undyed, greyish-wool tunic of a slave.

"Yes, *Magister*," he said. He kept his head bowed and his eyes downcast. I was beginning to think everyone in this place was frightened of the Stick.

"Dion, this is a new . . . er . . . *ward* of the senator, Gaius Marius Something-or-other," Stephanos addressed the newcomer. "He has no letters. I want you to work with him and get him reading for my classroom. That's all!"

"Yes, *Magister*," Dion complied. "Are we excused, *Magister*?"

"Yes," the Stick stated. "Get out of my office. I have important work to do."

Dion tugged at my tunic sleeve. "Follow me, young sir," he said softly and led me to his cubicle across the atrium, which was much smaller than the Stick's. A single, large worktable practically filled the middle of the room. On top was a pile of wax slates and some papyrus. I could see near one edge where Dion seemed to have been copying a document from one of the slates onto expensive reed paper.

"Please excuse my disorder, *Domine*," Dion muttered. "My function is to copy the *magister*'s thoughts and essays onto paper."

I noticed Dion refused to make eye contact with me. I had had little contact with slaves before that point in my life. A few worked in Avus Lucius' forges. When we visited, I had seen them scurrying about from a distance, but that was as close as I had ever come. I knew slaves had no rights in Roman society; they were considered mere property under Roman law. As poor as we were, we couldn't afford to buy one, so none worked on our "estate." But, Dion looked like a man to me, and from what I saw strewn across his worktable, a man with skills and a better education than I had.

"Dion, I'm no one's *dominus*. I work on a farm, and now I'm your student. Just call me Gai. *Bene*, okay?"

"That is kind of you, *Domine*," he answered, still not meeting my eye, "but the *magister* does not permit—"

"*Pediceatur*! Screw him!" I interrupted, rubbing the welts he had left on my arm. "What the Stick doesn't know, he doesn't know! This'll be our deal. In this room it's 'Gai' and 'Dion'! *Bene*?"

"'The Stick'?" Dion queried. I thought I saw a slight grin flee across his face. He quickly recovered, though. "Very well. *Bene*! If that's what you want, *Domi* . . . I mean, Gai."

"*Bene*! It's a deal," I said, offering him my hand.

Dion stared briefly at my proffered hand, then hesitantly grasped it.

Dion explained to me that I should come to his room each morning at the third hour of the day. He would set aside three hours each day to work with me. We could start the next day, if I desired, and begin with my "ah-bay-kays," as he called them. He said that since I already spoke the language, once I learned the sounds of the letters and began to recognize words I already knew, I'd be reading in no time.

Since I didn't even know what "ah-bay-kays" were, I was not as optimistic about my prospects as was Dion. But, since I believed this reading stuff would get me out of my daily chores around the farm, I pretended to be excited about the whole prospect of sitting in a mansion and playing games with paper.

Dion led me back toward the *peristylium*. As soon as I could find my own way, he faded back into the gloom of the house like a wraith from the underworld.

When I entered the garden area, Mama and the senator stood up suddenly, as if I had startled them.

"Ah, he returns," Gabinius said. I noticed that the fat man was a bit more flushed than before I had left. "Has Stephanos taken good care of you?"

"Yes, sir," I answered. My upper arm still smarted. "Thank you, *multas gratias*, for this, Senator."

"Good . . . good," he responded. "Your mother and I have concluded our business, I think." He looked over to Mama, who gave him the slightest smile and nod. "Regrettably, I must get back to my own affairs. *Officium pro re publica*, the demands of duty for the state, do not cease because I am in the country. Let me have my man drive you back to your estate in my carriage."

"That is most kind and thoughtful of you, Aulus," Mama agreed.

Suddenly remembering that we had left our farm cart hidden about a mile down the road, I was about to say something when Mama's sandal, again driving into my ankle, silenced me.

We took our leave of the senator. As we were following his *maior domus* back out toward the vestibule and the senator's waiting carriage, Mama hissed in my ear, "Not a word! I'll send you back for our wagon when we get home."

IV.

De Doctrina Romana

MY EDUCATION AS A ROMAN—
AND A FEW OTHER THINGS

*I*f I thought that my education as a Roman gentleman was going to relieve me from my daily chores, I was soon disabused of that notion. Papa, as always, agreed with Mama's arrangements—whatever they were—on the condition that I had my chores finished before I left for the senator's estate.

I calculated that if I had to meet Dion at the third hour and needed about one summer hour to cover the distance between our places, I had to be on the march by the second hour of the morning. I could get through my chores in a little less than three summer hours, so I calculated that I had to roll out of bed and have my ass moving by the eleventh hour of the night—what we in the legions called "the hour when the whores go home and soldiers go to work."

On my first day as a student, I learned the full extent of Mama's arrangement with the senator. In exchange for my "liberal education," I was expected to do chores around his estate, too, so not only did I fail to escape my own chores by agreeing to become a "young Roman gentleman," but I had doubled them! I was so exhausted by the end of each day, that I don't remember ever seeing the sun set that entire summer.

Dion was right, though. Once I learned my letters and the sound each one made, recognizing words came along quickly. Dion scratched basic words into a wax slate and had me sound them out.

"*Bene*, very good, Gai!" he encouraged. "Let's try this one next."

"Em ah tay eh air," I named the letters. "Em says mmm, so that's . . . mmm . . . ah . . . teh . . . air . . . *mater* . . . mother!"

"*Bene*," Dion agreed, scratching down my next word on his slate. "See what you can do with this one!"

"Let's see . . . pay . . . ah . . . tay . . . eh . . . air . . . pay says peh . . . ah . . . teh . . . air . . . *pater* . . . father!"

It wasn't all clear sailing, though. I had to learn the difference between sounding like some Gallic hick from the Padus Valley and a real Roman nob.

"This one's going to be a bit tricky," Dion warned, scratching down another word.

"Just bring it on, Dion," I boasted. "Let's see . . . u . . . ee . . . day . . . eh . . . oh . That says . . . we . . . day . . . oh . . . *wideo*. I don't get that one. Oh, wait . . . that's *video*, meaning 'I see.'"

"That's the way the word's pronounced up here," Dion warned. "Down in Rome, it's pronounced *wideo*. Don't let the Sti . . . I mean, the *magister* . . . hear you say *video*. He won't like it . . . and you know what that means."

Unconsciously, I rubbed my upper arm.

Within a couple of weeks, Dion had me reading elementary sentences.

"MAH tair Pah trem WEE det, *mater patrem videt*," I read. "Mother sees father."

"*Bene*," Dion prompted me. "Now, the next one."

"Uhhh . . . PAH tair MAH trem WEE det, *pater matrem videt*. That's 'father sees mother.'"

Again, there were some "cultural" issues.

"Dion . . . I don't understand something here. Why does the sentence read, '*Pater matrem videt*' with the verb, *videt*, coming after what is seen? Up here, we'd just say, '*Pater videt matrem*,' just like in Gallic, '*Tah gweld mam*.'"

"Hmmm . . . two things, Gai," Dion advised. "First, you're thinking too much like a Gaul. Latin's different . . . and don't ever use Gallic in front of the *magister*. He thinks he's a Greek and barely tolerates Latin. The sound of Gallic will push him over the edge. The other thing is, down in Rome, they like to place their verbs at the end of their sentences. They call that 'rhetoric.' It's supposed to build up anticipation in the hearer. You'll learn all about that from the *magister* when the time comes."

"Wait a minute," I responded. "The *magister thinks* he's a Greek? I thought he was a Greek. His name's Stephanos, isn't it?"

Dion actually snorted at that. "The *magister* has never even seen the coast of Attica. He's from a city down in Italy called Neapolis. They used to be a colony of the city of Syracuse in Sicily, which itself was merely a colony of Corinth in the Peloponnese. Neapolis was taken over by some hill tribes in Italy, then the Romans. Now they spend their time pretending to be Greeks and playing the whore to rich Romans. The senator has a villa down there, on the great bay. That's how Steph—I mean, the *magister,* attached himself to this *familia*."

"But, you're a Greek, aren't you, Dion?" I blurted out. I had not yet learned that one never asks slaves about their origins. Most don't know. For the rest, it's too painful.

Dion looked at me for a long second, then sighed. "My mother was brought back as a slave from Athens when your general, Sulla, captured the city. I was born a slave and will probably die a slave. But, in my heart, I'm an Athenian—not a puffed-up, strutting Neapolitan Greekling who writes garbage and thinks it's wisdom." Dion inclined his forehead in the direction of the piles of wax slates that cluttered his table, the *magister*'s writings.

A few weeks after this conversation, Dion demonstrated his knowledge concerning *Romanitas*, "things Roman." We were doing our regular reading drill when he presented a new word to me.

"*Bene*, Gai," he said, scratching on his wax slate. "Let's see how you do with this word." He extended the slate toward me.

"Ahhh . . . peh ee ah tay ee ah es . . . puh yay tas . . . *pietas*," I recited.

"*Bene!*" Dion encouraged. "What does *pietas* mean to Romans?"

"Duty," I answered.

"*Bene*," Dion continued. "Duty to what?"

The question confused me. I had never questioned duty before. "Duty's just . . . duty . . . an obligation . . . something you got to do," I essayed.

"Gai, you are a free man and a Roman citizen," Dion corrected. "There are no 'obligations.' 'Duty' is a virtue, *virtus*, as you Romans say, a strength in you. Does that make sense?"

"Uhhh . . . sure," I hesitated. I wasn't at all sure. I understood what Dion was saying. I just didn't know what he meant. "But, when I fail in my duty, like my chores, I get punished."

"That is true," Dion agreed, "but you are *free* to shirk your chores, if you want. Right?"

"I guess," I wavered.

"So, when you *choose* to do your chores, even if it is to escape punishment, are you not in effect exercising a *virtus*, the virtue of your labor, for your family?" he asked.

"Uhhh . . . if you put it that way . . . I can see that," I agreed.

"*Bene*," he continued, "now which do you think the gods love more: when you do your chores to escape punishment, or when you do your chores to help your family?"

"When I work to help my family?" I offered.

"*Bene*," Dion went on, "that is what the Athenian philosopher Plato suggests. But, his student Aristotle argues that it makes no difference why a person does something, as long as it benefits the *polis*, the society in which the person lives. Who do you think is correct, Gai?"

My head was beginning to spin. I wasn't sure what Dion was up to, but we had drifted miles away from simply reading the word *pietas*. "I'm not sure," I admitted.

"*Bene*," Dion said, "a school of Athenian philosophers called the Sophists teach that doubt is the first step toward *sophia*, wisdom, what you Romans call *sapientia*. As long as we doubt, we think; as long as we think, we grow intellectually; as long as we grow intellectually, we pursue wisdom."

"Dion," I asked, "I'm not sure what this has to do with *pietas*."

"*Bene*! Let us return to our discussion of *pietas*," Dion offered. "Do you agree with me that *pietas*, duty, is not only a virtue, but a virtue you share with others?"

"Sure," I agreed. By this point, I was willing to agree that up was down in order to help Dion get to the point.

"With whom is the virtue of *pietas* shared?" Dion asked.

"Uhhh," I hesitated, "my family, I guess . . . like when I do my chores to help them?"

"*Bene*!" Dion agreed. "To whom else ought the virtue of *pietas* be given?"

I thought for a few seconds, then essayed, "To the gods? When I make sacrifice?"

"*Bene*, Gai," Dion stated. "*Optime*, excellent! That is your *pietas* to the gods. Are there others?"

I was a bit stumped now. When I didn't answer, Dion suggested, "Perhaps not now, but to whom will you owe *pietas* when you assume your *toga virilis*?"

"To Rome?" I guessed.

"Yes," Dion agreed, "to Rome. To the *res publica*, the commonwealth, as you Romans describe it. For Romans, then, *pietas* is a hierarchical trinity—first the gods, then the state, then the family."

"What about me?" I challenged.

"Romans believe that only when one has satisfied one's duty to the gods, the state, and the family does one attend to one's own needs. Did not the great Roman hero, Aeneas, the one you Romans actually call *pius*, the devoted one, plunge back into the flames of Troy to rescue the *penates*, the family gods, and his blind father? Did he not abandon Dido's bed and the luxury of the Carthaginian royal court to obey the will of Iove and sail across the inner sea to establish the Roman state? This is true Roman *pietas*—gods, state, and family."

At this point, I was so out of my element, I could only nod in agreement. At that time in my life, I had no idea that duty to the gods, the eagles of Iove, the state, the Tenth Legion, my *familia*, the *gens Iulia*, and the interests of Gaius Iulius Caesar himself would soon become the focus of my life.

After my morning sessions with Dion were finished, I was given a light meal in the kitchens, usually bread and cheese left over from the household breakfast and some watered wine. After that, I completed my chores on the senator's estate. Since it wasn't a working farm and there seemed to be three slaves for every tree and blade of grass growing on the place, my tasks were light compared to what I had to do at home. Since I had some experience with horses, I soon settled in to a routine in the senator's stables. Although the senator kept over a dozen horses, the work still proved to be light. Even the horses of noble Romans didn't have to work for a living: no pulling wagons, no turning grinding stones. Gabinius' horses were used only by members of the *familia* and their guests for occasional rides through the surrounding countryside.

Every day, I mucked out the stalls, provided the horses with clean water and fresh fodder, and checked their hooves for bruising, cracks, or loose shoes. I inspected the fences around the paddocks for broken rails, protruding nails, and loose gates. Every couple of days, I cleaned the manure out of the paddocks and scrubbed the water troughs and feed buckets. In all, it meant about three hours of work each day, which I easily stretched into four. I was usually on my way back home for my dinner by the ninth hour. If I needed to stretch out my "work" time, I pretended to clean and repair the saddles and bridles hanging in the tack room behind the stables.

It was once while stretching time in this way that I met Gabinia and began my lessons on an entirely different aspect of *Romanitas*.

That afternoon, well into the seventh hour, I was sitting at the equipment table in the tack room with my back to the door. I was rubbing up some leather bridles with oil to keep them supple when I noticed some fleeting shadows suggesting that someone had entered the shack. I didn't pay much attention to this. Slaves were always coming and going, and they never called attention to themselves.

Suddenly, from behind me, I heard a girl's voice, "Oh! So this is where you're hiding, you lazy, good-for-nothing slouch? Get my horse saddled! I want to go for a ride!"

I did not imagine for a second that I was being addressed, but the novelty of a girl's voice in the tack room made me turn to look. There, just within the doorway, stood a goddess! Venus herself! The sun was behind her, transforming her white, woolen tunic into a translucent cloud barely disguising the softly rounded curves of a woman's maturing body. A teenager at the time, I had a natural and immediate reaction to this vision. I was mesmerized.

From somewhere beyond my trance, I again heard her voice, "How dare you look at me, *Serve*, Slave!" The slap on my face brought me out of my reverie.

I heard her say, "I'll have you whipped for this insolence! Now get my horse saddled."

"*Quiris sum!*" I stammered.

"What did you say?" she asked.

"*Quiris sum!*" I repeated, rubbing my cheek. "I'm a citizen, not your slave!"

"A citizen!" she stammered in turn. "Then, why are you—wait. You must be that Gallic boy from down the road, the one who's studying with Dion. I've heard about you."

While the girl was working through this new revelation, I was taking the opportunity to disguise my noticeable reaction to her and, in what was proving to be a somewhat contrary effort, get a better look at her.

She was no more than sixteen, maybe seventeen, tall for a Roman girl, just over five Roman pedes. Her light brown hair, streaked with flashes of blond by the summer sun, was pulled back into a ponytail for her ride. Her eyes had a slightly Asian cant, but they were the deepest blue I had ever seen. They seemed to glow with a light of their own. Her nose was straight but soft, with a slight upturn at the end. Her lips were red, and very full. There was a slight rouge in her cheeks from her anger upon encountering an apparently insolent slave. She was the most beautiful vision I had ever beheld in my fifteen years of existence. I almost wished I had been her slave.

I heard her say, ". . . you can understand . . . when I saw you here working, I assumed you were one of the slaves . . . we have so many . . . who can keep track . . . I must apologize for striking you . . . a lady doesn't . . ."

"If you tell me which horse is yours," I interrupted, "I'd be glad to saddle him for you, Miss . . ."

"Oh thank you . . ." she responded, "I'm Gabinia . . . the Senator's daughter . . . just call me Gabi . . . and your name is . . ."

"Gai," I interrupted again. "I'm called Gai . . ." I gathered up a saddle blanket, saddle, and the rest of the rig. "Show me which horse is yours."

"Oh, thank you so much for this, Gai," she flirted, laying her hand on my shoulder as she followed me out of the tack room "And after I was so mean to you . . . slapping you like that."

I began to realize that Gabi's response to anxiety was to talk, nonstop. How I could make a goddess nervous was beyond me. My way of dealing with the shock of having a chatty Venus appear before me was to shut up completely, so I said hardly anything. We were actually a good pair.

As I saddled her horse, she stood outside the stall, continuing to chatter on, "We've heard that Papa . . . I mean, the senator . . . had taken on a new ward . . . but we knew nothing about you. My older brother, Aulus . . . that's, of course, Aulus Iunior . . . said that you must be one of Papa's little indiscretions. He can be so mean sometimes. My little brother, Marcus, said he wanted to meet you . . . especially if you were his new brother. I told him you'd be no more than a half brother, at most. Say! What do you have left to do this afternoon?"

I was just tightening the cinch on her saddle, "Huh? What am I doing?"

"Yes . . . what are you doing this afternoon? Papa doesn't like it when I ride out alone. He says Roman ladies shouldn't bounce about the countryside unescorted. It isn't . . . *decet*. Yes, that's the word he uses . . . *non decet*. It isn't decorous. Besides, it's dangerous . . . bandits . . . runaway slaves."

"There aren't any bandits down here in the valley—" I began. Then, I realized where my interests lay, "But, your papa . . . I mean, the senator, is right. It's dangerous for a beautiful girl to be out by herself."

"*Bella?*" she interrupted, "*Bella?* You think I'm beautiful? You're so cute! Yes . . . you *must* come with me. I'd feel *so much* safer."

I didn't know how all this fit in with Dion's sense of Roman *pietas*, but at that moment, I knew exactly where my duty lay. I quickly saddled another horse and accompanied Gabi on her afternoon ride.

Such afternoon rides soon became our routine for the rest of that summer. We'd ride out, sometimes beyond the cultivated fields in the valley up to the wooded foothills of the surrounding mountains. I took to carrying one of the saddle knives in my belt. I told Gabi I had it just in case we ran into any villains in the hills. When I said that, she reached over and squeezed my arm. I felt my heart stop for a brief moment.

Soon, Gabi was visiting my dreams, and I would wake up in the middle of the night, sometimes in an embarrassing state.

I even mentioned it to Dion, who explained to me that the Greeks believe an immoderate *contemplatio* of an object of desire could have an effect both on the body, the *soma*, he called it in Greek, and on the *psyche*, the mind. The latter seizes on the vision of the desired one as captured by the eyes and creates a *phantasma* in the mind. Such *phantasma* can appear in dreams. As for the body, such an *obsessio* causes an imbalance of the four essential bodily humors: the hot, the cold, the dry, and the wet. The occurrences I was experiencing in the night were not shameful at all. They were merely the body's natural way of discharging the superfluity of the hot and the wet humors.

I don't know if any of this helped much, but as I listened intently, my vocabulary was increasing in leaps and bounds.

One afternoon, I decided to show Gabi my special, secret place in the foothills. Up in the hills, there was a spring in a hidden valley. Gran'pa had told me that it was a place where the old ones used to come to worship. The spring was sacred to one of the water goddesses. If you went there and called her name aloud, she would appear and grant you immeasurable riches. When I brought Gabi to the spring for the first time, the midsummer flowers under the green shade of the forest trees were blooming purple, white, and yellow. As we led our horses into the fold in the narrow valley, we could hear the spring playing over the mossy river stones. Her horse shuddered and whinnied. I told her that it was a sign that the goddess was near.

I never saw the goddess, but I did have Gabi at my side.

It wasn't long before our "enchanted grove," as Gabi called it, became our regular destination for our afternoon rides. Gabi began packing little picnic bundles, usually bread, cheese, and some fruit. Occasionally, she'd smuggle some wine from the kitchens, which she hardly bothered to mix with water. We became quite giggly at times—not a condition that Gran'pa would condone for "a warrior of the Gallic *fianna*," but had he seen Gabi, I'm sure he'd understand. The wine seemed to loosen many of the bonds that constrained us, but we didn't do anything more than hold hands while we talked. Occasionally, Gabi would give my arm a playful squeeze, or she would allow her hand to rest high up on my shoulders, giving the back of my neck playful rubs. I lived for those moments. I suppose I was falling in love with her, but only the way a boy of fifteen can love, with no inkling of what it meant or where it might lead. It was a pure and innocent love.

Conversation with Gabi really meant listening to her stories about living in Rome. She would share with me what her girlfriends thought and who was doing what to whom in Roman society. It made sense, really; having lived in the boondocks of the Padus Valley left me with little that would in any way interest such a sophisticated and worldly Roman noble woman.

Sometimes, while we sat in our enchanted grove and drank the golden, honeyed ichor of the gods from a leather bottle she had snuck out of the kitchens, she would read from the letters sent to her by girlfriends down in Rome. The letters were filled with gossip: who was dating whom, who got betrothed, whose baby so-and-so was really carrying, which of the nobility were bed-hopping. All of it was pretty much silly girl-stuff as far as I was concerned, but it seemed to interest Gabi, so I pretended it interested me.

From her stories, I learned that all the girls in Rome were mad over a rogue named Clodius. At one time he had been a patrician, named Claudius, but he fell deeply and hopelessly in love with a beautiful commoner, a freedman's daughter, named Chloe. His father refused to let them marry and threatened to disown Claudius if he didn't abandon Chloe, his true love. Claudius defied his father and became a commoner so he could marry his beloved. But, alas, a villain named Milo, who was the hireling of Clodius' father, kidnapped the beloved Chloe and imprisoned her in a secret dungeon somewhere deep within the bowels of the *subura*, a villainous area in Rome where Milo and his gang of cutthroats held sway. Clodius formed his own band of noble villains, good-hearted rogues who stole only from the rich so they could feed the poor. With them, he waged an unceasing war against Milo and his evil band in order to rescue his beloved, Chloe.

"Aurelia says that Clodius is so handsome that he is called *Pulcher*, the Handsome One," Gabi sighed, putting down the latest missive from her girlfriend in Rome. She was holding my hand so tightly that I was beginning to lose feeling in my fingers—and I loved it.

"*Pulcher* . . . Perhaps I should be known as *Pulchra*," she sighed, taking my numbed hand and actually placing it between her breasts. "What do you think, Gai? Am I *Pulchra*, the Beautiful One?"

It was at this point I fully appreciated Dion's grammar lessons.

"No, not *Pulchra*," I said. I delayed for a heartbeat or two to let that sink in, then employed the full force of my juvenile, Gallic charm. "You are *illa pulchrissima*, the *Most* Beautiful One!"

Those bottomless blue eyes bore into me for a few heartbeats, then she squealed, "*Si dulce*! You are so sweet!" She kissed me on the side of my mouth. "*Dulcissime*!"

I did not sleep much that night.

A week or so later, Gabi and I were again hidden away in our magic grove. We had finished our meal of bread, cheese, and a strange, brown, shriveled but sweet fruit that Gabi called *ficus*, figs. She said that her father, the senator, had obtained them from the Greek lands in the East, through a political associate of his named Pompey. She had managed a skin of a light, sweet wine, she called *Lunense*. I was beginning to feel myself drift a bit into that happy, detached state of mind that a few swallows of unwatered wine brings on. A fly was lazily buzzing in and out of the dusty sunbeams that reached down to the forest floor. A faint perfume of summer flowers wafted on a gentle breeze as Gabi read a letter that had just arrived from Marcia, a friend of hers in Rome.

"Marcia says all the girls are just mad about this poet, Catullus. He's so . . . so . . . wicked, the way he writes. Marcia sent me a copy of his latest poem. She calls it *Basia*, "Kisses." He wrote it for his pitiless and uncaring mistress, Lesbia.

I don't think that's her real name. Do you want to hear it, Gai? Should I read it to you?"

"Yes, Gabi . . . please," I responded. The last thing in the world I was interested in was some syrupy poem about kisses by some preening poet and his make-believe girlfriend. But, it excited Gabi, so it was alright with me.

"Oh, I just knew you'd want to hear it, Gai," she said, squeezing my hand, "Listen."

Gabi coughed slightly to clear her throat and began:

Vivamus, mea Lesbia, atque amemus,
Rumoresque senum severiorum
Omnes unius aestimemus assis.
Let us live and love, my Lesbia;
Let not all the empty words
Of dour old men deter us from desire.
The sun can set and rise again;
When our brief light is gone,
We'll sleep in eternal night.
So, kiss me a thousand times!
Then give me a hundred more!
A thousand more!
Hundreds after those!
Cover me, cover me
In thousands
And hundreds,
And thousands again!
When we have kissed countless times,
Kiss me, kiss me anew!
We dare not stop,
We dare not speak
In the heat of our desire!
The world could only envy us,
And cool the fire of our kisses.

When I knew she was done reading the thing, I opened my eyes. Gabi's face looked pink—flushed. She seemed to be having difficulty breathing—panting a bit. I sat up.

"Are you okay, Gabi?" I asked.

"Oh . . . okay? I'm more than okay, Gai," she said somewhat breathlessly. "*Quam Bella*! How beautiful . . . '*Da mi basia mille, deinde centum*; Give me a thousand kisses, then a hundred.' How he must love her!"

Suddenly, she turned to me; she took hold of my arm. "Do you know how to kiss, Gai? Would you like to kiss me?" she breathed.

I felt the ground falling away from beneath my feet. "I . . . uhhh—"

"Kiss me, Gai . . . *da mi basia . . . mille . . . dien centum* . . . kiss me." Her fingernails were digging into my arm.

I puckered my lips and began to bend into her.

"Not that way, silly," she said bringing her hand up to my lips. "Don't pucker like that. Relax your mouth. Yes . . . now . . . don't clench your teeth. Open them slightly for me."

I had no idea what she was talking about. Her hand moved under my chin, softly caressing the side of my face. She moved into me. Her lips pressed gently against mine. I pressed back softly. "That's good . . . good," she murmured.

Then I felt her tongue dart into my mouth. I recoiled a bit, but she now had her hand behind my head. "No . . . no . . . silly," she whispered, "play with me . . . with your tongue. Play with me."

Our tongues began to wage a mock battle. Suddenly, she thrust into me, then quickly withdrew. I pursued, reengaged, teased. She thrust again. Somewhere deep inside me a heat was building—the wet and the hot. It kept building. Gabi's fingers were raking my arm. Her other hand was tangled in my hair, pulling it slightly. Our tongues dueled: thrust, retreat, pursuit, thrust again. Gabi was panting, "*Basme*. . . kiss me . . . yes . . . yes . . . *basme*."

I felt Gabi's hand move down from my arm. She moved down and under the hem of my tunic. Her hand rested on my loin cloth. "Ah," she seemed to growl, "I must be doing this right." Her hand began to caress me gently.

"Touch me . . . touch me," she breathed.

When I didn't react, she reached up, took hold of my hand, and placed it on her breast. "Stroke me. Stroke me like this," she murmured.

I began to fondle her. She pressed herself more deeply into my hand. "*Dulce, dulce*, gently, *caro . . . dulce.*" She pressed her lips harder into me.

Gabi thrust herself into my hand, more insistently, urgently: "*Dure! Dure!* Rub Harder! Harder!*" She pulled away the folds of linen under my tunic. The fingers of her other hand were raking the back of my neck. "*Dure! Dure!*"

Suddenly, our lips parted. Gabi was falling back, away from me. She lay back, crushing the moss and flowers of the forest floor. Her hand, tangled in my hair, pulled me down to her. I was Orpheus dragged by Eurydice down into terrifying depths, yet I wanted to pursue. I did not want her to release me. Her eyes were closed. She was panting. She fumbled with something under the hem of her tunic, lifted her hips from the ground, and quickly lay back down.

Suddenly her eyes opened. They stared up at me. I felt as if I were staring into the depth of an endless, blue abyss—a cold, bottomless sea. It was as if she were looking at me for the first time. Then came the recognition, the realization. She let go of me and brought her hand up and placed her palm in the center of my chest. She pushed gently, "No . . . No . . . this is not right."

She pushed back harder. "No, this cannot be," she stated. "Gai . . . get off me . . . please. Get off me!"

I pulled myself back onto my knees. My hand lifted away from her breast as she untangled herself, lifting her leg over my knees and sitting up. She pulled the hem of her tunic down and fussed with its bodice.

"This was a mistake," she said, to no one in particular, as she reached up and brushed leaves and crushed moss out of her hair.

Without another word, she stood up, walked down to where we had left our horses, and began to lead her horse down out of the valley.

I was still kneeling on the ground with the evidence of her caresses still quite apparent in my body. I straightened out my clothes as best I could in my condition. I began to pick up the remains of our picnic and stuff them into the leather sack we had brought from the villa. By the time I got to my own horse and hung the sack across the saddle horns, Gabi was out of sight down the valley.

Although I did my best to catch up, I caught sight of her only at a distance as she approached her father's estate. By the time I reached the stables, she had already given her horse to one of the stable boys and retreated back into the house.

I had no idea what had just transpired.

I did know that what we had done in some way displeased the gods, for within less than an hour, I was in agony. The place under my tunic where Gabi had touched me felt as if it had swollen to three times its normal size. In pain, I made my way home.

V.

De Amice Novo
A NEW FRIEND

*G*abi did not show up for her ride the next day. I was a bit relieved when she didn't. I hadn't really gotten over what had happened the day before. It confused and frightened me.

But, when she didn't show again the next day, I became concerned. Had she decided she no longer wanted anything to do with me? What had I done wrong? Was it my inexperience in these, these things? Was she embarrassed by what happened? Did she consider me unredeemably awkward? Ugly? Too much an unsophisticated bumpkin to bother with?

When she didn't appear on the third day, I decided to march over to the main house and see if I could straighten this thing out. As I approached the house from the rear, near the entrance to the kitchens, I saw the senator's *vilicus*, his estate bailiff, a rough-looking character named Macro. When he spotted me, he quickly ended his conversation with a slave and walked over to me.

"Hey, lad!" he called with a somewhat lopsided grin. "I was wondering how long it would take you to show up!"

As he approached, I got a good look at him for the first time. His lopsided grin was caused by a jagged scar that ran down the side of his face from his right eye to the side of his mouth. He advanced with a wobbly gait as if his left leg was constantly trying to turn slightly to the right. His working tunic showed the signs of hard labor, mended rents and tears, frayed hems, and faded stains. The skin on his face, arms, and legs was stained brown by years of exposure to sun and wind, brown except for a number of thin, irregular white lines running along both his forearms, and the serrated tear of the white scar that ran down his face.

He caught me looking at his scar and unconsciously reached up and rubbed it. "*Ista mentula*, the prick who did that, was left-handed. Snuck in on my open side with one of those curved *sica* those Thracian *cunni* like to carry. Can't come at you like a man with a *pugio*, a real soldier's blade. Those *cunni* got no *virtus* . . . no hair on their balls. You're here looking for the Lady Gabinia, right?"

This was more information than I could process all at once, and Macro was now standing within two palms of me. To my surprise, I noticed that he was no taller than I was; he just seemed bigger. "I . . . er . . . yes . . . I came to see if Gabi, I mean the Lady Gabinia, wanted to go for her afternoon ride, sir."

"I bet you did!" he laughed "I bet you did! And, don't call me sir! I still have to work for a living. Just call me Macro. The Lady Gabinia won't be takin' no more rides up into the hills with randy young lads like you. She's gone back to Rome. She's living in her husband's house."

"Her husband's house?" I stammered "She's married? That can't be. She's too young."

"I don't know if the torches have been lit yet," Macro interrupted, "but the dowry's been decided and the gifts exchanged. That's the way the nobs down in Rome do it. She's been bundled off to her husband's house . . . some purple-striper with three names who's tied to her father in the senate. Easy duty for a girl. The old fart probably hasn't gotten it up in years . . . but she's got to be delivered *intacta* . . . *whole*, if you get my drift. So no more riding out into the hills with the likes of you."

"We never did—" I started.

Macro raised his hand for me to be silent. "I don't give a shit what you did or didn't do! It's the girl's reputation, get it? Once she's married, she can shag every gladiator and actor in Rome. Then it's stylish . . . but until she's married, she's as much a virgin as if she were toasting her breakfast roll on Vesta's flame. That's the way it is, boy. Just be glad nobody knows you're involved. Get it?"

I was dumbfounded by all this. "What they got you doing over in the stables?" Macro asked, changing the subject abruptly.

"Uh . . . feeding the horses . . . mucking out the stables—" I started.

"Pah!" he interrupted. "I got slaves to shovel horse shit. From now on, you work for me . . . after that Greek *fellator*, Dion, is done with you—"

"*Fellator* . . . Dion?" I interrupted.

Macro looked at me for a long second. "He's a Greek, ain't he?" he challenged. "They're all *fellatores*. Even that *mentula* who calls himself *magister*, the master . . . pah. All of them . . . *fellatores*. Why do you think the boys called Alexander 'The Great'?" He chuckled at his own joke. "Anyway . . . when you're done with Dion and have had something to eat, come find me. I keep my *mensa*, my office, in the back of the main house, next to the kitchen. Just ask the cook. He'll show you."

So began my apprenticeship as an assistant *vilicus* under the tutelage of Macro.

Macro wasn't a bad sort, a little rough around the edges, but not a bad sort at all. He didn't push the slaves on the estate too hard. In fact, he treated them pretty much the same way he had treated his men when he was an *optio*, an under-officer, in the Third Legion in Syria. He gave his orders, clear and simple, and expected them to be carried out. If for any reason he didn't like what he saw, he said something. If the correction wasn't made, he placed his boot firmly up the ass of the offender. That usually did the trick. Under Macro, there hadn't been a beating or flogging on the estate in years. And, most of the slaves knew an easy berth when they saw it. Cooperate and life was good. That was Macro's motto.

Macro had been cashiered from the legions for combat injuries some ten years before. As he told it, some Greek son-of-a-bitch got in under his shield during a skirmish up in the hills near Armenia and hamstrung him, which explained

Macro's limp and his attitude toward Greeks. It had been a meaningless fight. Mithridates had already been defeated and had run off over the mountains into Colchis. A band of his Greek mercenaries, who had become tired of running, decided it was nobler to die together than to surrender—something right out of an epic poem. So, Macro's cohort accommodated their wishes, but the endeavor ended Macro's career. There was nothing the legionary *medici*, the medics, could do for him. On a damaged leg, he couldn't hump all the equipment, weapons, and armor of a legionary for the expected twenty-thousand *passus* a day of marching. Fortunately, his tribune, a young purple-striper named Aulus Gabinius, took him into his *familia*, giving him the job as the *vilicus* on his country estate in the Padus Valley.

So, Macro's *pietas* necessitated his loyalty to Gabinius, his *patronus*, and to his *familia*.

Besides, Macro knew a good deal when he fell into it. The estate he supervised was mostly decorative. He had no annual crop quota to fill. He only had to ensure that the household was ready and operated smoothly when the *familia* was in residence. Additionally, he had to see to it that the lawns were cut, the trees trimmed, and the horses healthy and ready to ride. The slaves were well fed and not overworked, so they were content. The only recent crisis in Macro's life was that some local, wet-behind-the-ears, half-Gallic teenager began sneaking off into the hills with the patron's betrothed daughter and skins full of unwatered wine. Nothing good could come of that.

On my first day under Macro's tutelage, he took me on a tour of Gabinius' estate. Macro rode a horse like most Romans I had seen—all legs, no balance, bent at the waist, and trying to cling to the horse with his lower legs. He was in a constant struggle to keep his balance, even at times grabbing handfuls of the horse's mane to stay onboard.

I already knew most of the estate, including the stables, paddocks, and the lawns leading up to the house. To the west, a stream that ran through the property had been diverted into a network of channels and sluices to keep the vegetable gardens irrigated. The gardens grew mostly cabbages, carrots, lettuces, cauliflower, and broccoli, some onions, radishes, and cucumbers. Although mainly used to feed the slaves, the gardens also supplied fresh vegetables for fancy dishes when the *patronus* and his *familia* were in residence.

Past the garden on the other side of the stream was a small grove of fruit trees, of which Macro was quite proud. He told me the *patronus* had brought the original trees back with him from the East. They had been a gift from his mentor and commander in the war with Mithridates, Lucullus *Imperator*. They produced a fruit called *cerasa*, cherries. Being a few days passed the Calends of Quintilius, the fruit was just beginning to ripen. Macro showed me the small, round, reddish-green fruit hanging from the shady boughs of the trees. He plucked one and bit into it, quickly spitting out the meat. "Pah! Not ripe enough yet," he grimaced. "Another week or two and then we have to be quick with these to beat the birds. I expect to see the *patronus* up here soon after we harvest the fruit."

Then he turned to me and said, "Follow me. There's something special I want to show you." He wobbled along atop his horse, following the stream in the direction of a small ridge in the distance.

When we reached the ridge, I noticed a small, cleared area facing south. Macro managed to dismount without any incident and walked toward the clearing. "*Veni mecum.* Come on with me," he called over his shoulder.

I followed him to the cleared area. Then, he gestured to some short plants growing alongside the hill and said with some seeming pride, "So! What do you think of that?"

I had no idea what I was looking at.

"Those are grapevines," he said, or rather, insisted. "Grapevines! Growing up here in Gaul! The Padus Valley! This is the third season they've come back!"

"Uh . . . great," I agreed, not knowing why it was great.

"Don't you get it?" he asked. "Grapevines! If we can cultivate grapes up here, we can make wine."

He saw the blank look on my face.

"Wine's a valuable commodity," he explained. "Liquid gold. Romans love it. They can't get enough of it. There's always a market."

"But, we've always grown wheat—" I started.

"Exactly!" Macro insisted. "Wheat for bread. But, the Romans import tons of wheat from Sicily and Africa . . . even from Egypt . . . so that keeps the prices low. Now they're building these huge plantations down in Italy. *Latifundia*, they call them . . . all slave labor. You independent farmers up here won't be able to compete with them. Pretty soon, if you keep growing wheat, the Romans'll be up here buying your land for bronze *asses* on the denarius in order to consolidate all these little farms and start *latifundia* up here. It's inevitable. That's what they did down South in Italy. But, if we could start cultivating grapes . . . producing our own wine, we could break the cycle. You see?"

I wasn't sure I did, but I knew I had heard my father complaining about the prices he had been getting for his crops—and that with all the debt we had taken on to build Mama's Roman dream house.

Macro continued, "I was sure we could do this. Look. See this tree here? It's an *ilex* . . . a holly oak you Gauls call it. A buddy of mine in the legion, his family grew grapes. He said wherever the *ilex*'ll grow, the grapes'll grow. Just keep the plants high on a ridge or a hill. The winter mists that form in the valleys poison them. On a hill or a ridge that faces south, the grapes'll grow. I never forgot his advice, and look. He was right. Look at my babies here. Three years they've been coming back. This is the year I should start seeing more fruit."

Macro pulled back one of the leaves and exposed a large, thick cluster of small, green grapes.

Macro went on, "The *patronus* is behind me on this. Says if I can make it work, it's mine. He only wants a small percentage for the use of his land and slaves. But to really make it big, I've got to bring in a few of the local farmers . . . kind of a partnership. We could build a common press . . . share the storage facilities where we ferment and age the wine . . . a cooperative where we all share in the labor and in the profits. We could work under the patron's protection. Our first market could be Mediolanum. Do you think your old man'd be interested in joining in?"

My head was spinning: wine, grapes, *ilex* oaks. It all sounded very Roman, so Mama would probably love the idea, and Papa'd hate it—which meant we'd do it. "I . . . uh . . . could ask him," I stammered.

"Good . . . you do that. Let me know what he says," Macro encouraged. "Better yet, let me talk to him. We could bring him up here to see my plants. I'm telling you, kid, we could make a fortune, and the patron's behind us."

Later that night, at dinner on our *peristylium*, which was merely a patio on the south side of our house, I broached the subject with Papa.

"Grapes!" Papa exclaimed. "You can't grow grapes here. Winters are too cold."

"Grapes," my older brother muttered, shaking his head disapprovingly.

"Let's hear this out," Mama said. "I'm interested."

"Hear what out, Valeria?" Papa challenged. "You can't grow grapes here."

"Grapes," my older brother snorted.

"Well," Mama came back, "the man is obviously growing *something* up there on the ridge. Gai saw it."

"I don't know what Gai saw . . . probably some weed that looks like grapes. The woods here are full of them," Papa said.

"Probably weeds," my older brother snickered. "Gai thought they was grapes."

"*Were* grapes," Mama corrected. "Don't start talking like some *paganus* who just rolled off his hilltop, Luc. You're a Roman! Act like one!" Then back to my father, "If you're so sure that grapes can't be cultivated here, why don't you go over to Gabinius' estate tomorrow and see for yourself?"

"What's the point?" Papa challenged.

"What's the point?" Mama came right back. "Aren't you paying attention? That man is right! If the price of wheat goes down any further, I don't know how we're going to make ends meet. The point is . . . don't dismiss an opportunity until you've at least examined it! That's the Roman spirit. That's what made our people great!"

"Our people—" Papa started, then realized that it was a fight he was not possibly going to win. He surrendered quickly. "Alright, Valeria, I'll take a ride out there tomorrow." Then to me, "What time are you finished with your schoolwork?"

"*Meridies*, the middle hour of the day, Papa," I said.

"*Bene*! I'll come over after the middle hour. You think your friend, this Macro, will have time to show me his *grapes*?" Papa asked with just enough sarcasm to slip past Mama.

"Grapes," my older brother chortled, then stopped suddenly as he felt Mama's full glare. Sarcasm about something Mama thought important was a privilege of the *pater familias*, not the oldest son.

"He'll make the time for you, Papa. I'm sure."

The next day, at about the seventh hour, Macro took my Papa and me up to the ridge to see his grape plants.

"*Mercule*," Papa said, looking down at the immature, bright-green clusters of fruit. "By Hecules' arse! They're grapes! You say that this is their third growing season?"

"*Sic*,'" Macro confirmed, "and we look to have a pretty decent crop this year."

"Are you sure they'll ripen?" Papa asked.

"Can't see why not," Macro shrugged. "We had bits of fruit growing last year—not enough to call a crop, but they all ripened. Was not as sweet as the stuff that grows down in Italy, but good."

"*Mercule*!" Papa repeated. "This could work if the fruit ripens before the frosts . . . and we have at least until after the Ides of October before we have have to worry about that. Tell me again about this plan of yours."

"Simple," Macro replied, "we enlist local farmers to grow the grapes, and we harvest together and press them for the juice. We can press the pulp for the cheaper stuff. We might have to boil the juice to make it sweeter."

"Wait," Papa interrupted. "I know this guy in Mediolanum. He's a freedman who runs a tavern near the East Road Gate. Says he worked making wine down in *Tyrrhenia*, down in Italy. Claims he knows everything there is to know about making wine. If we could convince him to come in with us—and that tavern's a real dive. He can't be making much at it."

I was mildly shocked to learn of Papa's knowledge of Mediolanum's dives, but not enough to miss his reference: *nos*, we. Macro noticed too.

"*Euge*!" Macro interrupted. "Great! But first things first. We've got to grow a crop. Do you have any land where the grapes'll grow . . . high ground . . . facing south . . . with a good source of water?"

Before Papa could say anything, I interrupted, "*A Brin o Der'oo* . . . the Hill of the Oaks . . . the ridgeline north of the house where the pigs root for acorns. There's a small stream that runs down off the ridge."

"*Bene*!" Papa chimed in. "We could grow the grapes up there and still bring in all the wheat."

"Is the ridge clear?" Macro asked me.

"No," I said.

"That's not a problem," Macro replied. "I could send a gang of my boys over to your place to do the clearing and plant the vines. Luc, do you have an ox?"

"Sure," Papa said. "We use it for the spring plowing."

"Good," Macro said. "We'll use your ox to clear the stumps. When do you think we can get started?"

"Right away," Papa chimed in. "We're only busy with cleanup and repair around the farm until the time the crop comes in in September."

"*Optime*!" Macro said. "I can get the boys to do most of the chopping and digging. We can split the lumber and firewood between us. All you've got to do is make sure that the plants are well watered 'til the roots take. Make sure you keep the deer away. Mix up some garlic and dog piss in water. Spread it out around the plants—no closer than three, maybe four paces. I found that works well enough. Just make sure my boys get plenty of water while they're working . . . and maybe some extra food during the day—nothing fancy, maybe some bread and a little cheese. That'll keep them happy. I'll provide the tools."

So it was in this way we were launched into the wine business. Papa talked up the deal with a couple of our neighbors, who then threw in with us. Macro's "boys" were going to be busy all summer. In fact, when Mama told him about it, Avus Lucius liked the idea so much that he promised to build the press and the storage sheds for a "small piece of the action."

The thought occurred to me that, with all the money we were going to bring in with the wine business, I could probably stop being a Roman schoolboy and stay on the farm as Macro's assistant. But, I soon discovered that the Fates had a different plan for me.

After matriculating from Dion's instruction to the *magister*'s classroom, I studied with the senator's younger son, an eleven-year-old named Marcus.

Gabinius' older son, Aulus Iunior, had already assumed his *toga virilis* and was down in Rome being groomed by his father for his public career. Gabi, the Lady Gabinia, was, of course, also down in Rome, living with her husband's family, her reputation secure from the wild Gallic boys who roam around the Padus Valley. Romans don't waste effort on educating girls—at least not in anything more complicated than weaving and spindling, which is what proper Roman matrons do when they're not "shagging gladiators," as Macro so eloquently put it.

According to the *magister*, Roman gentlemen had to master three skills or *artes*: grammar, dialectic, and rhetoric. Grammar is the mechanics of Latin; dialectic is the proper method of thought and analysis; and rhetoric is the elegant use of language to persuade, praise, and entertain.

When I joined the lessons, we were reading Asellio's histories on the last war with Carthage, a good text for a fifteen-year-old Gallic bumpkin who had just learned his "ah-bay-kays." I knew most of the vocabulary, and the sentences weren't all that confusing. I discovered three things very quickly, though. First, the *magister's* instruction was for the benefit of young Marcus; I was just along for the ride. Second, young Marcus wasn't the brightest torch in the room. And third, when Marcus made mistakes, the *magister* took it out on me. The *magister's* goal was not Cato's call to arms, *Carthago delenda est*: Carthage must be destroyed. But rather, *Paganus delendus est*: The bumpkin must be destroyed! There were days after class when I could hardly raise my arms after the many swipes of the *magister's* stick, most in response to Marcus' errors. I began to wonder if the little shit got a kick out of seeing me caned.

Ever since my rides with Gabi, I had taken to carrying one of the saddle knives in my belt when I was working around the estate. I guess it allowed me a bit of a swagger to wear the thing. One day, while I was with Macro supervising some of his "boys" as they set up a sluice to water the grapevines, he noticed the knife in my belt.

"What's the pig-sticker for?" he asked nodding toward the knife.

"Uhh . . . oh . . . you never know when it'll come in handy," I stammered, realizing my subtle affectation with the knife had been noticed.

"Pah . . . the only thing a dress pin like that is good for is picking your teeth," Macro chuckled. "In the legions, the guys carry a real blade, a *pugio.*"

Macro pulled a blade out of the sheath hanging from his thick, leather soldier's belt. It was leaf-shaped, double-edged, a good three palms long and almost two wide. The steel was flawlessly polished, not a spot of rust, and the razor-sharp edges caught the sun as Macro drew it.

"This is the mark of a soldier, Gai," Macro was saying. "No legionary would go anywhere without his *pugio.* You could shave with this thing. Here! Feel that edge."

Macro handed me the *pugio,* handle first. Gingerly, I touched one of the edges; it was like a razor. Quickly, I handed it back to him, so as not to cut myself with it and prove myself even more of a wet-behind-the-ears hick.

Macro slid the *pugio* back into its sheath. "That's a Roman soldier's blade, Gai," he said. "It'll protect you in a tight spot."

I was soon to find out how right Macro was.

VI.

De Natale Sexto Decimo

I TURN SIXTEEN
AND LEARN A TRADE

*O*n the Ides of Quintilius, during the consulship of Gaius Iulius Caesar and Marcus Calpurnius Bibulus, the sixteenth anniversary of my birth was celebrated.

I expected it to be the beginning of the most auspicious year of my life. Not only was our erstwhile *patronus*, Caesar, the lead consul of the Roman state, thus increasing the *auctoritas*, the prestige, of our entire family, but the very next month of *Martis*, two days after the Ides, on the feast of *Liberalia*, I would be receiving my *toga virilis* and become a man in Roman society!

A most auspicious year!

There's a saying among soldiers: "Be careful what you ask the gods for because you might get it." In several months, I would get my first lesson in the truth of the saying.

But, that was still some months away, and there was a birthday to celebrate.

Mama had a maid by this time. She was the youngest daughter of one of our neighbors who had a small place up in the hills. She had been fostered out because her family just couldn't feed her, and she was little use around the farm. So, Mama took her in as a house servant and maid for the cost of three meals a day, a cot in one of the pantries, and Mama's cast-off clothes. Her real name was Aiofe, but Mama gave her a Roman name, Amanda. She was twelve or maybe thirteen. Even she wasn't quite sure.

Mama and Amanda spent my birthday morning preparing a feast for the family and making the special sweet cakes that are traditional for a birthday. Avus Lucius did not come. He claimed his business interests wouldn't allow him the time away from the city. But, he had sent a package several days earlier that I was anxious to open.

Around the fifth hour, I was surprised to see a horse, with Macro precariously balanced on its back, approaching the house. I had been excused from my duties on Gabinius' estate, despite the *magister*'s sour dismissal of birthdays as some decadent Roman carnival. I would have told him that we Gah'el celebrate birthdays too, but that would have resulted in an extra caning, and I had already had enough of those with Marcus' mispronunciations and his misuse of the subjunctive in clauses of purpose. But, Macro's arrival was a real surprise—especially considering that he had not fallen off the horse as he tried to balance the large parcel under his arm.

The start of my birthday feast was lubricated by a large tub of beer, and Papa broke out a couple of pitchers of his precious wine hoard. Thinking that wine was much too expensive, Macro pretended he liked Gallic beer. The first cup caused his eyes to water, but by the third cup, he had gotten into the swing of it. Mama, like any proper Roman matron, sat stiffly upright in her chair and drank water.

Dinner was sumptuous by our rustic standards. There was meat, mostly chicken, and Mama and Amanda had concocted some sort of dish with pork, some carrots, onions, and *garum*. There were hard-boiled eggs for good luck and a long life, and plenty of vegetables: a thick cabbage soup, chopped broccoli, cucumbers, carrots, and even a few olives.

The entire *familia* sat down around the large wooden table on our outside *peristylium*. After she was finished with her chores, even Amanda joined us, along with her brother, a blondish kid called Gwin, who had started working as a field hand that season—same deal as his sister, three meals and a bed.

Finally, Mama lit the birthday torch, and Amanda brought the sweet cakes out of the kitchen together with a cream sauce thickened with eggs and sweetened with honey. In a bowl, there was some kind of small, deep-red fruit.

"*Cerasa*," Macro choked through his beer, "cherries! The patron will never miss 'em. Be careful when you bite in. They have pits."

We all enjoyed the cakes slathered in the sweet cream, but the cherries were even more delicious. Before I knew it, there was a small mountain of pits piled up in front of me.

Papa walked into the house and came back out with a small, brownish jug. Mama's eyes shot javelins at him.

"Something to toast the birthday boy with!" he announced. "It's something special we brew up from grain," he said to Macro. "We call it *Dur uh Bee'wid*."

"Door uh what?" Macro tried to repeat.

"*Dur uh Bee'wid*," I repeated. "*Aqua vitae*, in Latin . . . water of life. But, we just call the stuff *Dur* . . . Oh, and be careful. It packs a punch."

Papa poured a little of the *Dur* out for each of the men around the table, even Gwin. The liquid poured out clear into our cups, just like water.

Then, Papa raised his cup, "To my son . . . to Gai . . . on reaching manhood!"

Then, Papa downed his drink.

The rest of us followed.

Macro gave his a suspicious sniff, then seeing that it hadn't killed any of us, downed his. I thought his head would explode! First his eyes widened, round as coins. Then, they turned red and seemed to pop out of his skull. He grabbed his beer cup and started draining it to extinguish the fire. Then, he realized what he was drinking. He looked at Mama and knew he couldn't spit it out, so he swallowed, then swallowed again. He seemed to be on the verge of gagging when he noticed some cake left on the table. He grabbed and stuffed it into his mouth. Eventually, he began to breathe again. His eyes receded back into his skull and found again their normal size and color.

The rest of us tried not to laugh. Mama was watching, but was not smiling.

Papa couldn't resist. "Would you like another wee taste of the *Dur*, Macro?" he asked, innocently holding up the brown jug.

"*Non volo. Non gratias*," Macro croaked. "I never was much of a water-drinker."

At that, we all lost it—even Mama smiled.

Finally, it was time for the gifts. I opened Avus Lucius' package first and discovered a large, white, irregularly shaped piece of cloth. Not knowing what it was, I held it out in front of me.

"It's a toga!" Mama almost squealed. "A *toga alba* . . . it is the white toga of your coming-of-age as a Roman!"

Mama got up from her chair and fingered the fabric. "It's so finely woven. It must have cost a fortune." She began collecting it up in her arms. "I'll put this away somewhere safe so it will stay clean for the *Liberalia*, when you will be able to wear it." Mama retreated back into the house with her treasure.

When she returned, Papa and Mama presented me with a gift, a sturdy pair of boots for working around the farm. My brother Luc gave me a pair of woolen stockings. "They go with the boots," he said, "for when it gets cold."

Macro then presented me with the parcel he had brought with him at such great risk. I pulled apart the cloth wrappings and discovered a wide, leather soldier's belt. The leather was worn, but well cared for. I noticed its large, well-polished brass fastener with a staring Medusa head. But, it was when I lifted it to try it on around my waist that I noticed a sheathed *pugio* fastened to it.

"If you're going to carry a knife, you might as well carry a man's knife!" Macro said.

I pulled the belt around my waist and fastened the buckle in the last hole punched through the leather. The belt clung to one of my hips, but on the other side it drooped down almost to the top of my leg.

"We can punch another hole for you in the saddle shop," Macro was saying, as I drew the *pugio* from its sheath. It was almost an exact replica of Macro's: dark iron and razor sharp. I looked over to Mama. Her lips were puckered as if she had just bit into something sour.

"I'll show you how to take care of the blade," Macro went on. "It's good iron. It'll keep an edge, but I'll show you how to keep it sharp. Who knows? Maybe in a couple years, you'll need the thing to shave."

It was well into the first hours of night before the gathering broke up. By then, Macro had developed a bit of a taste for *Dur*, so we put him back on his horse and pointed the horse in the direction of Gabinius' place. Ironically, the *Dur* seemed to have improved his horsemanship. Sometime during the evening, Macro had made the observation that although *dur* meant "water" in Gallic, it meant "tough" in Latin. The next morning he discovered the truth of his observation.

After my birthday, the days of summer seemed to fly by. It was early in the month of *Sextilis*, a couple of days past the Calends. I was swaggering around the senator's place, wearing my soldier's belt with its shiny, Medusa-head buckle and the *pugio* hanging from my waist when Macro commented that, if I were trying to look like a tough guy, I should learn how to use the soldier's knife, not just show it off.

After school the next day, Macro took me behind one of the storehouses, where he had set up three upright stakes, approximately three to four palms around and six *pedes* in height. He tested the middle one by trying to shake it, but it didn't move a bit. Then, he went over to a storage box next to the wall of the shed, opened it, and seemed to search for something.

Finally he grunted, "*Bene*," and pulled out what appeared to be two pieces of wood. He walked back over to where I was standing and handed me one. I realized that it was a toy *pugio* with leather covering the hand grip. Strangely, it felt a bit heavier than the actual knife.

"This is *not* a toy!" Macro began, as if he had read my thoughts. "It's called a *rudis*, a training knife, a foil. The army trains its *tirones*, recruits, using these. It's heavier than the real thing, so it will build up your strength and stamina. Believe me, if you can practice for a day with one of these, the real thing will feel as light as a feather. First, the proper grip! The *pugio* is held in the right hand, gripped across the palm, just below the base of the fingers," he demonstrated. "Then, the fingers fold over the grip, thumb over the top, parallel, below the hilt. Now, you try!"

I mimicked what I had seen Marco do with his wooden *pugio*.

"*Bene*," Macro approved. "Not too tight. A lot of guys grip the handle with all their strength because they don't want to lose the thing in a fight, but holding the *pugio* too tightly binds up the arm muscles and slows your arm motion. *Bene . . . bene . . .* just like that. This is called the 'palm grip.' It's the basic grip—not just for the *pugio*, but also the basic legionary sword, the *gladius*. Now for the basic fighting stance."

Macro demonstrated as he talked me through it.

"Place your feet shoulder-distance apart. Little more . . . little more . . . *bene . . .* right there. Now. . . place the right foot slightly to the rear of the left. No . . . no . . . right toes to left heel . . . like so. *Bene . . . bene . . .* now . . . loosen the knees . . . lots of bounce in the knees. You got it. Your center of balance is in your hips and ass. *Bene. . .* stand straight up from the waist . . . like so. Knife hand low . . . at the hips. No . . . not touching your body. Keep it loose . . . *bene.* Left hand high and a little forward . . . *bene.* Gives you balance. In the legion, this is called 'first position.' . . . It's also the starting point for fighting with the *gladius*, except then you'd have your shield, the *scutum*, in your left hand. Get used to the feel of it. Keep those knees loose . . . flexible."

Macro moved around to face me.

"Looks good. How's the balance?"

He continued his instruction. Then, suddenly, he pushed my shoulders with both hands, and I stumbled back a step. "*Male*! No good! Stay loose! Absorb the blow and recover. Flex with the knees. Let the upper body absorb the hit." He pushed me again. "Yeah . . . *bene . . .* that's it. Then recover. I'll teach you how to back-step later . . . *bene.* That's it." Macro continued to test my stance by shoving me from different directions. Finally, he said, "*Bene . . . Laxa*! Recover! No, I mean, relax."

I sensed Macro had slipped into some kind of an army mode with this drill.

Macro continued. "The next thing we're going to try is getting into first position quickly. I will give a preparatory command: 'First position!' Then the command of execution: 'Move!' On the preparatory command, you will do nothing. When you receive the command of execution, only then will you assume the first position. Do you have any questions?"

"No, *Optio,*" I answered. Now I knew Macro was falling into military-drill mode. He didn't react at all when I used his former military rank.

"*Bene,*" he began, "first position . . . MOVE!"

I assumed the position as best I could. Macro poked, pushed, and made some adjustments.

"*Bene*! *Laxa*!" he ordered.

As soon as I came out of my stance, Macro began again: "First position . . . MOVE!"

Again, poking, pushing, correcting. Then, "*Laxa*!"

We repeated the drill until Macro could find no fault with my stance. But, then he kept going.

"First position . . . MOVE!"

"Recover!"

"First position . . . MOVE!"

"Recover!"

It seemed we had repeated the drill for an entire summer hour, and I was sweating freely. Small rivulets were flowing down between my shoulder blades. Salty sweat stung my eyes. My muscles, especially my upper legs, began to scream. Still we drilled.

"First position . . . MOVE!"

"Recover!"

"First position . . . MOVE!"

"Recover!"

I was beginning to wonder what all this had to do with using a *pugio* when Macro finally called a halt to the drill. He took my wooden *pugio* and returned it to the storage chest, from which he brought out a piece of cloth and tossed it to me.

"Wipe yourself down!" he ordered. "You look like you just came out of a *laconicus*, a steam bath."

I unbuckled my belt and removed my sopping tunic to rub my chest, back, and under my arms. I tossed the cloth back to Macro. He hung it on the fence in the sun to dry.

"You might want to throw your tunic on the fence, too!" he suggested. "You walk around here smelling like that and all the sheep are going to fall in love with you."

I threw my tunic over the fence next to the cloth and kept my belt hooked over my shoulder.

"Let me explain why I'm drilling you like this," Macro began. "These are basic combat moves, the ones we use in the legions. In combat, you don't have much time to think. You have to react instantly. If you have to think about where your hands go or which leg goes in front of the other, you'll be dead before you can work it out. So, we drill these moves . . . over and over and over . . . until I can sneak up on you while you're dead asleep and yell, 'First position!' and you'd be in it before you even wake up. Make sense?"

"*Constat*," I replied, "I get it!"

"I'll start teaching you other combat moves tomorrow," he continued. "One at a time, and you must master each before we go on to a new one. One at a time, until you can do each in your sleep."

"*Stat*! Directly, *Optio*!" I shouted, assuming the position of attention.

"Once you have the moves down, then we'll start with some fighting techniques," Macro said, ignoring my exaggerated role-playing.

"Sounds good," I agreed.

"In the meantime," Macro went on, "anytime I say 'first position' to you, I expect you to assume it . . . *immediately* . . . anytime . . . any place. *Compre'endis tu*? You understand?"

"*Compre'endo*," I agreed.

"Go get your tunic back on. The sheep are starting to get horny," Macro told me.

I walked over to the fence, grabbed my tunic, and had just noticed that it was still a bit damp when I heard Macro's voice from behind me, "First position!"

"Huh—" I started.

"First position!" Macro shouted.

I dropped my damp tunic and assumed the position, right there in the yard under the sun, in nothing but my loin cloth.

"A delay like that could get you killed in combat," Macro yelled. "Remember . . . anytime . . . any place. Now, recover. .. . . Pick up your tunic and get dressed!"

I picked my tunic up out of the dirt and shook it a few times. Big clods of dirt fell off the damp cloth. Macro was walking away saying, "Come on! Get dressed! Unless you are planning to stay back here and make the sheep happy."

The next day, at the seventh hour, we were at it again.

First, Macro ran me through the first position drill a few times until he was happy with my performance. I was just beginning to work up a sweat when we went on to something new.

"This is the basic attack move," Macro started. "It's called the front thrust. Watch me."

Macro assumed the first position, then said aloud, "Front thrust. . . Move!" When he said, "Move," the wooden *pugio* in Macro's right hand exploded forward to a position level with his eyes, then it froze. "Recover!" and the *pugio* withdrew, and Macro was back in first position.

"Any questions?" Macro asked.

"No," I said, trying to piece together in my mind all the moves.

Macro sensed my uncertainty, and said, "Stop thinking about it, and watch!" He then repeated the drill a few more times.

"Front thrust . . . Move!"

"Recover!"

"Front thrust . . . Move!"

"Recover!"

"Front thrust . . . Move!"

"Recover!"

I noticed that every time Macro executed the drill, his wooden *pugio* struck in the exact same place.

"Now you try it," Macro ordered.

My first attempt at the front thrust was a disaster. I never realized that so many body parts had to work together. Macro told me again that I had to stop thinking about what I was doing and instead let my muscles do the work. So, he continued to drill me.

"Front thrust . . . Move!"

"Recover!"

"Front thrust . . . Move!"

"Recover!"

"Front thrust . . . Move!"

"Recover!"

Soon, the move began to feel comfortable, natural. Then, Macro started teaching me the finer points of the strike.

"Gai, before you recover the *pugio*, twist your wrist like this," Macro demonstrated. He twisted his wrist so the flat blade of the *pugio* was parallel to the ground. When he was back in the first position, the blade was again perpendicular to the ground.

"Now, you try," he said. "Front thrust . . . Move!"

"Recover!"

"Front thrust . . . Move!"

"Recover!"

"Front thrust . . . Move!"

"Recover!"

I remembered to twist the *pugio* a few times, but then I reverted to pulling it straight back. Macro stopped me.

"Okay," he said, "I'm going to help you remember to twist the blade."

He modified the drill.

"Front thrust . . . Move!"

"Twist!"

"Recover!"

"Front thrust . . . Move!"

"Twist!"

"Recover!"

"Front thrust . . . Move!"

"Twist!"

"Recover!"

When we finally took a break, Macro reminisced. "When I was learning that move, I did it with a *rudis*, a wooden *gladius*. Heavy bastard . . . built up the arms and shoulders. Every time that I forgot to twist that damn wooden sword, the training officer would whack my wrist with his *vitis*, his vine staff, and I was expected to respond, '*Cedo alteram, centurio*! Hit me again, centurion!' Sometimes he did. He was a right bastard . . . a damn good soldier . . . good officer, too . . . but a right bastard."

"Macro," I said, still catching my breath. "I got a question."

"Go ahead," he responded.

"Why the twist?" I asked. "Wouldn't it be quicker just to pull the *pugio* straight back?"

"It gets stuck sometimes," Macro answered.

"Stuck?" I started.

"Yeah . . . the front thrust's a killing blow. It's supposed to go deep," Macro explained. "Sometimes your aim's off . . . or you just don't have a good target. If the *pugio* goes into your enemy's belly . . . or high up on the chest . . . it might get stuck, hung up on some bone or gristle, or it just won't come out. The twist frees it . . . like pulling your boot out of mud." Macro's eyes seemed to drift. Whatever he was seeing was not in that practice yard.

"What do you mean by a good target?" I asked him.

"What? Oh . . . yeah . . . the optimal target for the forward thrust is the throat . . . either low, where it joins the body," Macro pointed to a concave spot at the base of his throat, "or to the sides." He pointed to the sides of his neck. "Put your hand there. You can feel a throbbing."

I did, and I did.

"The throbbing you feel is from the ducts that carry the blood through your body," he said. "Cut 'em, and it's a quick kill. Messy as hell . . . but your man goes down quick."

"Why's that?" I asked.

"A *medicus*, one of the legionary medics, once told me the heart works like a pump, pushing blood through the body. The body needs the wet humors of the blood to stay alive. Cut one of the big lines, the body dies quickly. Cut some of the small lines, the body dies slowly. You want to avoid that. An enemy can kill you while he's slowly bleeding to death. But cut him right," Macro pointed to the side of his throat, "and your man goes down swiftly and stays there. Your knife won't get caught. Of course, blood spurts like a fountain . . . but that's your best shot."

Macro walked over to one of the poles, picked up a stone, and scratched an X at what would be throat-level on a man of average height.

"When I start you on the *palus*, the practice pole, that's your target," he told me. "You have to train your body to hit it at will . . . any time it's exposed. That's what you hit!"

Then Macro drew another X at mid-chest level. "That's your secondary target. It's right here on a man's body." Macro thrust his thumb up under his sternum and continued, "It's a quick kill . . . right into the heart . . . but sometimes the *pugio* gets stuck. Then you twist and pull. Should pop right out. Make sense?"

"Yes," I gulped. All this made me realize that, despite the wooden knife I was holding, this wasn't a kids' game Macro was training me for.

"*Bene!*" Macro continued. "You're not yet ready for the pole. We need to get back to our drill. First position! Move!"

"Front thrust . . . Move!"

"A little higher, Gai! Aim for the throat! Twist!"

"Recover!"

"Front thrust . . . Move!"

"Good . . . right on target! Twist!"

"Recover!"

"Front thrust . . . Move!"

"Good . . . Good . . . Twist!"

"Recover!"

Later, as we were walking back to the house, Macro saw me rubbing my right arm.

"The workout getting to you?" he asked.

"Uh . . . not too much . . . I'm okay," I hedged.

"Look," he said, "I saw those bruises on your right arm when you thrust the *pugio*."

"Uh . . . it's nothing . . . really," I continued to evade.

"That *cunnus* is left-handed, isn't he?" Macro accused.

Before I could respond, Macro had reached over and lifted my tunic sleeve to look at my right shoulder.

"*Cacat*! Shit!" he whistled through his teeth. "I've known centurions who couldn't do that much damage with a whole forest of vine cudgels! *Fellator*! I'll have a talk with that *mentula*! I'll put a stop to that shit!"

The next morning in school, I didn't notice any difference in the *magister*'s teaching style. While he read out to us from one of Cicero's orations against the infamous traitor, Catalina, he did his best to impress upon young Marcus the various ways the dative case could be used in Latin.

"Please listen again, Master Gabinius, '*Hos libros dono mihi misit.*' *Mihi* of course is the dative form of the first-person pronoun, *ego*, and in this sentence it indicates the indirect object of the verb, *misit*. 'He sent these books *to me.*' *Dono,* on the other hand, is the dative form of the noun, *donum*, and here the dative indicates the purpose of the verb, *mittere*, 'as a gift': 'He sent them to me *as a gift.*'"

Marcus showed no sign of comprehension. I braced myself for a blow . . . none came.

The *magister* sighed and tried again. "Listen to this phrase: '*Puella, non tibi est vultus mortalis.*' Here, *tibi* is the dative of the familiar form of second-person pronoun, *tu*. In this phrase, it refers to the noun, *puella*, and it indicates something possessed . . . actually not possessed as indicated by the adverb, *non* . . . by the girl being addressed, *vultus mortalis,* the appearance of a mortal."

Still no comprehension.

In an attempt to distract the *magister*, I was about to ask if it was an example of the trope, *ironia*—anything to distract him from Marcus' apparent impenetrability to the finer points of Latin grammar and from smacking his cane into my shoulder.

Finally, Marcus grabbed a handful of grapes from a bowl on the table and dismissed the *magister*'s whole effort. "I don't see what difference it makes . . . dative of possession . . . dative of purpose. I understand what the sentences means . . . and that's all that matters. I only need to understand what people are saying to me." And, with that, he stuffed the grapes into his mouth.

I saw the color build up in the *magister's* face. I braced for the blow, but again, it didn't come. Then I noticed that the *magister* wasn't even holding a rod. In fact, there were none to be seen in the room! Slowly, the color drained from the *magister's* face, and he attempted to go on with the lesson despite Marcus' chomping and pit-spitting.

Macro had worked his magic.

Later, in the training yard, Macro asked, "So? How was class today?"

"Nothing special," I quipped, "unless you're interested in the five uses of the dative case."

"No . . . not especially," Macro responded. "Let's get some work done."

We started with the first position. Then Macro had me execute some front thrusts until he was satisfied with what he saw. Finally, he said, "*Bene*! It's time to start you on the *palus*, the training pole. You don't know it yet, but you're going to learn to hate the *palus* worse than that Greek *fellator* with his five different uses for the dative."

Macro led me over to the pole on which he had X'ed the throat and the heart. "Here is how we do this drill," he announced and assumed the first position about two *pedes* in front of the pole.

"Front thrust . . . Move! Recover!" he yelled.

Faster than a viper's strike, Macro's wooden *pugio* had struck. It seemed to have hit the center of the upper X. It had been a blur. I could have convinced myself I hadn't seen it, but the pole quivered from the strike.

"That's how the killing blow, the *percussus*, the punch, is delivered to the throat," Macro instructed, relaxing from his fighting position. "My bad leg slows me down a bit . . . but a knife-fighter strikes fast. Your opponent's a dead man before he can even register your attack. Any questions?"

I just shook my head.

"Need to see it again?"

Again, a shake of the head. "No."

"*Bene*," he said, moving away from the training pole, "you try it."

Macro's invitation was, of course, a trap. I was not ready for the *palus*, and his little demonstration had intimidated me. I assumed the first position.

"Front thrust . . . Move! Recover!" Macro suddenly yelled.

The command to recover was useless. My first thrust at the training pole was off the mark. The *rudis*, the weighted, wooden *pugio*, slipped to the right, and I almost followed my arm into the *palus*. If I hadn't managed to stop myself with my left hand, I think I would have kissed the X, not killed it.

"Recover!" Macro ordered again.

I resumed first position. I could feel my cheeks burning.

"Not bad for a *tiro*," Macro commented. "We're going to concentrate on two things today: first accuracy, then power. Relax. Watch me."

Macro assumed first position in front of the training pole and executed the forward thrust at half speed. "The knife follows the eyes," he said, as he executed the move. "Fix the center of the X in your eyes and train the entire body to follow the eyes into the target." He hit the center of the X a couple more times. Then, he had me do it at a slow pace. Soon, with his coaching, I was hitting the X close to the center. As soon as I was hitting the target consistently, Macro had me speed up. As soon as I was accurate at that speed, he had me speed up again. It took most of the afternoon, but I was hitting the X, more or less in the center, at a fairly quick speed.

I was soaked with sweat when Macro finally called a halt to the drill. "*Bene*," he said. "For every thrust a Roman soldier makes in combat with a real weapon, he makes a thousand into the *palus* with a *rudis*. If you're going to make a mistake, make it here in the training yard. That way you stay alive in combat, and it's your enemy who crosses with the boatman. *Compre'endis tu?* You understand?"

"*Etiam*," I panted, "yes, I understand; *compre'endo*."

"*Bene*," he responded. "Catch your breath. We have more work to do before we're done for the day."

When I finally managed to get my heart down out of my throat, Macro began. "Next thing we're going to work on is getting some power into your strike."

Macro assumed the first position in front of the *palus*. "The power doesn't come from your arm. It comes from your body, especially your legs, hips, and shoulders." He struck the pole, right on target. Again, the pole quivered with his strike.

"When you attack, you actually trigger the release with your trailing foot, the right one. You twist on the ball of your foot, and that brings your right knee toward the center of your body, the center of your balance." He demonstrated this, twisting his foot and knee a couple of times for me to see.

"The knee coming across triggers the hips." With that remark, he opened his hips parallel to the target. "This swings the weight of your lower body, and the power of your legs, toward the target." He demonstrated the coordinated foot and hip movement to me a couple of times.

Then, he had me assume first position and run through it a couple times. "Feet . . . hips," he coached. "Feet . . . hips." The movement felt awkward, and girlish, to me. It didn't help when Macro put his hands on my hips to "guide them through the zone" as he put it. "*Bene*, open your hips. They should end up facing your target."

When Macro was satisfied, he demonstrated the rest of the technique. "Now the upper body movement. After the hips come around, then the shoulder. You trigger the thrust with this part of your shoulder." Macro put his hand on the front part of my shoulder. "You should feel muscle and a roundish bone. Feel it . . . right there. It's right where your arm ends. You push that part of your shoulder at the target. That pulls your arm around like a whip. Then the hand comes through and strikes the target."

Macro demonstrated the move a couple of times, then had me try it.

"Square your hips to the pole . . . *bene*. Now, thrust with the shoulder. Let the arm follow . . . the hand . . . *bene*. Now do that a couple of times . . . *bene*."

Then, he had me try putting it all together slowly while he coached me to the cadence: "Foot . . . knee . . . hip . . . shoulder . . . arm . . . hand . . . again . . . foot . . . knee . . . hip . . . shoulder . . . arm . . . hand . . . again . . . foot . . . knee . . . hip . . . shoulder . . . arm . . . hand . . . again!"

Then, he sped it up: "Foot . . . hips . . . shoulder . . . strike . . . again . . . foot . . . hips . . . shoulder . . . strike . . . again . . . foot . . . hips . . . shoulder . . . strike . . . again . . . foot . . . hips . . . shoulder . . . strike !"

Eventually, he was just giving the basic drill we had started with, "Front thrust . . . Move! Recover! Front thrust . . . Move! Recover! Front thrust . . . Move! Recover!"

He finally stopped to give me a chance to catch my breath again. I was so winded I had to bend forward, steadying myself with my hands on my knees. I watched the sweat pour off my head and face into the soil.

"Good workout, eh?" Macro said, hardly breathing heavily. "Catch your breath, and we'll try it on the *palus*. Go get yourself a drink if you need it."

I walked over to a wooden trough under the eaves of the storage shed. I threw some water up in my face, then bent further over and soaked most of my upper body and chest. Although the water had been sitting out in the summer heat for some time, it felt cool, refreshing. I picked up a mouthful in my hands, swashed it around my mouth a little, and spit it out. Water resting in a trough is full of demons. No point in getting myself sick.

Macro handed me a leather skin. "Here! Drink some of this. It's straight from the well." I must have emptied half the skin before Macro snatched it back. "Don't want you puking on my nice, clean dirt here," he laughed.

When I had finally recovered a bit, Macro had me back in front of the training stake in first position.

"You ready?" he asked.

I nodded, locking my eyes on the X.

Immediately, he commanded, "Front thrust . . . Move! Recover!"

Another disaster—even worse than the first time I tried. I missed the X *and* the pole!

"Okay . . . recover . . . recover," Macro directed. "You're thinking too much about it. Your brain is trying to direct your body. We've got to practice this. Train your muscles to make these moves automatically. Let's slow it way down again . . . walk through it a couple times until it feels right."

So, I went right back to the slow-motion drill with Macro coaching me. Soon, I was hitting the target again, and this time, I could feel more power in the thrust.

Macro called a halt. "*Bene!* That's enough for today." He looked up to see where the sun was. "Looks like it's getting to be the ninth hour. Let's take a quick tour of the place and see what the rest of these lazy bastards have been up to. Then you can go on home. Tomorrow we'll pick this up where we left off."

"*Bene*," I croaked, looking up at Macro from a bent-over position, my upper body seemingly supported only by my hands and arms wedged between it and my knees. My tunic was soaked, as if I had been swimming in it. "*Bene*," I choked out again, then puked half a skin of water all over Macro's nice, clean dirt.

The next morning, at Macro's suggestion, I tried to "double-time" the distance between my house and the senator's estate to "improve my wind" for my weapons training.

As Macro explained it, the normal army marching pace, "quick time" he called it, was three thousand *passus*, paces, each summer-hour. That allowed a unit to cover its daily twenty thousand paces in approximately six to seven hours, giving the legionaries plenty of time to construct their marching camp, the *castrum*, at the end of the day's march.

One full legionary pace, Macro clarified, was "right foot to right foot." Soldiers always stepped out right foot first, so when the right foot hit the ground again, that counted as one pace. A single stride, right to left, was approximately three *pedes*, so, on a Roman road over flat ground, the full pace was six during daylight; going uphill or over rough terrain or with limited visibility, the pace was shorter. But, a unit always did its twenty thousand each day's march.

In the front of every marching unit was a group of veteran legionaries whose job it was to pace the unit—the timing of each stride, the length and the count. During the march, the centurions ensured that the centuries or cohorts were keeping up with the pace element and that no gaps opened up between the marching elements. Roman army units didn't use drums to time their march. They didn't have to. They were constantly drilled, and if their training faltered, the centurions "motivated" the troops with their *vites*, vine cudgels.

The troops that were marching far enough forward could actually hear the count and, when the pace-count got over nineteen thousand, could anticipate the end of the march. Near the end of the march, the soldiers would pray to all the gods that the *legatus*, the legionary commander, or the senior tribune would not be feeling his oats that day and cry out, "*Infantes*, boys, can you do another thousand for me?"

In the Roman Army, the only acceptable response to such a challenge was, "*Alia duo mille passuum eamus, capu*'! Let's go another two thousand, chief!"

During a forced march, the army marched double-time. The length of the pace was the same, but the timing was quicker, almost six thousand paces an hour. A well-trained legion could keep this pace up for at least the six to seven hours of the normal day-march.

That was one of the tests of a Roman soldier: how long could he keep that pace up under arms, equipped for battle? It was shameful to fall out—and dangerous. If the enemy didn't pick you off, your centurion would when you finally stumbled into camp. After a session with the vine stick in front of your mates, you would be double-timed around the camp in full-kit for a couple hours to "improve your wind." Then, your centurion would allow you to stop in order to clean out the latrines before camp broke the next morning.

So, at Macro's suggestion, I began "double-timing" to the senator's estate to "improve my wind."

That morning in class, the *magister*, again unarmed, was using his beloved Cicero manuscript in an attempt to impress young Marcus with the elegance of proper Latin, specifically, a grammatical gymnastic called the "loosened ablative." It seemed fairly straightforward to me, but Master Marcus was having no part of it.

"Listen again, Master Marcus," the *magister* entreated, "it's a phrase constructed from a noun in the ablative form and a verbal participle, also in the ablative. Its relationship to the independent clause is loose. That's why it's called *absolutum*, 'free from'."

Marcus picked his nose, then picked through the fruit bowl, looking for something more interesting than Latin grammar.

"Let's try another example," the *magister* continued. "*Consule imperium tenente, nihilum timemus*. The independent clause in this sentence is *nihilum timemus*: we fear nothing. The clause *consule imperium tenente*, with the consul possessing official command, loosely indicates why we fear nothing. The noun *consule* and the present active participle of the verb *tenere* are both cast in the ablative case. The word *imperium* is in the accusative because it's the direct object of the participle, *tenente*."

Marcus selected a ripe-enough peach and shrugged slightly before biting into it.

The *magister* sighed. Then he looked at me and asked, "Gaius, can you construct a sentence using a loose ablative clause?"

"*Certe*," I responded. "Certainly, *Magister*! *Magistro fustem non habente, nihilum timemus.* Since the teacher does not possess a stick, we fear nothing."

The *magister* stared at me for a long second, then looked over to Marcus, off in his own world, his lips and cheeks smeared with the meat of the peach. The *magister* shrugged and said, "*Bene*! *Quod est rectum.* Good! That is correct!"

Then he started explaining something he called the passive periphrastic, while Marcus finished his peach and spit the pit out into the fishpond.

Later that afternoon, Macro picked up our drill where we had left off the day before. He put me in first position in front of the *palus* and commanded, "Front thrust . . . Move! Recover!"

It took me a couple of repetitions to get back into it, but soon my *rudis* was hitting the mark with some power.

When he was satisfied, Macro told me to keep going, but without his commands. He watched me work for a little while, then said, "Keep it up! I'll be back in an hour."

So, there I remained, slamming a wooden knife into a wooden pole in the summer sun.

Macro wandered back about an hour later. He nonchalantly watched me repeatedly killing the training poll before telling me to halt. "Take a break! Get some water if you need it!"

My wrist, arm, and shoulder were on fire. I soaked them in the water of the nearby trough before throwing some water onto my face.

"Hurts, doesn't it?" I heard Macro saying behind me. "That's good. Means you're training and building the muscles in your arm, shoulder, and back. If you're doing it right, your legs'll hurt, too, especially the right one. After you get some water, stretch them out. Easy with the water. Don't want to puke on your boots . . . again."

While I was stretching the knots out of my legs, Macro continued, "Better to feel the pain in training. You don't want to get a case of 'dead arm' in combat."

"*Bene*," he said, looking up to see where the sun was, "time waits for no mortal. Back to the *palus*. Assume the first position. Front thrust . . . Move! Recover!"

Macro watched a while, then said, "If it helps, imagine the training pole is me. Remember that bastard of a centurion I told you about? I must have killed him thousands of times in training. Stuck my *rudis* right down his throat. Give that anger a focus. That's it. Harder!"

Finally, Macro said, "Keep it up!" and walked away.

By the end of training that day, I was a wreck. I could hardly lift my right arm, and I walked like a man with two wooden legs. Macro seemed pleased, though.

"It's starting to look good," he began.

Almost glaring at him, I thought, *starting*?

"Couple more days of this, and you'll be hitting the *palus* like a real soldier."

I was beginning to realize that "like a real soldier" was Macro's highest praise.

"Then we can move on to some combat techniques. I'll make a fighter out of you yet, Gai."

And, that's what I did for the next three days. I pounded that training stake until it should have begged for mercy. But it didn't. It just stood there like I had never hit it, daring me to try again. I named the damned thing "Macro," and I killed it over and over again.

On day four, Macro had me hitting the lower target—*heart*, he called it. He called the upper target *throat*. Then he mixed them up as I struck.

"Throat," he yelled. I struck.

"*Bene*! Throat!"

I struck.

"*Arduor*! Harder! Heart!"

I struck. The *palus* quivered.

"*Optime*! *Iterum*! Again! Heart!"

I struck, yelling, "Die, you stinking *cunnus*!"

"*Optime*! Relax! Take a break! I almost felt that one myself."

Good, I thought, trying to catch my breath; it's working.

"Let's try something different," Macro announced. He went over to my training stake and began carving target X's around it with a flat stone.

When he was done and I was finally breathing again, he said, "Knife-fighters don't stand in one place waiting for the other guy to stick them. They tend to circle each other." Macro assumed first position. "Always circle to your right; protect your open side," he said, circling my *palus*. "First, move your back foot about three to four palms to the right. Then your left . . . back into first position . . . always ready to strike. Be careful not to cross your feet. You'll get them tangled up. First right . . . then left . . . always in position to strike. Always keep your eye on your opponent!" Macro continued to circle my training pole.

Finally, he said, "You try it!"

I did. I felt a bit awkward at first, but soon my body seemed to adapt to the movement. I was circling the *palus* for the third time when suddenly Macro commanded, "Throat!"

Without thinking, I struck. My *rudis* hit the upper X before me.

"Keep circling. Eyes up. Eyes up. Keep moving," Macro said. "Throat!"

I struck again, hard, on target.

"*Bene . . . bene,*" Macro coached. "Keep moving. Eyes up. Keep circling. Heart!"

We kept this up for the better part of an hour. Then, Macro suddenly commanded, "Throat! Throat! Heart! Throat!"

I struck at his command. My *rudis* darted out: high, high, low, high. Each time I hit, the *palus* quivered.

"*Optime!*" Macro congratulated. "*Optime!* Your muscles are doing the work now! *Optime!* You're beginning to look like a soldier!"

After that compliment, I was feeling pretty good about myself: "You're beginning to look like a soldier!" That is, until the next afternoon, when Macro pulled a stunt on me worthy of the devious Greek schemer, Ulysses.

The *magister* was actually trying to teach young Marcus the rudiments of Greek. We were transitioning from "ah-bay-kay" to "alpha-beta-gamma." The only effect it seemed to have on Marcus was that he transitioned from the peaches to the pears.

Later, in the practice yard, thinking I had mastered first position and the forward thrust, I was all ready to learn the more advanced combat moves, which was why I was confused when Macro told me, "Grasp the *rudis* in your left hand."

"What's the idea?" I challenged him. "I'm right-handed!"

"All soldiers are," Macro answered. "We train them that way so they fit into the legionary battle line."

"That's what I'm saying," I persisted.

"Think about it, Gai," Macro persevered. "How are you going to fight— survive—if your right hand isn't, isn't available?"

Macro's use of the phrase *tu' dextra manum non ad manum* confused me at first. How could a *manum* not be *ad manum*? Macro was beginning to talk like the *magister* in rhetorical circles. Then I got it.

"The long-sword barbarians, like the Gauls," Marco was saying, "or the ax-swingers, like the Krauts, like to kill with an overhand blow, over the shield, straight down on a poor grunt's skull. If their aim is true, it doesn't matter whether the poor son-of-a-bitch was righted-handed or left-handed; they only care about handing the coin to the boatman. But, the Roman infantry helmet, the *galea*, is designed to deflect an overhand blow. Normally, the edge of the weapon slides down the side of the helmet and hits the shoulder. So, not only does the grunt get his bell rung, but he probably has a broken collar bone: left shoulder and he loses his shield; right shoulder and he loses his sword. His fighting partner, his *geminus*, is supposed to pull him back off the line when that happens. But, combat is messy; what's supposed to happen rarely does. So, a *mulus* may have to fight for his life with one hand. And if that hand's the left hand, he better know how to use it. We train all our soldiers to fight with both hands. A grunt can survive losing his hand . . . even his arm. But he's not going to last three heartbeats on the line if he can't use his sword."

So, with the *rudis* in my left hand, Macro placed me in front of my *palus* and adjusted my first position for a left-handed attack. Then he commanded, "Throat!"

My body didn't move. It couldn't; it didn't know what to do. My brain didn't even know what commands to issue.

Macro wasn't a bit surprised. "Let's take it one step at a time. Left foot steps three palms toward the pole. Left hand comes forward and through."

I had to relearn the forward thrust, step-by-step, as if I had never done it before. My entire body seemed to resist what it felt was a backward move. By the end of the day, though, I was doing a reasonable parody of the forward thrust with my left hand.

A reasonable parody, however, was not at all satisfactory to Macro. I had to be able to perform as well using the left hand as I did using the right. So, we kept at it every day for over two weeks. I again found myself striking at an image of Macro's face floating before me where the target X was scratched.

Finally, Macro was satisfied.

Then, he started me on a series of drills in which he had me circle the *palus,* right-handed, hitting targets at his command.

"Throat!"

"Throat!"

"Heart!"

"Throat!"

Then he'd command, "*Sinistra!*" I'd flip the *rudis* from my right hand to my left, continuing to circle, striking at his command.

"Throat!"

"Heart!"

"Throat!"

Then, Macro would yell, "*Dextra!*" I'd flip the practice knife back to my right hand and continue the drill.

The Calends of September came and went, and we were still at it. I didn't realize it then, but in a few short weeks, that drill would save my life.

VII.

Inter Iliadem et Lupinarium

BETWEEN THE *ILIAD* AND THE BROTHEL: MY FINAL LESSONS IN BEING ROMAN

he harvesting of our crops began around the Ides of September. Even though I was in the third generation of "Romans," we still believed that all crops must be harvested by the day before the Calends of November, a day we Gah'el call the *Samon'win*.

According to the legends of our people, countless generations ago, when we first descended from the high places of our god, Lugh, we fought a seemingly endless war for sovereignty of the middle lands, which lay between the sky and the dark places of Lugh's sister, Danu. Our enemies were a people called *Uh Thloo uth uh Doo T'wil*, The People of the Dark Goddess. Although we Gah'el were by far the better warriors, the people of the dark goddess were magical. They possessed *Uh Crochan uh Deh Ga'th*, The Cauldron of Rebirth, in which, at the dark of the moon, when there is no light on the middle lands, they would place their battle dead to be revived at the next dawn. The cauldron could rouse the bodies, but it could not retrieve the souls of the dead warriors from the underworld. So, the reanimated warriors could not speak, nor could they quicken a woman's womb, but they could take their place in the line of battle and kill.

So, the wars continued.

According to some versions of the tale, Arth Mawr destroyed the cauldron. Others say he captured it and hid it in a place so secret that even the magic of the people of the dark goddess could not find it. Eventually, the two peoples agreed on a treaty that divided all the lands in two. The Gah'el would possess the high places, where we could worship Lugh; the Dark Ones would possess the underworld with their goddess, Danu. The middle lands, they would share. From the Calends of November until the day before the Ides of April, the Dark Ones would possess the middle lands; from the Ides of April until the day before the Calends of November, the *Samon'win*, the Gah'el ruled the earth. After the *Samon'win*, anything left in the fields would belong to the Dark Ones by right. In fact, during the *Timor T'wil*, the Dark Time as the old ones called it, it was customary to leave offerings of cream, fruit, and cheese on the threshold of the house so that the Dark Ones would not enter to snatch away one of the young children of the Gah'el and leave one of their own in its place, *uh dirp w'ol*, the Changeling.

So, despite all our Roman sophistication, which didn't allow for such superstition, Papa was determined to have the crops in by the Calends of November. He told me that between my older brother, Lucius, and the hired boy, Gwin, they could probably get it done—as long as I continued tending the animals. In that way, I could continue with my schooling, but I was sure that Mama had something to do with it—just as I was sure that she would not be leaving offerings on our doorstep for *Uh Thloo uth uh Doo T'wil*.

The *magister*'s attempts at teaching Master Marcus the refinement and elegance of the Greek language were resulting in very little progress, except for the times when the young scholar was focused on his fruit bowl. *Tah mayloh*, he would say, presenting an apple before eating it, or *mereka stap'ulia*, for a bunch of grapes, or *tah rodakivo* for a peach. Then, he would devour his vocabulary lesson. As for me, I was struggling with the Greek verbs. But, I consoled myself with the thought that perhaps a rich wine merchant from the Padus Valley would have Greek-speaking customers in Neapolis and all the cities of *Magna Graecia*— maybe even Athens itself. So, knowing when to say *tah krasi* instead of *vinum* for wine might just be important to me someday.

I even allowed myself to dream that I might become so rich, so sophisticated, quoting Sappho and Homer in Greek, and so dashing, being able to hold my own with my flashing *pugio* against vicious and brutal villains in the worst *subura* dives, that Gabi would come back to me. We then would have to flee Italy because that jealous old senator husband of hers would hire Milo's thugs to murder me and bring her back. In due course, we would live in gentile exile in Athens, where I would spend my days in the *agora*, where all the Greeks gathered, arguing philosophy with the scholars of the stoa, the legendary porch of Plato and Aristotle. I would be admired and envied as *ho keltos ho sop'os*, the Wise Gah'el.

The *magister* suddenly brought me out of my reverie, back into my real world.

"Well, Gai?" he demanded.

"Uhhh . . . *tohn logohn* . . . uh . . . genitive plural of the noun, *ho logos* . . . means . . . *verborum* . . . of the words . . . so the passage reads, "The sense of my words is this."

"Is that all?" the *magister* persisted. "Is that your only translation?"

"*Ho logos* . . . uh . . . of course . . . it can also indicate *ratio*, reasoning, meaning, thought. So the speaker is not only referring to the actual spoken words, but also to their meaning . . . or the thoughts behind them . . . *rationum*."

"*Bene! Est rectum.* Marcus! Now will you please put down that pear and pay attention?"

Later that day, Macro was teaching me various fighting techniques, both right-handed and left. First, the defensive parries: high sweep, high block, low-reverse sweep, low-stabbing block. Then, various attacks: reverse thrust, overhand thrust, underhand thrust, front-hand side thrust, reverse-hand side thrust. These he associated with various foot movements: the advance, the retrograde, the reverse circle. Each one he drilled until he felt that I "looked like a soldier."

Soon, Macro began drilling me in various combinations of movements. "Forward thrust! High block! Low-sweeping block! Retrograde! Retrograde! Low-reverse sweep! Advance! Advance! Forward thrust! Throat!" If I thought spending hours stabbing at a *palus* was exhausting, these "dance recitals" around the practice ground soon taught me the error of my thinking.

A few days past the Calends of October, when the trees on the higher mountains were beginning to shift from green to an autumn mosaic of reds and oranges, Macro finally called a halt to my individual drills.

"You know everything I can teach you, Gai," he started, "and you execute well—fast and clean. Tomorrow, you and I start sparring."

"Sparring?" I questioned.

"*Certe*! Certainly!" he responded. "You didn't think you were learning these moves so you could entertain the crowds in the forum with your grace, did you? None of this is worth a bronze *as* unless you can fight and win. So, tomorrow you fight me. Hey! I'm old, and I'm damaged. You should be able to finish me off in no time. Right, *Tiro*?"

I knew when he called me *tiro*, rookie, he was setting me up for one of his little traps. And, I was right.

The next afternoon, Macro brought out two different *rudes*. These wooden knives were lighter than the one I had been training with, approximately the weight of my own *pugio*. I also noticed that the edges and points were exceedingly blunt.

As if reading my thoughts, Macro said, "Don't want any accidents. I'm too old to show up at some *medicus* with a wooden knife stuck in my chest." He seemed to laugh under his breath.

Macro began rubbing the points and blunt edges of both *rudes* with white chalk. "This marks the hits, so there are no mistakes," he said absently.

He tossed one of the *rudes* to me and explained, "No rules. We're trying to kill each other . . . but when I say stop, we stop. The safe word's *garum*, fish sauce. If either of us says that, the fight stops. Don't want either of us getting carried away."

"*Bene*," I agreed.

"Let's go!" Marco said.

We both assumed the first position and started circling. The first time Macro feinted at me, he was amazingly fast; I almost tripped over my own feet retreating.

Without breaking his position, Macro said, "Watch your opponent's eyes. They'll usually give away his intention. It's a 'tell.' . . . Also watch his shoulders. You can't thrust without changing the position of the shoulders. Watch."

Macro made a couple of halfhearted feints at me. Each time, I saw a movement, or what looked like added tension, in his shoulder the instant before he struck.

"But, it's the eyes that give it away," he continued still circling. "It's like a squint, or a more intense look—piercing almost—right before a strike. If you ever find yourself fighting a guy who has no 'tell' . . . nothing in his eyes . . . make sure you kill that guy the first chance you get. He's not human. He's a monster. His soul's already with Demeter in the underworld."

As we circled, Macro seemed to drop his guard slightly, open up a bit. I had a target, his throat. I struck. Front thrust. Macro seemed to know. He simply sidestepped. My *rudis* stabbed air. But, before I could recover, Macro slashed my forearm with his wooden knife.

"Stop," he commanded.

I relaxed.

"You saw me drop my guard . . . open up . . . so you thrust . . . right?"

I nodded. My arm stung where he had slashed me. There was a clear chalk mark just above my wrist.

Macro saw me looking. "That could be a killing blow," he said. "There's a major blood vessel right there. You'd bleed out in a few heartbeats. At a minimum, a couple of slashes on the wrist like that and you wouldn't be able to use that arm anymore."

I nodded.

"But, you can win a fight like that," Macro continued. "You don't always have to go for the kill. Now, what do you think went wrong?"

"I was too slow," I started.

"No," Macro interrupted, "you were fast enough. You didn't even give much of a 'tell.' That part you did well."

"Then what?"

"I set you up," Macro stated. "I actually used your strength against you. I knew you'd see me drop my guard, and I knew you'd strike hard once you had a target. So I let you see what you wanted to see. Then, I sidestepped the thrust that I knew was coming and hit the target you offered . . . your arm. That's the difference between practice and fighting. In practice, you work against a *palus*, a stake in the ground that doesn't think and just takes the beating. In a fight, you're against another man who thinks and who wants to kill you. You've got to think too! Your body's quick; you're mind has to be quicker. Make sense?"

I agreed, but I realized that Macro had just dropped me back to the beginning, like he did when he made me use my left hand. I was a *tiro*, a rookie, at this.

"*Bene*," Macro said getting back in his fighting stance. "Let's have another go."

By the end of the afternoon, I had taken a pretty good beating. I had more chalk marks on me than a wall in the forum during elections. Each time Macro struck, he'd stop us and explain what had happened. My only comfort was that he didn't get me the same way twice. But, despite the unsharpened training knives, I had more than a few bruises to deal with.

As we were walking back to the main house, Macro asked me, "What's my weakness?"

"What do you mean?" I asked.

"We just went round and round in that yard for over two hours. What is my most obvious weakness?" he persisted.

I thought for a second, then I said, "Your leg . . . your left leg . . . you can't go back on it. You have trouble circling into it."

"*Recte*," he agreed, "that's right. So, why didn't you take advantage of it?"

"That wouldn't be fair," I started.

"*Inique*," he mocked me, "wouldn't be fair? This isn't a game, *puer*, boy! This could be your life. You see a weakness in an opponent, you use it! You exploit it! If some guy's stupid enough to take you on with a bum leg . . . or one eye . . . or half his fingers missing, he deserves to die!"

I bristled a bit at Macro calling me *puer*. That's what he called his slaves, his boys, *pueri*. I was determined to make him eat that word the next day.

But, I wasn't able to. At least not at first.

Despite his leg, Macro seemed to be able to avoid most of my attempts to mark him. I did manage to put some marks on the back of his left arm and even one high on his right shoulder. Each time I marked him, he grunted, "*Bene!*" Then, he made me pay for it. At one point, he tricked me into thinking his left leg was collapsing. When I went in to take advantage of it, he instantly recovered and gave me such a thrust to my midsection that it knocked the wind out of me.

"That's the oldest trick in the world, *boy!*" he taunted, as I bent over trying to catch my breath. "And, if this were the real thing, it would've gotten you killed. You got any idea how long it takes to die from a stomach wound like that? It ain't pretty, *boy*! Now, get your head out of your ass!"

Macro assumed the fighting position and gestured me to come at him.

The air was barely back in my lungs, but now I was angry. *Puer, is it? Boy,* I thought to myself. I wanted to kill that gimpy old son-of-a-bitch. This *puer* was about to shove a wooden *rudis* right up that old man's *culus*. He'd be shitting splinters for a month!

I assumed a fighting position in front of Macro, and we began circling. After a few halfhearted feints, I struck. I came in high and hard, toward the left side of his throat, forcing him to counter with a high, sweeping block. This move caused him to shift some of his weight onto his damaged left leg. As soon as I saw his weight shift, I kicked his left leg out from under him. He went down in a heap onto his left side; he had to use his right hand, the one holding his practice weapon, to keep from rolling. I locked his right hand to the ground, and brought my *rudis* to his throat.

Macro must have seen the rage in my eyes. He immediately called out, "*Garum! Garum!*"

It took a few heartbeats for the safe word to penetrate my anger. I pulled back my *rudis* and straightened up. Macro held out his right arm for me to pull him up to his feet. I didn't move for a few heartbeats, but eventually I pulled him up off the ground.

"*Optime!*" he congratulated me when he recovered his feet. He squeezed my shoulder, "*Optime!* That was a good move! That's how it's done!"

I wasn't quite ready to surrender my anger to his praise. "Don't you ever call me *puer* again!" I practically hissed at him.

Macro looked at me for a long heartbeat, then laughed. "*Puer*! If that's all it takes to make you want to kill, you'd better stay out of any soldiers' *caupona*! After a few cups of cheap wine in those places, I've heard a lot worse from guys who liked me." That made him laugh harder.

"I think that's it for today," he said, putting his arm around my shoulder. "This old man's got to go and lick his wounds."

As we walked off the training ground, I realized that Macro was limping heavily on his left leg.

The last days of October rushed by. Each day, the hours of daylight were getting shorter. Even the trees in the lowlands and valleys were turning red and orange. A hard rain would come through one day, and the trees would be stripped bare, like skeletons. With the morning frosts, the grasses would soon turn brown, and the fields would be dark brown, empty of crops. Such was the earth as she prepared herself for the "dark times," the return of the people of Danu from the underworld.

The *magister* was reading out to us from Homer's tale of the destruction of Troy. It's curious, really. The Greeks celebrate their great heroes of that struggle—Achilles, Aiax, Odysseus—while the Romans see them as childish, brutish, and deceitful. The Romans believe that they are descended from the Trojans, through Aeneas, a hero and prince of the House of King Priam.

According to the tales that Mama told me, Aeneas led the survivors of Troy to Italy, where they defeated the Italians under their war chief, Turnus. Aeneas slew Turnus and married Lavinia, King Latinus' daughter. Ascanius, Aeneas' son by his first wife, Creusa, who was killed when the Greeks burned Troy, founded the city of Alba Longa. Eventually, Rhea Silvia, a Vestal Virgin and daughter of King Numitor of Alba Longa, was visited by the god Mars and gave birth to twins, Romulus and Remus. Numitor's brother, Amulius, who had overthrown the king and usurped his throne, ordered the twins exposed on the Tiber River. But, they did not die. Instead, they were nurtured by a she-wolf until a shepherd named Faustulus and his wife, Acca Larentia, raised them as their sons. When Romulus and Remus became adults, they killed Amulius and restored their grandfather, Numitor, to the throne of Alba Longa. They then decided to establish a city on the Tiber where they had been nurtured by the she-wolf. However, the brothers quarreled. Romulus killed his brother, Remus, and named the city after himself, Rome.

Mama also told me that one of Ascanius' names was Iulius, and he is the founder of the *gens Iulia*, the family of our *patronus*, Gaius Iulius Caesar. Even more importantly, Aeneas himself was the son of the goddess Venus. So, the *gens Iulia* claimed descent from the goddess, which added great esteem, *auctoritas*, to Caesar, and through his patronage, to us.

I would have been greatly impressed by all this had I imagined that the great Gaius Iulius Caesar, descendant of Venus and Consul of the Roman Republic, had any idea at all about our existence.

Macro had no respect at all for such old fairy tales. In fact, he sneered at them. He once told me that Romulus and Remus were nurtured by a she-wolf, a *lupa*, which is what soldiers call a whore. So, according to Macro, Rome was nurtured by the breasts of a whore!

Whatever the story may be, the Romans believe their conquest and domination of the Greek cities to be retribution, divinely inspired vengeance, for the Greeks' burning of Troy. Romans believe that their conquest of the Greeks was sanctioned, if not obligated, by their sense of *pietas*, devotion to their ancestors.

Caesar himself would soon teach me a lesson in what Romans believed they must do in order to be *pius*.

Getting back to the *magister*, Homer told a much different story, one in which the Greeks were brave and noble and the Trojans cowardly and deceitful. According to Homer, the war had been caused by the rape of the beautiful Spartan queen, Helen, by a weak and craven Trojan prince, Paris. The war was merely an outraged husband's revenge.

The *magister* read, actually intoned, the Greek text to us:

μῆνιν ἄειδε θεὰ Πηληϊάδεω Ἀχιλῆος
οὐλομένην, ἣ μυρί᾽ Ἀχαιοῖς ἄλγε᾽ ἔθηκε,
πολλὰς δ᾽ ἰφθίμους ψυχὰς Ἄϊδι προΐαψεν
ἡρώων, αὐτοὺς δὲ ἑλώρια τεῦχε κύνεσσιν
οἰωνοῖσί τε πᾶσι, Διὸς δ᾽ ἐτελείετο βουλή,

ἐξ οὗ δὴ τὰ πρῶτα διαστήτην ἐρίσαντε
Ἀτρείδης τε ἄναξ ἀνδρῶν καὶ δῖος Ἀχιλλεύς.

The *magister's* eyes seemed to lose their focus as he sang these sacred words, and he seemed to drift back into the mists of time.

When he finished, the *magister* gradually returned to the reality of the classroom. He asked, "Master Marcus, can you translate the first verse?"

Marcus stopped chomping his apple and actually looked thoughtful for a moment. "I hear the word *sing*," he struggled. "Is someone named Peleus singing?"

The *magister* blanched a little. A Roman chopping up Homer's verse was cutting a bit too close to home. But, he quickly remembered who was footing the bill for his scholarly lifestyle and recovered.

"Good start, Master Marcus," the *magister* managed. "Could you continue, Gaius?"

"Sing, goddess, the anger of Peleus' son Achilleus," I recited.

"*Bene! Quod est rectum*, Gaius! And, who is the θεά, the goddess, whom the poet addresses?" he asked.

"Kaliope, daughter of Zeus and Mnemosyne, the muse of epic poetry, *Magister*," I answered.

"*Euge!* Let's hear the second verse again: οὐλομένην, ἣ μυρί᾽Ἀχαιοῖς ἄλγε᾽ ἔθηκε." Would you like to try that one, Master Marcus?" the *magister* continued hopefully.

Finally, we generated a translation of the entire passage, without disturbing Marcus' snack much at all:

Sing, goddess, the anger of Peleus' son Achilleus and its devastation, which put pains thousand fold upon the Achaians, hurled in their multitudes to the house of Hades, the robust souls of heroes, but gave their bodies to be the delicate feasting of dogs, of all birds, and the will of Zeus was accomplished, since that time when first there stood in division of conflict Atreus' son, the lord of men, the brilliant Achilleus.

The *magister* reviewed the fine points of the grammar and rhetoric for us, spoke a bit about the "elevated style" of the diction and allusions, introduced and explained two verbal tropes he called "euphony" and "cacophony," and told us to memorize the entire passage for the next class.

Macro and I continued our sparring, but now I was beginning to give as well as I got. At the end of our matches, we both had our share of chalk marks, mostly slashed on our forearms and the outer part of our shoulders. Neither of us seemed able to land any "killing" blows on the other. Our sessions were being cut short by the diminishing length of the winter hours and Macro's need to supervise his "boys" in getting the grapevines ready for the winter.

One afternoon, we were cooling down after a match in one of the storehouses. It was getting too cool to be standing around out of doors after sweating. Macro brought out a brown clay jug and poured into two cups a liquid that looked slightly yellow but sparkled in the lamp light. He then poured a bit of water into each.

"Go ahead!" he told me. "Try it!"

As he began to sip from his cup, I lifted mine to my lips. It was wine.

"So, what do you taste?" he asked almost eagerly.

"Wine," I answered.

"No . . . no . . . what does it taste *like?*" he asked insistently.

I had no idea what to say.

"Do you taste the apples," he asked smiling, "and a slight hint of pear?"

I looked at him blankly.

"Here," he said, ripping a piece of bread from a loaf left over from breakfast, "eat a bit of this, and taste it again."

I complied and took another sip of the wine.

"Let it rest for a few seconds on your tongue; then spit it out," he told me.

I did, but I was beginning to think that Macro may have been tippling from the jug since lunch.

"Well?" he demanded.

"Yes," I hedged, tasting what I thought was *mere* wine again, "Apples . . . and something sweet . . . a bit like . . . honey."

"Indeed," Macro said happily, refilling my cup. "It's from the vines we're growing here! If the new vintage is half this good, they'll lap it up down in Rome. We'll make a fortune with it!"

I liked the sound of *nos*, we, in that sentence. He held his cup up to me. We clinked and drank.

"I'm sending my boys out to your place tomorrow to get the vines ready for winter," he continued, again topping off our cups. "I really like the way the plants took this summer. The roots seem to have taken to the soil. They're strong. According to your father, there are two more farmers in the valley who want in. We're on our way, Gai!"

Again we clinked and drank. I noticed that Macro had stopped reaching for the water pitcher, and I had a long walk home in the twilight. But, I was beginning to think I could taste a slight hint of apple in the golden liquid. My thoughts drifted: *a rich wine merchant . . . a townhouse near the agora in Athens . . . snuggling with Gabi every night.*

My dreams of Gabi and a life of idle wealth began to unravel the very next week.

Ironically, it was while I was hurrying home on the evening of the *Samon'win*, the day before the Calends of November, the day the Dark Ones return from the underworld. This is not a good time for a member of the Gah'el to be wandering about the countryside at night.

Even the Romans were careful about this day of the year. Macro, after a thorough sampling of his new vintage, had told me the country folk down in Latium believe that on the Calends of November, Pluto, the god who rules the underworld, releases the *lemures*, the spirits of the restless dead, from their prison for one day to seek appeasement. Although Macro claimed he didn't believe in these old wives' tales, he said that it's never a good idea to be caught out at night while the *lemures* are prowling about. In fact, the superstitious *pagani* down in Italia leave small offerings of food and cream on their doorsteps to ward off these malicious spirits of the dead. When he said that, Macro spilled a few drops of his wine and muttered some incantation under his breath.

So, that evening I was doing my best Roman legionary "double time" to get home before dark because night comes quickly down in the valley.

The sun had dipped below the ridges to the west, and I was only about halfway home.

Suddenly, I spotted a dark, shapeless mass on the side of the road. No sooner had I seen it than it made a sound, a soft moaning. For a heartbeat, I believed that it was one of the *Uh Thloo uth uh Doo T'wil*, the People of the Dark God, just escaped from the caverns of the underworld, trying to lure me into some kind of trap as punishment for daring to be away from my hearth on the night of *Samon'win*.

But no! I quickly realized that it was a man, a seemingly badly injured man lying alongside the road. I broke my pace and approached the shape.

"Are you alright?" I called.

A moan, some seemingly inarticulate speech, answered me.

I moved closer. I started to bend down on one knee, reaching out toward the dark shape with my right hand.

I sensed movement behind me. I turned to my left to look. The blow that was supposed to crush my skull missed and struck a glancing blow to my right shoulder. I spun away from the danger into the middle of the road. I saw the other man, the one who struck me, dark in the twilight. He held a heavy cudgel, *uh sal ayleh*, in our tongue, the weapon of a thug.

"I missed the little bastard, Win," he was saying.

"Well, finish him, you stupid son-of-a-bitch," the other was saying, rising from the side of the road. "I want to get back to town before it gets too fookin' dark."

Win! I thought. *They're Gah'el! Thieves? Town? Why would thieves from Medhlán be way out here on the night of the Samon'win?*

The one with the club came at me.

I couldn't feel my right arm. With my left hand, I reached under my cloak and pulled my *pugio* out from its sheath hanging under the Medusa buckle of my soldier's belt. It was reversed. I flipped it in my hand, but the club was coming down toward my head. I pulled my head back and stepped back with my right leg. The club whistled by, less than a palm from my face. I pushed it toward the ground with my *pugio*, and the thug came forward toward me, slightly off balance following his own blow. I delivered a backward slash with my knife. I felt a slight tearing resistance as the blade cut through his face. He dropped the club and staggered back while I recovered into first position, looking for a target for a killing blow. My right arm still refused to move. The man continued to backpedal. His hands went to his face, and he screamed.

"I'm cut," he seemed to gurgle into his scream. "The fookin' little bastard cut me, Win! I'm bleedin'!"

"Shut yer gob," the other ordered, standing up. "Let a man do 'is work!"

The other reached down toward his belt and pulled out a knife, a long, curved dagger, a *sica*. He slashed the knife through the air at me as he approached. He was an amateur, a *tiro*. He was trying to intimidate me with the movement, distract me.

It didn't work.

I waited, and I watched. His dagger crossed in front of me to my right, then my left. I saw my target, his throat, and I struck. At the last instant, I raised my strike; my *pugio* tip hit him in the mouth. I felt it go in, felt teeth brake. Then it hit something hard, bone. I twisted it, withdrew, and recovered to first position.

The man howled! He spit blood. Gagged. He fell to his knees.

I didn't finish him. I just got out of there. Maybe there were more of them out there in the lengthening shadows. I ran as best I could with my damaged arm. I was a thousand paces down the road before I stopped to catch my breath and take inventory of the damage. I cleaned the blade of my *pugio* using dead leaves and grass. I returned it to its sheath under my cloak. I could feel some tingling in my right fingers. My shoulder was beginning to ache. I tried to move my arm. Pain lanced up my neck and across my back.

I walked quickly the rest of the way home. It was soon dark. I was no longer worried about the Dark Ones leaping out at me from the shadows. If they did, I'd cut them to shreds.

By the time I got home and got my clothes off, I had recovered some movement in my right arm. My shoulder had turned black and purple where the club had hit me. Mama was horrified. I told her it was nothing, a minor accident. I had fallen from a horse at the senator's estate.

Papa looked at the bruise. "You fell from a horse?" he asked.

"That's what happened," I lied. "The horse stumbled . . . went down on his front knees. I couldn't grab the mane in time."

I don't think Papa was buying my story, but he didn't press me. Maybe it was for Mama's sake.

"I don't think anything's broken," Papa said. He probed around my injury as I tried to move the arm. It felt worse than the torments of Tartarus. "But, that's one hell of a bruise you got. It's going to hurt for a while. I'll mix up one of Gran'ma's compresses to draw the poisons out of it. You're going to have to sleep sitting up for the next few nights. Only way the poison will come out. I'll give you a little *Dur* to drink tonight to help you sleep."

The *Dur* didn't help at all. The pain kept me awake all night. The next morning, Papa rigged a sling for my arm. It seemed to help with the pain. At least it kept my arm from flopping around every time I moved.

When I got to the estate, rather than go to the *magister's* class, I went and sought out Macro in his *cubiculum* at the back of the main house. When I arrived, he was briefing his "boys" about the day's assignments. When he saw me in the sling, he sent them off.

"What happened to you?" he asked. "Did one of those little, Gallic fairies of yours kick your ass on the way home last night?" Just to get a good dig in, Macro used the word *nympha*, a girl fairy.

I told him the story about the club and the two Gallic thugs from Mediolanum, who had no business being that far out of town at night—and about the *sica*.

Macro whistled through his teeth. "That's quite a story!" he commented. "The whole thing stinks! There're enough people to rob at night in town. Those *cunni* had no business being out on the road like that . . . not city boys. It sounds like an ambush; they were waiting for you."

I agreed.

"I know a couple of guys in town I can talk to . . . ex-soldiers . . . good guys," Macro said. "The way you marked them, your thieves won't be hard to track down. Maybe it's a good thing you didn't kill them. Dead men are hard to talk to . . . and these are two guys I definitely want to hear from."

I went back to the windy plains of Troy with the *magister*. He didn't like my being late, but when he saw the sling, he didn't ask any questions. A couple of days later, Macro called me into his office after class.

"Got the word back from town," he said. "Seems your two friends were pretty well-known around town as enforcers, cheap muscle for hire. Most of their work was bouncing drunks out of *cauponae* and cheap *lupinaria*. Taverns and whorehouses were their natural habitat, but sometimes they busted heads collecting debts for the bankers around the forum. An occasional murder wasn't beyond them."

"So, what's it got to do with me?" I asked, grimacing, as I flexed my injured arm. I had finally recovered full movement, but it still hurt like the blazes. It hurt so bad that I didn't catch on to Macro's use of the past tense.

"I'm getting to that," Macro said. "These two boys told my mate that a few days ago some guy with a Roman accent showed up in the *caupona* where they hung out, bought them a pitcher of the best wine in the house . . . the vinegar instead of the piss . . . and offered them fifty *denarii* each to off you. Even told them where you would be that night."

"Off me?" I questioned. "You mean kill me?! Who'd want me dead? Why?"

"They didn't know," Macro continued, "didn't care really. Silver's silver. If some nob down in Rome wants you dead and is willing to pay to have it done, that was all they cared about."

"Does your friend still have them?" I asked. "Maybe if he pressed them they'd tell."

"Pressed them?" Macro chuckled. "That's going to be a bit difficult. They aren't talking to anybody anymore."

Not talking to anybody? I wondered for a second. "You mean, they're dead? Your friend—"

"A message had to be sent," Macro said. "Next time some Roman *cunnus* tries to hire somebody to come out here, it's going to cost a hell of a lot more than a few coins. In fact, the *cunnus* will probably end up swimming in the sewers with the rest of the rats."

"So, we're just going to leave it?" I pressed. "They were hired to kill me! They knew where to find me."

"Calm down, Gai," Macro said. "You're right. This was an inside job. Whoever it was who gave the order knew exactly where you'd be and when. I'm willing to swear on the *manes* of my dead parents it wasn't any of my boys. And, I don't think that Greek *podex*, arse, of a *magister* has the balls to get involved in something like this. Besides, the *mentula* who set this up has plenty of silver to throw around. And, we know he's from Rome. Let me send word down to the senator's household in Rome. Most of his bodyguards are all ex-soldiers, most of them good guys. Someone should be able to sniff this out."

A couple weeks later, Macro received a message from one of his army cronies down in Rome. When I found Macro, he had the letter unrolled on his desk in his *cubiculum*.

When I entered, he asked, "Have you ever heard of Marcus Calpurnius Piso?"

"No," I said. "Who the hell is that?"

"He's the guy who wanted you dead," Macro said, rather too matter-of-factly for my comfort. "Perhaps this will help you remember. He's old. He's a senator. And, until recently, he was affianced to one Gabinia, only daughter of Aulus Gabinius."

"Gabinia," I stammered, "Gabi . . . the senator . . . but how?"

Macro raised his hand to silence me. "It seems that the young Lady Gabinia—*Gabinia Pulchra*, as she styles herself these days—has been telling tales to her harebrained, giggly girlfriends about her adventures in Gaul this summer."

"Adventures in Gaul?" I repeated. "But, she was here . . . wait . . . nothing happened."

Again, Macro silenced me. He read from the letter, his finger tracing the text. "It seems, according to the Lady Gabinia Pulchra, that one sunny afternoon, while out riding through the wild hills and forests of Gallia, she was accosted and kidnapped by a wild, Gallic brigand, a handsome war chief, outlawed by the Roman authorities. He spirited her away to a secret valley, high in the hills. There, in his hidden grotto he . . . he . . . well . . . the Lady Gabinia just cannot talk about it. But, he was wild and madly handsome with long, fiery-red hair, Gallic mustachios down to his chin, a broad chest and shoulders, and his . . .

I love this part . . . long, shining Gallic sword." Macro stopped reading long enough to regain control of himself.

He continued, "The brave Lady Gabinia found herself falling for this rogue. But, realizing that she was a Roman noble and had responsibilities to the *res publica* and her *familia*, she was able to escape by flirting with the brigand's dimwitted servant, an ignorant peasant farmer's boy, who was supposed to guard her while the brigand was away doing whatever it is that brigands do. She stole back her faithful mount and rode with all her might back down into the valley to safety. Unfortunately, the brigand saw her riding away from the secret valley and gave chase. He would have caught her, except that the Lady Gabinia could ride like the Gallic horse goddess . . ." Macro seemed to struggle with the word.

"Mahk'a," I suggested.

"Yes," Macro continued, "like the Gallic horse goddess, Mahk'a. She barely reached her father's estate safely, the handsome brigand in hot pursuit . . . but he dared not follow her there. The estate was guarded by a faithful, but grizzled, old Roman legionary, whose life her father, the noble senator, had once saved in a desperate fight against thousands of wild Parthians. I guess that's me. But before the brigand rode off, from the top of the ridge, he reared his black stallion up on its hind legs in the setting sun, and—oh, this is rich—twirled his long, Gallic sword above his head three times to show his undying love for the Lady Gabinia Pulchra, whom he knew could never be his. Then he escaped back into the hills. The faithful, old Roman soldier organized armed bands of militia to hunt the brigand, but he easily eluded them in the forested hills and valleys of Gaul, where no Roman dares to venture. *Quam merda!* What shit! Finally, her father, the senator, decided to return his precious daughter to Rome to protect her from this handsome and brave Gallic warrior, who had fallen so desperately and hopelessly in love with her."

I was stunned, but finally asked, "Who am I? The handsome brigand or the dimwitted peasant?"

"Who the hell knows?" Macro answered. "Either . . . neither . . . both—it doesn't matter. What matters is that this little fairy tale finally reached the ears of her esteemed fiancé, the noble Senator, Marcus Calpurnius Piso. Seems some of the younger set, a bunch of noble, ne'er-do-wells, who group around a drunken rogue named Marcus Antonius, made a very public joke about it at the old man's expense. All of Rome was howling about the Gallic brigand and the senator's child bride. To make matters worse, the Lady Gabinia's older brother, Aulus, is very chummy with this Marcus Antonius character. Piso actually got the news from Marcus Licinius Crassus himself, Caesar's partner, at some drunken dinner party with all the other senatorial nobs. Seems Piso sits with Cicero, Cato, and the rest of the conservatives in the senate, so Caesar and the *populares*, the progressive set, made full use of his embarrassment. Piso decided to put on a show of his *pietas*. He put two and two together . . . long afternoon rides with a Gallic stable boy . . . and sent an agent up here with a bag of silver to fix the problem. That is, fix you. He probably planned to deliver your head to Caesar's doorstep."

"*Cacat*! Shit!" I cried. "Do I have to worry?"

Macro held his hand up and stopped me. "There is a happy ending to this farce! It seems that on her wedding night, the Lady Gabinia Pulchra played the part of the virgin well enough to convince her husband that these tales about wild, Gallic brigands were just that. So, all's right in the Piso household. He's no longer interested in dispensing good silver to a bunch of cheap, Mediolanum tavern thugs to whack some horny teenager in the wilds of *Gallia Cisalpina* to protect his *auctoritas*. Besides, the smart set in Rome has already found some other reputation to devastate. With their attentions diverted, you're in the clear for now!"

"What about the senator . . . our senator?" I asked.

"Gabinius?" Macro chuckled. "Seems he knows his daughter well enough not to take her romantic daydreams seriously. He was concerned about her riding up into the hills with a randy teenage boy and what that could do to the marriage and all the political plans and maneuvers that rested on it . . . hence, her hasty removal to Rome. Since the marriage came off and he's successfully dumped the fair Lady Gabinia Pulchra on poor old Piso, he doesn't really care about you. His *auctoritas*, his reputation, wasn't affected at all. In fact, now that he's pulled in Piso and his influence with the *Optimates*, the real nobs in the senate, with the marriage, he expects, with Caesar's support, to be elected one of the consuls for next year. So, not only does his *pietas* for the reputation of his *familia* not urge him to act, but he doesn't want to do anything that might offend Caesar's *patrocinium*, his protection for you and your family, so close to the election. Looks like you're home free on that one, too."

Despite the fact I was fairly certain that Caesar had no idea that I, or my family, existed, I indeed wanted to believe that I was home free.

We were soon past the Calends of December. It was the "dark time." I walked to the senator's estate before the sun rose and returned home after it set. Not only were the daylight hours getting shorter each day, but the air was also getting colder. Mama sewed long sleeves onto my Roman *tunica*, and I tucked the thing down into my woolen, Gallic *bracae*, trousers. Then, I tucked the bottom of the *bracae* into a thick pair of woolen socks and then shoved my feet into a thick pair of leather boots for the long walks back and forth to the senator's estate. I had pulled my *laena*, my winter cloak, out of the wooden chest where Mama stored our winter clothes. It had belonged to my Gran'pa and had a nice *cucullus*, a hood, attached to protect my head and ears when the frigid winds blew down into the valley from the mountains to the North. The first time Macro saw me in this get-up, with my Gallic trousers and woolen socks, he made a crack about me looking like a fine Roman-maiden-stealing brigand from the wilds of *Gallia comata*, long-haired Gaul. I had the satisfaction of watching him turn blue as he tried to "bare-leg it" through a Gallic winter like a true Roman.

The *magister*, when he saw my *bracae*, went off on a long tangent about how trousers were invented by Persian barbarians and were brought into the cultured world of the Greeks by the semibarbaric Maecedonian veterans of Alexander's army returning from his conquest of Darius' empire. No Greek, he sniffed, would ever cover his legs in such a barbaric fashion. I'm sure Macro, had he heard this, would make some crack about Greeks allowing easy access to their kilts.

Every morning the fishpond had a thin sheet of ice before the sun finally hit it, so we moved class in from the *peristylium* to a large *cubiculum* near the kitchen. The *magister* huddled close to a large brazier, which, together with the kitchen fires nearby, kept the room warm enough. At least our supply of ink wasn't frozen when we began each morning. Unfortunately, Master Marcus' academic resolve was sorely tried by the smells of food being prepared in the kitchen and the fact that all he could find in his fruit bowl were the wizened remnants of that year's harvest: some prunes, raisins, and a few wrinkled apples.

In our studies, Homer's war against Troy was going badly for the Greeks. No surprise there! The Trojans gave the Greeks a pretty good thumping when they attacked the city, driving them back to their encampment. Their main hero, Achilles, refused to fight and sat pouting in his tent because of a disagreement he had had with the Greek king, Agamemnon, over a captive girl. The king tried to make amends, but Achilles refused to come around.

From such behavior, it's pretty obvious to me why the Romans were able to rout the Greeks just about every time they met them in battle. Achilles! *Quam primo*! What a prima donna! If a Roman soldier acted like that and refused an order to go into battle against the enemy, his general would have his comrades beat him to death in front of the whole army. The only thing the Greeks seemed to have done right in the war was to fortify their camp with *fossa* and *vallum*, parapet and ditch. The Roman army was smarter, according to Macro, even fortifying its daily marching camps this way. The Greeks only got the work done after the Trojans had kicked their butts and were breathing down their necks. They damn near lost their ships and their camp! *Quam amentes*! What idiots!

The *magister* considered the trouserless Greek clowns to be heroic role models of his race, so we continued to plow through his Homer, word by word, line by line—a whole ten years' worth of a story! A Roman army would have had the walls down and the city burned to ashes in ten days!

We were quickly approaching the annual festival of *Saturnalia*. Mama told me that before the wars waged by Iove and the other gods against the Titans, Saturn ruled the universe. At that time, there was no winter, no dark times. Humans enjoyed the bounties of the earth without having to labor. So, at the darkest part of the year, when the sun begins its journey back from the underworld, we celebrate those bountiful, brighter times with lights and reverie. As a kid, this was my favorite time of the year. There was no work to be done on the farm—we still had plenty of food in our larders—and there were mischievous tricks to be played. It was a complete breakdown of discipline, and it was a time of gifts, especially gifts.

About two days before the Ides of December, Macro had a surprise for me. I was sitting at the large table in the kitchen of the senator's estate, wolfing down some bread with olive oil, my head still spinning with Greek preterits and Patroclus going off into battle dressed in Achilles' armor—no good was going to come of that, I was sure—when Macro burst into the kitchen and told me to come with him. I quickly grabbed a couple of small loaves with one hand and my woolen cloak with the other, and I followed him out the back door into the yard.

There I saw two horses, saddled and ready to go.

"If you're done stuffing yourself," Macro said, "hop on and come with me."

Macro mounted one of the horses and headed in the direction of the road leading off the estate. I did a quick juggling act with the loaves and my cloak, not wanting to drop either, and then tried to figure how to get my ass up on the saddle. Finally, the loaves went down the front of my tunic, the cloak went around my shoulders, and I managed to mount.

When I finally caught up with Macro, I asked, "What's the rush? Where're we going?"

"Town," he answered, "and I want to get there before I'm too old to care."

I reached down into the front of my tunic and pulled out one of the loaves, offering it to Macro. "Want one?" I asked.

"Not after where that's been," he said and picked up the pace to a canter.

When Macro's horse sped up, mine did too, without any urging from me—or any warning. My loaf and I almost ended up going over backwards. But, I managed to save myself, and the bread, and followed Macro down the road toward Mediolanum.

About three miles past my place, we picked up the Roman road, called the *Via Nova*, the New Road, even though it had been built during the Germanic invasions in my grandfather's time. It was smooth, paved, and ran as straight as an arrow across the plain toward Mediolanum, straight to the western gate of the city. Built so that the Romans could move their legions around quickly, it ran basically south and west until it connected down in the Padus Valley with the main Roman road, *Via Aemelia*, a few miles south of the Roman *colonia* at Placentia.

Just as we passed a carved, granite stone that marked one mile from the town forum in Mediolanum, I noticed that limestone and marble tombs were being built along the road. Gallic Medhlán was becoming more Roman over time. We

Gah'el bury our dead in the ground. In the old days, we'd erect mounds over the graves of our kings. But, we never burned them, poured their ashes in jars, and built little stone houses for them like the Romans.

The German invasions had terrified the merchants so badly that they mustered their civic duty and poured some of their profits into rebuilding the city walls and maintaining the *Via Nova*. The new western gate was a masonry building of granite. It was topped with a crenelated parapet and guarded on each side by round towers over thirty feet high. The gate had three portals. The center one was wide and broad enough to accommodate the two-way traffic of large farm carts and merchant wagons that stocked the city markets and shops. On each side of the center entryway was a smaller gated portal for pedestrian traffic. Members of the city militia stood outside the gate, collecting tolls from the farmers and merchants entering the city and taxes on goods sold from those leaving the city.

Macro and I dismounted and walked our horses toward the center portal. I was just wondering whether the guards would charge us to enter when Macro called over, "Io, Galene! That money's supposed to go into the toll box, not into your pockets!"

A guard inspecting a merchant's cart looked over, then called back, "Macro! It's a dark day, indeed, that I see your ugly kisser approaching my gate!"

The guard, Galenus, waved the cart through the gate and walked over to us. "*Quomo' vales, m'amice?*" he said to Macro. "How's it goin', buddy? What brings you to my town? Draining our winter supplies of wine or paying a visit to the *lupae*, the whores?"

The men shook hands. Macro asked, "How's your woman?"

"She's well! We're expecting in early March. Looks like a boy, the way she's filling out," Galenus responded.

"Great to hear, Galenus," Macro said. "I knew I picked a good provider for my son."

"If he looks anything like you, the midwife won't know which end to slap," Galenus chuckled.

"This is Gaius," Macro said, gesturing at me. "He works with me up at the senator's place. Thought I'd introduce him to Rufia as a Saturnalia offering."

"Rufia, is it?" the guard said. "You sure you're still welcomed there? I heard it cost her close to a hundred *denarii* to fix the place after your last visit."

"Of course I am!" Macro said, feigning indignity. "I was defending the lady's honor. Those two *mentulae* from down South called her a cheap whore. There's nothing cheap about Rufia, so I had to set them straight."

Both men laughed at that crack. Then, Galenus said, "*Bene*! You can leave those nags at my brother-in-law's stable. Usual friend-of-the-family discount. I assume you still know the way to Rufia's *lupinarium*."

"I can find that place blind drunk," Macro chuckled.

"I know that," Galenus countered. "I didn't know if you could find it sober!"

Both men laughed at that one. Macro clapped Galenus on the shoulder, and we entered the city.

"Galenus is a mate of mine from the Third Legion," Macro explained. "Mustered out after Mithridates bought it and things got boring. Brought his woman back with him from Asia. *Mulieres castrorum*, we called them, camp women. Doratheates is her name. We all just call her Dora. Took good care of Galenus . . . even followed him on campaign . . . a good woman. I'm glad the gods have finally blessed them with a child."

Macro seemed to get quiet, pensive, after he said that. I was about to ask him if he had ever had a woman, a *mulier castrorum*, while he was in the army. But, something warned me off asking.

We dropped the horses off with a slave at a stable near the gate. I assumed it was the place that belonged to Galenus' brother-in-law. Macro dropped a coin in the slave's hand, "Good brushing and some water . . . no feed. We'll be back for them in a couple of hours."

Macro led me up the main street from the gate to the town forum, but some seventy paces up the hill, he turned left into a side street. Clothing trying to dry in the feeble winter sun flapped over our heads. Macro said, "Stay in the center. You could get a shower if you're too close to the buildings."

I was about to ask him what he meant when a few paces down the street I saw a bowl attached to an arm appear out of a third-story window. The arm turned over, and the bowl emptied, splashing the pavement ahead of us with piss.

"Supposed to walk that stuff down to the sewer grate," Macro said. "Rarely happens in this neighborhood. At least it's only piss."

Macro led me into an even narrower street off to the left, an alley really, not enough room for us to walk side by side. I watched for bowls attached to arms in any of the upper windows and then ran right into Macro's back. He had stopped before a door painted bright blue.

"The color of Venus," he said, winking at me. Next to the door was a Priapus in faded blue paint. Its erect penis was so long and curved it ended almost at his nose. Underneath was chalked, "*Astrea Optima.* Astrea's the best." And below that, "*Rufia verpas rubefacit.* Ruby makes pricks grow red." I assumed that this must be the *lupinarium.*

As he knocked on the blue door, Macro rubbed Priapus' painted phallus. "Never hurts to get the god's attention," he said, then laughed at some joke lost on me.

The blue door swung inward, but the doorway was immediately filled by one of the largest human beings I had ever seen. In the shadows of the alley, his hair looked white, and he had a luxurious mustache down past his chin. Even in the cold of December, he wore the short-sleeved, grey, woolen tunic of a slave. His arms seemed like bulging tree trunks of human flesh, as if some god had brought an oak to life. His hands seemed large enough to hold an entire human head. If he were of a mind to break either of us in two like a couple of Roman twigs, then explaining to him that it was against the law to lay those hands on a citizen wouldn't do much good.

"*Wæs hæl*, Wulfgar!" Macro greeted the titan in a language I hadn't yet learned. "Almost time to burn the yule log for Wodin and the Modranicht . . . eh, my friend?"

"Macro," he grunted in response, "I no think see you after last time."

"Wulfgar here's a real, live Kraut, from up where the Rhenus meets Ocean," Macro explained to me. "'Bout as far as a civilized man can go before he falls off the edge of the earth . . . covered in ice and snow all the time . . . horrible place. The gods send soldiers there to punish them."

"Me no Kraut," Wulfgar interrupted. "Me Saxon people!"

"*Gens Saxona*," Macro corrected Wulfgar's Latin. "He's been Rufia's doorman in this *lupinarium* almost five years, and he still speaks Latin like some sheep-shaggin' Kraut from beyond the Rhenus. You gonna let us in? It's getting cold out here on the doorstep!"

"Cold?" the giant dismissed Macro's complaint. Then he turned his head and called into the room, "*Domina*! Lady! You boyfriend here!"

From out of the darkness behind Wulfgar, I heard a woman's voice call out, "Well, let him in, Wolfie, before he catches his death out there!"

The giant stepped back out of the doorway and allowed us to enter Rufia's *lupinarium*. I was immediately overwhelmed by the heat, the overwhelming smell of burning lamp oil, and something else, something I wasn't familiar with, some earthy aroma, like damp earth. As Macro led me down a short flight of stairs, I blinked, trying to clear the lamp soot from my eyes.

When we reached the bottom and "Wolfie" was taking our cloaks, a woman suddenly emerged out of the fog of lamp oil and lavender, swayed up to Macro, placed her hands on his shoulders, and kissed him noisily on the mouth.

"Macro . . . Macro . . . Macro . . . *me' miles gloriosus*, my glorious soldier!" she was saying. "Why have you stayed away so long?"

She stood about five feet tall, her lithe frame wrapped in a shimmering Greek chiton of bluish-green. She pressed her ample bosom into Macro as she kissed him. Then, she took him by the arm, asking, "And who have you brought for me?"

Her gown was draped over only one arm, leaving her right shoulder bare. The diaphanous material hung elegantly down across her bosom, leaving me with no doubt that she was the model for every statue of a goddess I had ever seen. No wonder Circe could turn men into dumb animals!

Suddenly, I realized she was talking to me. "I'm up here, *carrissime*!" she was saying, laughingly. "What's your name?"

I had to think about the answer. "Uh . . . uh . . . Gai," I finally managed to stammer out. Amused, she looked at me with eyes the exact same green as her gown, eyes that bore right into me with a piercing fire.

"Well, uh . . . uh . . . Gai," she laughed, "*beneventus a' me' domum*. Welcome to my place!" She placed her hands on my forearms, leaned in, and kissed my cheek. My head swam in the fog of lavender with just a hint of roses. Still in the background, there was another fragrance, an odor, really—earthy, damp.

"We better get this one some wine before he forgets how to breathe," she teased.

She clapped her hands to get the attention of one of her servants and led us over to a couch. In the lamplight, her hair shimmered like dark, red fire. When we sat, she leaned back into the couch and crossed her legs, letting the skirt of her chiton, which was split halfway up her thigh, fall aside.

"I'm flattered by your attentiveness, Gai." I heard her voice from somewhere far off. "But, I'm still up here, *carissime*. Maybe you should drink some of this."

I tore my eyes away from her legs and saw that she was holding out a cup. I took it and drank without taking my eyes away from her—and immediately choked. It was unwatered wine.

"*Lente . . . lente . . .* slowly, *carissime*," she said, patting my back. Then, she turned to Macro. "So, what can I do for you two boys?" she asked.

"The lad here just turned sixteen," Macro said, draining his cup. "So, as my Saturnalia offering, I brought him here to make a man out of him."

"Ah," said Rufia with a wry grin, rubbing my thigh, "this wouldn't require something with a toga, would it?" They both laughed at that. I was too busy trying to learn how to breathe again to participate.

"He looks like a sister man to me," she said after giving me the once over. "Let me see who's free in the back. Excuse me, gentlemen."

Rufia rose like shimmering green smoke and walked through a curtained doorway.

"Sister man?" I questioned.

"That's Rufia's little system for pairing off her customers with the right girl," Macro explained. "She says there are three types of men when it comes to sex—with women, that is. Rufia doesn't cater to the other stuff. Her types are mother men, sister men, and daughter men. That is, men who like older women, women their own age, or younger women . . . girls even. Rufia doesn't cater much to that, either, but she has a couple of girls who are great actresses. She believes the gods make men that way. Why, she hasn't a clue. Leave it to a woman to make a philosophy out of sex . . . useless stuff . . . but she believes it helps the business."

Rufia's return from the back interrupted Macro's lecture. "Gai," she was saying, "I have the perfect girl for you. Her name's Cynthia. She's waiting for you."

"Menander," she called over to a servant waiting by the doorway, "please show this young gentleman the way to Cynthia's *cubiculum*. While you are otherwise engaged, *carissime*," she said to me, caressing my cheek, "I will entertain *me' miles fortissimus*, my strong and brave soldier."

Menander held back the curtain for me. As I entered, I glanced back and saw Rufia sit down and snuggle into Macro on the couch.

Menander led me down a corridor. On each side were doorways, some open, others curtained off. Next to each of the open doorways hung a small, wooden sign with a name: Aegle, Arethusa, Erytheia, Hesperia. I imagined that I had stumbled into an inn that accommodated all the nymphs and naiads of Acadia.

The signs next to the curtained doors read, "*Occupatum*."

Finally, Menander led me to an open *cubiculum* whose sign read, "Cynthia." He gestured for me to enter, and as I did, he flipped the sign: "*Occupatum*."

Upon entering, I encountered a nymph, tall, about my height. Her long, loose hair shimmered like gold in the dim lamplight. She was draped in a flowing, light blue chiton, again covering only one shoulder. Even in the dimness, I could see the outline of her body and the places where her flesh lifted the shimmering blue fabric.

"*Beneventus, me' Domine*," she intoned, her eyes downcast. "Welcome, my Lord. Please, make yourself comfortable."

Only then did I realize that the only piece of furniture in the room was a bed.

I sat down on its very edge.

"Would my lord like me to unlace his boots?" the blonde divinity asked. As she kneeled before me and began unlacing my work boots, her gown fell forward, revealing her cleavage.

Jerking my head up, I stammered, "You aren't Roman?"

"No, my Lord," she said. My boots were about half undone.

"You sound Gah'el. Are you?" I persisted, trying not to look down at her.

"I will be whatever pleases you, my Lord," she said, removing my left boot.

"What is a woman of the Gah'el doing—?" I started.

Dropping my boot, the goddess reached up and placed a finger on my lips.

"*Bee'thaf un gath fee argloo'eeth?*" she asked in perfect Gallic. "Shall I be my lord's captive?"

"*Fee gath,*" I stammered. "My captive . . . no . . . not that."

She looked up at me. I was drowning in the blue seas of her eyes. She was saying in Gallic, "You are Gah'el? From the countryside?"

"*Shuh,*" I answered. "Yes."

She stood. "I have something that may make you more comfortable." She slipped through the curtained doorway and returned a few heartbeats later with another of the local nymphs, this one a brunette in a deep red gown.

"I need you as a witness, Meriope," she said in Latin.

"Sure thing, *cara,*" said the other girl, working on her nails with a small piece of pumice stone.

"Please stand, my Lord," she said to me. "And take my right hand in yours."

When I stood up, I realized I had a pronounced limp. I still had my right boot on. I awkwardly took Cynthia's right hand in mine, and we both faced the one called Meriope.

Cynthia intoned in Gallic, "I, Athvoowin, daughter of Gwili, of the Glas Sect of the Insubreci, do swear and affirm in front of this witness that I take . . . take—what is your name, my Lord?"

"Uh . . . my name?" I stammered, forgetting my own name for the second time that day. "My name . . . uh . . . Gaius Marius Insubrecus."

"I take Gaius Marius of the Insubreci as my husband for one course of the sun. Let no one dispute that this is my will and this is my oath!"

"There!" she said, turning to me. "Now we are husband and wife for one day, according to the laws of our people. No one can claim that you took me against my will, and no one can claim my head-price against you." She pecked me on my cheek. Her lips burned, fiery coals against my flesh.

"Thank you, Meriope" she said in Latin to the lady in red.

"Sure thing, *cara,*" Meriope responded. She blew on her nails and left, making sure our curtain was securely closed.

"Now, my husband," Athvoowin of the Insubreci addressed me, pressing her hand on my chest until I sat back down on her—our—bed, "I will remove this other boot for you."

Later, when I returned to the front room, Macro called out to me, "You were in there a lot longer than I expected." Then, he chuckled.

"Leave the poor boy alone, Quintus," Rufia, who was sitting across Macro's lap, scolded. "It's his first time."

"I know," Macro snorted again.

Quintus, I thought. I didn't know what surprised me more, the fact that Macro actually had a *praenomen*, or the fact that Rufia called him by it. By the look in Macro's eyes, he had, while waiting, made a fair sampling of Rufia's wine cellar.

"Here," Rufia was saying to me, holding out a cup of unwatered wine. "You just ignore that uncivilized lout. Was Cynthia good to you?"

I felt my face redden. "We . . . we . . . we were talking," I started.

"Talking?!" Macro burst out. "Talking! I'd like to have been a fly on the wall for *that* conversation!"

Rufia slapped Macro playfully on his shoulder. "Now you just ignore him, Gai. Sometimes, Quintus, I just don't know what to do with you!"

"I could make a few suggestions," Macro laughed.

"But, could you afford it?" Rufia shot back. And, with that, they both started laughing.

We stayed at Rufia's a little longer. Macro refilled my cup; I didn't remember draining it. As we sat, one of Rufia's girls walked over to me, gave me a sisterly kiss on the cheek, and giggled, "*Gratulationes tibi*, congratulations!" This happened two more times. Finally, one of the drunken male customers came over and shook my hand! With that, Macro decided that I had been adequately embarrassed and said, "Let's get out of here!"

I noticed that my second cup of wine was empty.

We got up and started toward the stairway, back up to the entrance of Rufia's *lupinarium*. I was already at the bottom of the stairs when I noticed Macro was no longer with me. Looking back, I saw him with his head leaning down toward Rufia's shoulder. He was whispering something in her ear. She was looking in my direction and nodding with a slight grin. The conference ended with Rufia pecking Macro on his cheek. Then, turning him toward the exit, she gave him a slight push to give him some momentum in the right direction.

"Our guests are leaving, Wolfie!" she called out.

As if by magic, the blond giant suddenly materialized beside me with our cloaks, like bath towels hung over his massive left arm. I'd hate to have this guy creep up on me in the dark from some German forest with something more lethal than a couple of raggedy cloaks in his paws. His right arm gestured us up the stairs.

We each grabbed a cloak as we negotiated the stairs. In Macro's condition, it was a bit like mountain climbing. When we successfully made it back out to the street, the blue door closed firmly behind us, and I was a bit surprised that it was still daylight. With a somewhat wine-induced, bemused look on his face, Macro looked around to get his bearings; then we marched back down the alley the way we had come earlier.

"To the baths!" he called out without turning around. "And be careful of the piss pots!"

I started to throw my cloak over my shoulders, then realized I didn't want to lose sight of Macro. I had no idea where I was. So, cloak half on, I hurried down the alley after him. We arrived back at the narrow street under the clotheslines, turned right down to the *via principalis*, the main street, then right again up toward the city forum. Just before entering the forum, Macro led me up another narrow street to the right and immediately down a short flight of stairs into a building. I immediately smelled the warm, slightly moldy smell of a *balnea*, a bathhouse.

The *balneator*, the bathhouse attendant, stood before a doorway at the end of a short corridor. Macro fumbled a bit in the recesses of his *marsupium*, his purse, finally producing an *as*, a bronze penny, which he tossed to the man.

"There's another one for you if we still have all our clothes on the way out," he told him.

The man bowed slightly, saying, "Of course, *Domine*!"

Immediately upon entering, Macro tossed me his cloak, saying, "Hold that for a second, will you?" Then, he entered a small doorway to the left. From the odor, it was obviously a *latrina*.

When Macro emerged, he was adjusting his clothes. "Better here than in the bathing water, eh?" he said with his lopsided grin and a wink.

We went down a short passage and entered a large rectangular hall with a vaulted ceiling. The feeble winter daylight illuminated the cavernous space through two clear windows high up under the ceiling arches in the two shorter, opposing walls. Long stone benches with a row of wooden pegs above them ran along both sides of the longer walls. The room was empty except for a *capsarius*, an attendant, who needlessly gestured us to seats along the right-hand wall. He placed two towels on the designated benches and hovered. Again, Macro tossed the man a penny, and said, "I've already greased your boss. No funny business, eh?" The man bowed and left us.

"Hang your clothes on the pegs," he told me. "But, if you're carrying any money, take it along with you. Better take your belt and *pugio*, too. No use tempting these bastards."

We stripped, and I followed Macro through one of the portals leading from the dressing room, towel over one shoulder, belt over the other. As soon as I walked through the door, the steamy heat hit me. It was mid-December, so Macro was dodging the cold bath in the *frigidarium* and going right for the hot water in the *caldarium*.

Before we entered the chamber, Macro turned to me. "Put on these wooden clogs," he said, gesturing with his head to rows of wooden shoes stored in recesses along the wall. "The floor's right above the *hypocaustum*, the furnace that heats the water. You don't want to scald the bottom of your feet."

We both put on the wooden clogs, dropped our towels and personal belongings in the vacated recesses, and walked over to a pool of steaming water. There were steps leading down into the pool. "You may want to take this slow," Macro suggested. "Get used to it before you go deeper."

Macro stepped out of his clogs and entered the water. I followed. It wasn't too hot, but such warmth on a cold, winter day felt splendid, luxurious. The chills that had tormented my feet and legs all winter were instantly forgotten. Soon, we were both up to our chests in the steaming water. I felt the heat penetrating into the depths of my muscles; my arms, legs, and shoulders began to loosen, almost flow, into the delightful, soothing waters that surrounded me.

"This is perfect," Macro almost sighed.

We found a perch on the stairs where we could sit and lean back with only our heads out of the water. The cavernous hall was quiet; we had the place to ourselves. I closed my eyes, and suddenly, I was choking and trying to blow water out of my nose.

"Fell asleep . . . eh?" Macro laughed. "It happens! The water gets to you . . . especially after a couple of beakers of Rufia's wine . . . which reminds me."

Macro got up and called out, "*Capsari!* Attendant!"

An attending slave materialized from the shadows, "*Domine?*"

"Bring me my purse," Macro instructed. "It's over there under the towels by the entrance!"

"*Stat', Domine,*" the man responded with a slight nod of the head. "Immediately, Lord."

The man returned with Macro's battered, leather *marsupium* and handed it to Macro.

"*Gratias,*" Macro muttered as he dug around in the leather bag, coins clinking. Finally, he pulled out a small, silver coin and tossed it over to the slave. "Run across the road to Grifud's *caupona* . . . the one with a green rooster painted on the wall next to the entrance. You know the place?"

"*Intellego, Domine!* I know it, Lord," the man responded.

"Good . . . tell Grif . . . or his wife, Telin—she's a big woman, a blonde, weighs almost sixteen Roman *saxa*, usually behind the bar keeping an eye on things—tell her you want a pitcher of wine . . . the good stuff. Tell her it's for Macro. She'll know. Got it?"

"*Intellego, Domine!* I understand, Lord!"

"You should get at least two pennies back from that coin. Leave one on the bar for the house. You keep the other. We'll be in the *trepidarium*, the sauna room. Got all that?"

"*Intellego, Domine,*" the slave responded and started moving toward the door.

"Oh!" Macro said suddenly.

The man stopped and turned back toward us, "Yes, *Domine*?"

"Two beakers, tell 'em," Macro said holding up two fingers.

"*Dicto pareo, Domine*," the slave said with a slight bow. "I obey, Lord." Then he continued on his way.

"Must be new," Macro muttered. "Too polite for this place . . . too polite by half. He'll learn." Macro rose from the steaming water, still holding his clinking *marsupium*. He slipped on his wooden clogs and wobbled over to where we had dropped our towels.

"Let's go over to the *trepidarium*, Gai," he invited. "I'm starting to wrinkle up like a raisin . . . ugly enough as it is."

I followed Macro through a portal to our right into a smaller room. This one had no pool, just a large basin filled with water standing in the middle. The air was delightfully warm, and I noticed that the floor was covered by a colorful mosaic of tiny fishes swimming in an aquatic jungle of sorts. The walls were divided into rows of small *cubicula*, open to the center of the room where the basin sat. I followed Macro into one. There was a stone bench covered with cushions along the three walled sides. Macro dropped his towel, purse, and belt on the bench and sank into the cushions with a sigh.

I dropped my stuff and settled down opposite him. Macro kicked off his wooden clogs. "You don't need them in here," he said. "The room's warmed only by the *caldarium* we were just in. Floor's warm, not hot."

An attendant appeared at the entry to our *cubiculum*, holding a bath strigil. "You ready for me?" he asked abruptly. I noticed the lack of the word *domine*.

Macro didn't seem to mind, though. "No . . . not now . . . but when the guy from the *caldarium* gets back with our wine, tell him where we are."

"I'll tell him," the slave responded and left.

"Now, that's a bathhouse slave!" Macro said shaking his head. "They usually have enough to buy their freedom in about twenty years—not my boys, though. No way of getting your hands on the money working on a farm. You people don't believe in slavery, do you?"

"There used to be something like it in the old days," I answered. "Under the old law, they were called *dar fu'thir*, something like 'tenants of air,' because they could own nothing, not even the clothes on their backs. They were usually war captives, sometimes criminals, and they were given the dirtiest and most dismal tasks in the tribe: mucking the pigs . . . cleaning out the latrines . . . handling the dead . . . those sorts of things. They had no honor-price; they were considered possessions of the king, so any harm done to them was an offence against the king. But, they didn't stay slaves for life. After a few years, if they worked hard, they became *sar fu'thir*. They still weren't members of the tribe and couldn't join the war musters, but they could own their own huts, get married, have children . . . and their children were full tribal members. They could bear weapons in the tribal musters, and thus were *cum'rodeer*, *cives* in Latin, citizens."

"What if these . . . these . . . dar foot'ers, you call them, tried to escape?" Macro asked.

"They'd be captured and put back to work," I answered. "If they persisted, they might be beaten. No other clan or tribe would harbor them. That would be an offense against the king to whom they belonged, against the high king, the *Brenna*, who ruled all the tribes, and against the laws of our fathers. No one would dare."

"Seems a messy way to run things, and we Romans don't hold much with kings," Macro started.

"It's never wise to leave a man without hope," I countered.

"What'ya mean by that?" Macro challenged.

"Roman slaves . . . born into slavery . . . die in slavery. Even their children are the property of their masters," I explained. "There's little hope for them, unless they're lucky enough to buy their freedom . . . just bondage, hard work, and oppression, generation after generation. It's no wonder that thousands joined up with that escaped gladiator when he marched through here. Spartacus, wasn't it? Sometimes, risking the cross can be better than accepting life as it is."

Macro seemed just about to say something when the attendant from the *caldarium* arrived with a pedestal table and the wine. He placed the table before us and poured some of the wine into the two cups he had brought.

Macro took a long taste. "Ah, *bene*," he said finally, with a small belch. "That's the stuff." Then to the attendant, "You can get out of here. We'll pour for ourselves!"

The "good stuff" was unwatered and so strong it almost brought tears to my eyes.

Before the *capsarius* got out of our *cubiculum*, Macro asked, "Did strigil-boy out there hold you up for your penny?"

I saw the slave's left hand tighten around something. "No, *Domine*," he answered.

"Good, lad," Macro congratulated him and went back to the wine.

Macro took another long drink of the wine, then said, "I treat my boys fairly . . . work them hard . . . but I treat them fairly." Then, he became silent, intent on the wine and his own private thoughts.

We remained silent for a while, basking in the warmth of the *trepidarium*. Time is difficult to measure in silence. Finally, Macro poured his third cup of wine, and said, "Maariam . . . her name was Maariam."

"What?" I responded, returning abruptly from my own reveries.

"My woman . . . my *mulier castrorum* . . . her name was Maariam. I saw the way you looked at me when we were talking about Galenus' woman, Dora. My woman was Maariam."

I noticed his use of *was*. "What . . . what happened?" I asked, not sure I wanted to know or wanted to encourage Macro to talk about it.

Macro took another long drink. "Dead," he said into his cup, "dead some ten years now . . . her and our child."

I looked up at him. His eyes were unfocused, more from the memories than the wine.

"She showed up in the *vicus*, the civilian settlement that grows up around the legionary camps, outside of Nicomedia. She was starving . . . all eyes and bones. Dora took her under her wing. It was when Mithridates swept down on the city and chased Cotta's boys down the coast. A riot broke out in the town. Supposedly the natives, the Greeks, were murdering everyone Roman . . . some sort of victory celebration. But there were always a few private feuds to settle. Maariam's father was a banker . . . wasn't Roman at all . . . not even a Greek. Came from some fly-speck of a place in Asia down near Egypt. The Greeks called it *Ioudaia*, or something like that. A lot of people in the town owed him money . . . so they decided to settle their debts the easy way. They killed the old man, his wife, his sons. They raped Maariam until they thought she was dead. Then they tried to burn the house down over the bodies . . . *irrumantes Graeci* . . . prick-suckin' Greeks. But she wasn't dead and managed to crawl out of the house before it burned down on top of her . . . eventually found her way to our camps. Dora found her living in a hole she had dug near the *vicus* . . . starving. Dora always had a good heart . . . took her in . . . fed her."

Macro finished off the cup of wine, then poured another.

He continued, "I was Galenus' *optio* . . . Lucullus' Third Legion . . . Second Century, Third Cohort . . . left flank of the first battle line. Dora took care of my cleaning and mending for me . . . so, of course, I met Maariam. Soon, after she got stronger, she was doing my cleaning and mending. Then she was keeping me warm at night, when I didn't have to sleep in camp."

Macro seemed to be staring up toward the ceiling of the *trepidarium*. Somewhere up there, his memories were alive again for him.

"Mariaam had a strange god. She clung to him despite what he allowed *ist' pedicantes* . . . those ass-loving Greeks . . . to do to her and her family. He had no name . . . strange . . . but she prayed to him . . . for her family every evening . . . like they were still alive somewhere . . . every evening. How'd it go again?" Macro began to chant, *"Yit gadal vyit kadash shmei raba balma di vra khirutei . . . amain . . . amain . . . amain."*

I looked over at Macro. In the dim light of the *trepidarium*, I could hear him chanting repeatedly that strange word: *amain*. Still staring up at something only he could see hovering above us in the shadows, tears were forming in his eyes. He seemed to be chanting a prayer for his lost Maariam.

Macro caught me looking at him. Quickly, he wiped his eyes and poured out some more wine, muttering something about the smoke from the lamps.

Then, he continued, "We were pushing up into the mountains, chasing Tigranes, the king of a shithole called Armenia. We had just dug our marching camps near some mountain river we had been following up into a valley . . . the Aratsani, I think it was called . . . something like that. We were pushing some recon units up the valley when Tigranes jumped us . . . came rolling down the valley like an avalanche. There must have been thousands of them. They pushed us back into our camps. Right then, our baggage train came up the valley. When those *cunni* saw that, they broke off and went after the loot. There was nothing we could do but hold our walls and watch. There were three cohorts with the baggage . . . the tenth out of each of our legions. They tried to form a battle line, but they didn't stand a chance. Tigranes' infantry hit them straight on, and his cavalry went around their flanks and right up their asses. The whole thing was over in less than half an hour. Then they went after the *impedimenta*, the supplies and equipment. As far as we were concerned, they could have that shit . . . but our people from the *vicus* were with the train. We heard the screams all night. There was nothing we could do. In the morning, Tigranes' people were gone. They knew without our supplies we'd have to retreat back down the valley. When we looked where the baggage train had been, we could see nothing but columns of smoke and the vultures. Galenus was lucky. We found Dora and a few other survivors hiding in a narrow side valley the bastards had overlooked. Dora said that they were being chased by cavalry—Greeks by their armor—when she and Maariam got separated. We found Maariam's group about an hour later. The Greeks had trapped them against the river. The lucky ones drowned."

There were no tears in Macro's eyes now. They were still seeing something, but they were alight with murderous hatred.

"I buried what was left of her. That's the custom of her people, so I honored it. I piled flat slabs of rock over her grave so the animals couldn't dig her up. Her god had no name, no symbol, so I didn't know what to carve on the rocks to protect her spirit. So I just carved, *MARIAM VX MACRONIS OPT LEGIII*, Maariam, wife of Macro, Optio, Third Legion. I realized then I didn't even know how old she was. When we were retreating back down the valley, toward the plain where we could resupply, Galenus told me that Maariam was carrying a child . . . my child. Dora had told him. Maariam wanted to be sure before she said anything to me. She told Dora if it was a boy, she was going to name it after one of the great heroes of her people . . . Ioshue . . . Ioshue Ben Macro . . . Ioshue, *filius Macronis*."

Macro put down his wine cup as if the taste suddenly revolted him. Abruptly, he announced, "I've had enough of this place. Let's get out of here before these bastards steal our underwear and sell it for towels." He got up and left the *cubiculum*.

We dressed quickly and were soon heading down the main street toward the west gate. There was less than a winter hour left of sunlight. We wouldn't get back to the senator's estate before dark.

When we got to the turnoff for Rufia's *lupinarium*, Macro stopped. "I'm a bad enough rider as it is," he explained. "If I try to get up on a horse with this much wine pickling my brain, I'll break my neck before we're a mile down the road."

I didn't need this much of an explanation for what was, by that time, quite obvious, so I just nodded.

"I'm going to spend the night at Rufia's," he continued, putting his hand on my shoulder and nodding toward the street with the clotheslines. "The livery where we left the horses is no more than thirty . . . maybe forty paces . . . down this street. When you see the livery, you'll see the gate. The gate's open until dark, and guards won't bother a single rider leaving at this hour. Just tell the boy at the livery you're with Macro, and I'll take care of it in the morning. They know I'm good for it. Don't go all the way to the senator's place tonight. Just go home. Bring the horse back in the morning."

With that, Macro gave me a wink and plunged into the shadows that had filled the narrow street leading to Rufia's place.

I was a couple of miles down the *Via Nova*, just before the farm road that led up to my family's farm and Gabinius' estate, when the sun finally slipped below the mountains. The winter chill was on me as soon as the sunlight slid away. I pulled my woolen cloak a little closer around me. My mind was still a bit clouded by all the wine I had drunk at Rufia's and at the bathhouse, but despite that, one thing was very clear to me: this was one adventure Mama could never hear about.

VIII.

De Fine Pueritiae
MY CHILDHOOD ENDS

*I*t was two days before the Calends of *Ianuarius*, the month of the two-faced god, the god of endings and of beginnings. The *magister's enarrationes*, his reading of the *Iliad*, had been suspended for the Saturnalia. Achilles had finally decided to get back into the fight, and in his rage over the death of his friend, Patroclus, had routed the Trojan army from the field. Only the intervention of the god, Apollo, had prevented Achilles from storming the city itself.

Mama had insisted that I make a Saturnalia offering to the *magister* and Macro, even though the day of gift-giving was past. (I didn't dare tell her of Macro's gift to me!) Mama had wrapped some of the season's fruit harvest, mostly dried apples and pears, and I was carrying them to Gabinius' estate.

Marcus had traveled down to Rome to be with his family for the festival. Their celebrations would be especially festive this season. We had recently heard that the senator had been elected one of the consuls for the coming year.

It would be the consular year of Lucius Calpurnius Piso Caesoninus and Aulus Gabinius, 696 years from the founding of the city by Romulus, the year that Gaius Iulius Caesar would become Proconsul of *Gallia Cisalpina, Illyrium,* and *Provincia*, the year that Caesar *Imperator* would launch his first military campaign north of the River Rhodanus to prevent a tribe called the Helvetii from migrating west. This was to be the most significant year of my young life— the year that I would have to flee from my home to save my life, the year I would become a soldier, and the year I would learn what *Caesaris patrocinium*, the protection of Caesar, really meant.

But, on that dark, cold, December day, as Nona spun the thread of my life from her distaff, and Decima measured it out with her rod, and Morta decided whether to cut it, I walked down a farm road in the Padus Valley with a parcel of dried fruit under my arm, and no other thoughts in my mind except whether Hector would survive his fated encounter with Achilles and the fact that my Saturnalia offerings were a couple days late.

I arrived at the senator's estate just after *meridies*, the sixth hour, the middle of the day. The sun was hidden behind a sea of dirty, grey winter clouds, and a damp, chilling wind whistled down from the mountains in the North. The first winter snows would soon be on us. I hoped the grapevines up on the ridges, the fuel for my dreams of riches and success, would be able to weather this year's snows.

I walked around to the back of the main house to where Macro's *cubiculum* was located. I imagined I'd find him in his office huddled over a brazier, or in the kitchens, where the cooking fires burned all day. I hardly noted the three horses standing outside one of the storage barns or the giant of a man in a black cloak standing next to them. I certainly didn't note his reaction to my sudden appearance. He immediately stuck his head through the door of the barn to warn someone inside.

When I walked into Macro's *cubiculum*, he wasn't there. His *scriba*, a slave he called Petros, was going over some figures etched into a writing tablet, sitting as close to the brazier as he could without melting the wax.

When I walked in, he said, "You just missed him, Gai. He went down to the paddocks with a couple of the boys to check on the fences."

I thanked him and quickly decided that I'd walk to the paddocks first. The *magister* could wait a little longer for his dried apples.

When I turned and walked back out the door, my world exploded suddenly into blackness and stars. My parcel dropped to the ground. Two steel-like arms locked themselves through mine. All the air seemed to have been punched out of my body; I couldn't seem to breathe. My feet were dragging behind me across the yard toward the storage barn. I tried to call out, say something, but all I could manage was a gasping rasp.

I immediately felt a sharp blow to the back of my head, then stars again and blackness. A voice from somewhere above me in the darkness: "Shut yer fookin' gob, ya shithole. I hears one more sound outta you, and I'll do ya meself."

I heard the door to the barn bang open and felt my feet dragging over the lintel. Then I was flying forward. I hit the dirt floor and was vaguely aware that someone had lit torches in a barn full of hay. I had to tell them that they would burn the place down; that was all my mind could grasp. I managed to get to my hands and knees. I heard a voice say, "Stand that little *cunnus* up! Get him on his feet!"

Again, the steel bands hooked under my arms, and I flew up onto my feet as if I didn't weigh a thing. My legs didn't seem to work. My knees wouldn't lock, but the steel bands under my arms kept me hovering upright. My eyes finally managed to focus. There was a man standing in front of me. He looked familiar and wore a long, expensive woolen *laena* of reddish-brown over a white winter tunic. The tunic was bordered with a broad purple stripe. *Roman*, I thought, *senatorial*. Then I recognized the face. It was the senator, but younger, thinner. It was his older son. "Gabinius," I croaked, "Aulus Gabinius?"

My head exploded again. I heard the voice behind me, "You address yer betters as *domine*, ya stinkin' *podex*!"

"No, Excelsior," Gabinius Iunior corrected, "he's quite right. No Roman citizen calls another man *lord*. That's only for slaves . . . and gladiators . . . like you two."

Then, he turned back to me. "So! This is my dear sister's wild, Gallic brigand. I must say . . . I'm disappointed . . . very disappointed. No wild black stallion . . . no bejeweled long sword. just a stinking, little Gallic farm boy . . . very disappointing."

"Gabi," I managed to croak.

Again, my head exploded. This time the blow came from in front of me. I tasted blood in my mouth where my teeth had raked my inner cheek.

"You never speak my sister's name, you *pagane* shit heel," Gabinius snarled. For the first time, I noticed he wore a sword, a military short sword, a *gladius*, hanging on his left hip, like an officer.

Gabinius was speaking again. "Do you have any idea how much trouble you have caused me? How much embarrassment to me, to my family?"

"Nothing happened," I managed to say. There was breath back in my body, at least for the time being.

Again, Gabinius punched me in the face. This time I saw it coming and managed to roll a bit with the blow.

"Nothing happened?" he snarled. "Nothing happened? You don't get it, do you? You stinking, Gallic *mentula*! A senatorial family . . . no . . . a consular family . . . must be above even a hint of scandal! Nothing happened? All Rome is laughing at us . . . laughing at me: '*Scortillum Gallo . . . fututrix barbaris soror eius.* His sister's some Gaul's little slut . . . a bitch for barbarians. How many blond, blue-eyed bastards are they hiding up there in Gaul?' . . . We're a damned laughingstock! I can't walk through the forum without hearing this shit . . . from plebeians . . . the *vulgus*!"

Gabinius was insane, over the edge with rage. I tried to squirm, but the two gladiators tightened their grip on my arms.

Gabinius drew his sword. "There's only one thing to do with you. My dignity must be avenged." He parted my cloak with the point of his sword and slapped my testicles with its blunt side. "I'm going to nail your *coleones* to the rostra in the forum under a sign that says, 'This, to all who dishonor the *gens Gabinia*.' That should settle things nicely, I think."

It was then that Gabinius noticed the *pugio* hanging from my belt. He removed his sword from my testicles and clicked its edge against the handle of my knife.

"What's this?" he sneered. "The little Gauling has a sting, does he?"

He dropped his sword and took a step back. "Release him!" he told his gladiators.

"But, *Domine*—" the one behind my right shoulder began.

"Shut your mouth and obey me!" Gabinius shouted at him. "Release him!"

I felt the steel bands around my shoulders release. I almost collapsed, but managed to get my legs to support me.

Gabinius dropped his cloak. "Draw that knife, *cunne*! Let's see how well a Gallic brigand fares against a Roman."

I felt my cloak ripped from my shoulders and saw it tossed aside into the hay piles.

"Draw that *pugio*!" Gabinius screamed.

I did and assumed the first position. A *pugio* against a *gladius*. Macro had told me that, with two fighters of equal skill, reach wins. A *gladius* had reach over a *pugio*. How well trained was Gabinius? I was about to find out. Anything was better than having my balls carved off while two thugs held me down.

"This is perfect!" Gabinius hissed. "A duel . . . the brave, older brother in single combat restores the honor of the family by killing the brigand who dishonored his sister. I may commission a poem . . . an epic."

Just then, the barn door crashed open. Macro came through. The gladiator to my left, a hulking monster, his long, red hair tied in braids halfway down his back, effortlessly pinned Macro to the wall.

"What's going on here?" Macro challenged.

"Ah . . . you're just in time to witness this, *vilicus*," Gabinius said mockingly. "I'm about to kill this boy in single combat and restore my family's *auctoritas*."

Macro hesitated for a second, then seemed to smirk. I thought he had lost his mind. Then he said, "You don't want to do this."

"He has no choice," Gabinius countered.

"No, Gabinius," Macro answered him, "not the boy . . . you. You don't want to do this."

The red-haired gladiator pulled his fist back to punch Macro's face, but something in Marco's eyes made him hesitate.

"Put your hand down, Slave! I'll have you up on a cross before sundown," Macro ordered.

"Release him!" Gabinius ordered. The gladiator let go of Macro. "You stay out of this, Macro, or I'll put you back on the road, where cripples like you belong!"

Macro just shrugged and seemed to smirk again.

Gabinius turned back to me. He brought his sword up and said, "Now to finish with you, *podex*!"

Gabinius thrust toward my belly. His move was slow, weak, and I easily saw it coming in his eyes. I blocked it.

"So, it has some skill," he sneered. Then, he tried the same move again, with the same result.

We danced around the barn for a bit. I realized that Gabinius had little skill with the sword. I also noticed that his henchmen began to grunt in appreciation each time I countered Gabinius' attacks. I even heard the red-haired one grunt something that sounded like, "Goot . . . Goot!"

Finally, I had had enough of this. There's only so long you should play around with a madman thrusting a sword at you. From the way he was breathing, Gabinius was getting winded. When I blocked one of his weak thrusts toward my throat with a sweeping block, I heard the gladiator to my right cheer, "*Bene gestum*! Well done!" With that, Gabinius lost it. He raised his sword up over his head to bring down a slashing blow on my skull. His weapons instructor seemed to have failed to teach him that a *gladius* is for stabbing, not for slashing.

As Gabinius raised his arm, he exposed his throat. I struck. At the last second, I raised my strike and raked his left cheek down to his teeth. Then, I recovered back into first position.

Gabinius at first did not realize the extent of his injury. He merely felt a blow to his cheek. He too tried to recover to first position. Then his brain signaled him that something was seriously wrong with his body. He looked down toward where he thought he was injured. He noticed the blood pouring down out of his face onto his once-white senatorial tunic. Then, he tasted it in his mouth, down his throat. He dropped his sword and both hands went up to his ruined face. He screamed—gurgled really— "Kill him! Kill him, you bastards!"

There was a dangerously awkward moment while his gladiators decided what to do. Then the one on my right, the one called Excelsior, said, "Yer honor knows that if we touch steel outside the *munera*, the gladiatorial combats, it's instant death. Ain't that right, *Optio*?"

"Absolutely correct," Macro nodded, "and, the boy here's a Roman citizen. We'd keep you alive on the cross for a week before we'd let you die . . . nasty stuff."

"Ya," the redheaded one agreed, somehow understanding the Latin.

Gabinius fell to his knees, bleeding onto the ground. I could actually see his teeth through the hole I had raked across his face.

Macro stuck his head out the door and yelled to Petros, who had gone to find him when Gabinius' two bully-boys had scooped me up earlier, "Run over to the barracks and get Tonsor. Tell him to bring his sewing kit. We got some work for him!"

Gabinius was now down on his hands and knees, exactly where he had me earlier.

Macro told the gladiators, "You might want to get him up on his feet . . . keep his head down. Don't want him choking to death on his own blood." The two thugs knew exactly what Macro meant; they had seen enough of this in the arena.

They went over to attend to Gabinius. As they walked by me, the redheaded one slammed me on my shoulder and said something that sounded like, "*Thas vas swa goot thoo art thas haileguh thrimma!*"

"What was that all about?" I asked Macro.

Macro shrugged, "I only know enough of that Kraut gibberish to get through Rufia's door. Sounds like he liked the show."

Then, he took me aside while the two gladiators got Gabinius back up on his feet. "Gai, get out of here now before these two change their minds about killing you," he whispered to me. "Go home! Whatever you do, don't come back here! Wait at home until you hear from me! Got it?"

I didn't need any more prompting. I sheathed my *pugio*, grabbed my cloak off the floor, threw it over my shoulders, and took off out the door at the double time. I was a good thousand paces down the road before I dared slow to a walk.

I didn't see Macro for almost a week. The festival was over, and Mama was asking me why I hadn't returned to the senator's place for my lessons. I told her Marcus hadn't returned yet from Rome. I hated lying to Mama, but I didn't dare tell her the truth.

Finally, two days before the Ides of *Ianuarius*, on *Dies Veneris*, the day of Venus—an impulsive and faithless goddess at best, her day is never auspicious, *nefas,* for business or making important decisions—Macro arrived around the ninth hour, barely clinging to the back of a bay mare. Papa, Lucius, and Gwin were out in the barn, trying to decide how to get another year out of the plow rig. Mama and Amanda were fussing about the house, arranging and neatening our rooms.

Mama greeted Macro in the vestibule with Amanda hovering behind her. Macro told her that he had something to say that the entire family should hear. I saw a brief shadow of concern flitter across Mama's face, but playing the role of the true *matrona Romana* of legend, she immediately recovered and continued in her role as hostess. She sent Amanda out to the barn to fetch the men and led Macro into our atrium, which was really just the rear of the vestibule, away from the winter drafts that came in under the entryway door. She invited Macro to sit near the brazier.

"Would you like some wine . . . or perhaps some beer?" Mama invited.

I saw yes in Macro's eyes for a second. Then he said, "No, thank you, *Matrona.* Perhaps some water?"

Macro refusing wine! This was serious!

I went out into the kitchen and poured a pitcher of water. When I returned to the atrium, Papa and Lucius were greeting our visitor. I guessed Gwin had been left out in the barn. Amanda assumed her station behind Mama's chair, where Mama was sitting as straight and as stiff as a pillar, a good inch from the chair back.

Soon, we were all settled. Macro had drunk enough of the water to get over the trauma of having to ride a horse five winter miles down a farm road, and he began: "Well it's not all good news, but it could have been one hell . . . Oh . . . forgive me, *Matrona* . . . it could have been much worse."

Mama raised her hand to stop Macro. "I'm sorry, Quintus Macro," she began, "but we have no idea of what you are speaking. What could have been much worse? And please, call me Valeria."

Macro glanced over at me, then shrugged his shoulders. "Of course, *Matro* . . . I mean, Valeria. And, just call me Macro. The other day, when the lad here came over to the estate, he was attacked."

Mama's eyes blinked twice. Papa exclaimed, "Was it more of those damned bandits on the roads?"

"No," Macro responded. "Worse! The lad was attacked by the senator's son, Aulus Gabinius Iunior."

"What would cause Aulus Gabinius Iunior to attack my son, Macro?" Mama asked.

"He thought he was defending the honor of his sister, the Lady Gabinia," Macro explained.

"Her honor?" Mama stated flatly, blinked twice, and stabbed me with a look. Papa's jaw hung open. Lucius grinned and gave me a brotherly punch in the shoulder, which didn't help Mama's attitude one bit.

"Nothing happened; I swear!" I defended myself.

"I believe the lad," Macro continued. "But, there's been a lot of gossip down in Rome about it, and the young Gabinius felt he had to avenge the honor of his family."

"So?" Mama literally hissed. "What actually happened?"

"Gabinius showed up at the estate with two thugs—a couple of gladiators he brought up with him from Rome," Macro continued. "I think he would have done for the lad here, but Gaius was able to defend himself and escape."

"Well, *that* explains why he hasn't been attending his lessons these last few days," Mama stated, stabbing me with her eyes again. "What about Gabinius?"

"Gabinius?" Macro said, as if surprised by the question. "Gabinius? He's still alive, but he won't be winning any golden apples for his beauty. The lad carved his face up a bit."

Mama blinked twice, then paused. "So, where does that leave things, Macro?" she asked.

Macro looked pensive for a second—quite a feat for him—then explained: "Since the young Gabinius is alive, the senator . . . I mean, the consul . . . does not feel obligated to avenge himself on your family. But, the lad did mark up a senatorial pretty good, and that won't go unnoticed. The young Gabinius will need at least a few weeks to recover. In the spring, once he's well enough to travel, he's expected to take up a post as a *tribunus militum*, a military tribune, under the Roman Proconsul in Greece. He'll be gone for at least a year. So, I don't think we'll be hearing from him for a while."

"And the rest of it?" Mama demanded.

Macro sighed, shrugged, and continued, "The consul cannot ignore this. It touches on his family. His *pietas* demands he do something. I received a message from Rome, from the consul's *ad manum*, his confidential secretary. Out of respect for your patron, the outgoing consul, Caesar, Gabinius has granted young Gaius here the *gratia* of "time to depart," three weeks to remove himself from the province. If he is found here after that time, he will be arrested on charges of *sacrilegium*, insulting the gods of Rome by attacking the family of the consul, which is sacrosanct. He will, of course, be found guilty."

"How can that be?" Papa interrupted. "The boy was only defending himself!"

Macro answered Papa in the manner of a weary schoolmaster with a headstrong pupil. "There's an old saying in the Roman forum, Secundus: 'The only honest jury's a rich jury.'"

"I don't get that," Papa countered.

Mama explained, "What it means is that since juries are called from the poor citizens, they're easily bribed. The only incorruptible jury is a jury comprised of rich men, and there's no such thing in Rome."

"That's about it. Gabinius' money will buy the verdict, and Gai here'll be condemned. Not even a Cicero could save him. The sentence is exile and confiscation. Since he's not emancipated, they'll come after your farm, maybe even your father's assets, *Matrona* . . . I mean, Valeria. But, he'll never get to trial. He'll be swimming in the Tiber long before that."

"But, Gai's a good swimmer," my brother interrupted.

Mama actually rolled her eyes at that.

Macro explained, "I can assure you that the young Gabinius and his friends in Rome will see to it that Gai doesn't live long enough to be convicted."

"Then, Gaius must depart," Mama concluded.

"I might have a suggestion, Valeria," Macro offered.

"A suggestion?" Mama invited.

"The army," Macro said.

Mama blinked twice. "The army!" she spat.

"Please . . . hear me out on this," Macro appealed.

I wondered briefly if anyone was going to ask me what I thought.

Macro continued his argument, "The new Proconsul, Caesar, is raising troops in the North, at least two new legions, they say. He's brought a few of Pompey's legions over from Spain. The Tenth is encamped just up the road at Aquileia. It's understrength, like most veteran legions, but a good, experienced outfit. So, the recruiters are looking everywhere for lads to fill up the ranks. There's even a rumor going around that Caesar plans to enlist Gauls without the franchise from around the province. The lad's a bit young, but he's tall enough and strong. With your connections to the *gens Iulia* and a recommendation from me as an ex-officer, he should have no trouble enlisting. It's only six years. And, once he's in . . . Gabinius won't touch him. He'll be under Caesar's protection. Besides . . . when his hitch is up, this whole thing will have blown over."

"What about our plans?" I finally pitched in. "The vineyards?"

"Six years is almost perfect," Macro answered. "We can't get much done now. We need to get this thing going . . . find more farmers willing to pitch in with us . . . get the vines in the ground. In six years, we should have a large enough crop to be distilling significant amounts of wine. That's where the money is. It's not like Caesar's going to start a major war up North. Who's up there to fight? The Germans have been quiet since Marius thumped them years ago, and the Gauls across the Rhodanus are mostly civilized. They even trade with us now. At most, Caesar'll fight a battle or two with some small tribes up in the hills, get his triumph from the senate down in Rome, and settle down to a couple years of lucrative extortion like any good Roman governor. In six years' time, you'll be back, a little tanner, a little leaner, and ready to take over our wine business."

It made sense. Even Papa was nodding at what Macro was saying. That should have been my first clue. Mama just sat straight-backed and still in her chair, her mouth like a bloodless knife slash across her face.

Finally, she said, "It is agreed. Gai must leave, and the army is his best option."

About a week later, everything was arranged. I had a letter from Macro saying that as a soldier, I was second only to the god Mars himself. I had a copy of my diploma of Roman citizenship from the *tabularium* in Mediolanum. Even Avus Lucius wrote a short note as a member of the Equestrian order and a major army contractor. I planned to present myself to the army recruiter in town the next day—not surprisingly, he was also a chum of Macro's. Mama decided to have a bit of a going-away observation for me. She couldn't get herself to call it a *celebratio*.

During the ninth hour, Macro arrived at our farm, clinging to a horse and a parcel. His arrival reminded me of my birthday last summer—less than six months ago, but so long ago, a different life.

We all sat down to dinner. We had freshly baked loaves, with oil and *garum* for dipping, along with cheese, salt, small radishes, cabbage leaves, and bowls of olives. Papa had offered up a pig and a couple of chickens, and Amanda cooked them in a *garum* stew with kale, cauliflower, onions, sprouts, and broccoli. She had also managed a hot, thickened broth of white carrots, cabbage, and random parts of the chickens that hadn't ended up in the stew. It was all washed down with strong brown beer. Even Macro seemed to be getting used to the brew.

When we were finished eating, Amanda cleared away the dishes. We picked over some raisins and dried apples, and Papa broke out the *Dur*. Finally, Mama stood, excused herself, and went back into the bedroom. I got up to follow her, to make sure she was alright, but Papa caught my eye and shook his head. I sat back down.

With Mama gone and Amanda busy in the kitchen, Macro began to tell a story that began with a centurion, a Greek philosopher, and a Vestal Virgin walking into a *caupona*. He was just about to wrap it up saying, "So the *cauponius* says to the Greek—" when Mama returned from her room with a parcel in her arms. She placed it down on the table and said, "Gai, would you please stand?"

I stood up. Mama reached around my neck and removed my *bulla praetexta*, the silver locket I had worn since I was a baby, which held the first cuttings of my hair. Mama placed the locket around her own neck. The locket was a potent talisman as long as Mama wore it. The baby hair contained the blessings of the goddess, Diana, protector of mothers, childbirth, and children. The goddess had brought my mother and me through the torments and dangers of labor and birth. She would now serve to protect me as a man from the dangers of the world.

Then, Mama unwrapped the parcel. It was the snowy white toga that Avus Lucius had given me for my last birthday. Mama removed the toga and began draping it around me. Amanda attempted to help her, but Mama shooed her away. Finally, after a few final pulls and tugs, Mama backed up a couple of steps to inspect her work.

After one final adjustment, she turned to Papa and said solemnly, "Secundus! I, Secunda, present to you your son."

Papa got up, walked around the table, and grasped my right arm with his, saying, "I, Secundus, greet my son, Gaius, for the first time as a man."

Papa stepped back, and Mama again stepped up to me. She placed each of her hands on my shoulders and kissed me lightly on my right cheek, saying, "I, Secunda, greet my son, Gaius, for the first time as a man."

Mama stepped back and said to my brother, "Lucius! Greet your brother as a man!"

Lucius bounded around the table and shook my hand while pounding me on the shoulder, "*Gratulationes*, congratulations, brother!"

Mama again retreated back into her room. I heard the door shut firmly behind her.

Macro was shaking my hand. I was beginning to feel a bit ridiculous all wrapped up in shapeless white cloth. I was wondering how Rome was able to conquer so much of the world without tripping over the folds of these ridiculous dresses.

"Can I take this thing off now, Papa?" I asked.

"Yes . . . certainly," he responded, sitting back down. "Wrap it back up. Your Mama would kill you if you got any stains on it."

I undraped the toga without entangling myself in it and carefully rewrapped it in the parcel. Then, for safekeeping, I placed the parcel on a side table, away from the beer and *Dur*, which I assumed would occupy the rest of the evening.

Macro bent down near his place at the table and came up with the parcel he had carried so precariously from the estate. He placed it on the table, unwrapped it, and brought out a large, reddish-brown woolen cloak.

He held it up to me, "This was my *sagum*, my military cloak. It kept me warm and dry in the worst weather . . . better than a wife."

When Macro said the word *uxor*, wife, he abruptly stopped talking. He seemed to stare at something back over my shoulder in the shadows of the room. Then, he thrust the cloak at me.

I took the cloak from him. It was unexpectedly heavy. I felt some lumps in the fabric. When I looked, I saw that it had been mended, stitched. I wondered if Maariam had done the work. I dared not ask. But, I realized how precious this piece of cloth was to Macro.

"*Mille gratias, m'amice,*" I stammered, "a thousand thanks, my friend."

"I have one more thing for you, Gai," Macro said reaching down into his *marsupium*. He pulled out an amulet. It was a dull, lead-grey medal suspended by a leather thong. He walked over to me and placed the thong over my head. I picked up the amulet and examined it. A human face with huge eyes was stamped on it—from its curls, a woman. She wore a peeked crown and her smile was as big as a crescent moon.

"This is an amulet of *Bona Fortuna*," Macro was saying. "All soldiers wear it. If you remain *fortis*, strong, she will never turn her back on you. Carve your initials on the back. That way she will know it's you. She'll remember your name. Whenever you need her, just take the amulet in your right hand and say her name, *Domina Fortuna*, and she will listen."

I felt a hand on my shoulder. I turned to see Mama there.

"Those are most generous gifts, Macro," she said. "I thank you for them and for your goodwill."

I learned later in the legions that the reason why the *Fortuna* amulet was made of lead was so no one would be tempted to loot it from a dead body left on the battlefield. Besides, most soldiers understood that taking a dead man's *Fortuna* was terrible luck, a curse, really. The reason why a soldier carved his initials on the back was so his body could be identified by his comrades if they could no longer recognize his features. That way he'd at least get a proper burial and have a coin for the ferryman. Soldiers believe that the spirits of the unburied dead cannot cross the river, but must wander the earth as *lemures*. Macro understood this. He also knew that I would soon learn this for myself. But, he would do nothing to upset Mama further. I think he rather liked her.

"Again, many thanks, *m'amice*," I said.

After that, the party was reduced to beer and *Dur*. Mama excused herself just after sundown, taking Amanda with her. Lucius hung in for about an hour longer. At some point, Gwin put his head on the table and began to snore. Macro abruptly announced, "*Amo dure mi Dur durum*. I really like my whiskey strong!" He laughed at his own linguistic cleverness, then joined Gwin in Morpheus' kingdom.

Papa and I threw blankets over the sleeping celebrants. Before he left me, Papa put his hands on my shoulders and said, "Take care of yourself up there with the army, son. If anything happened to you, it would kill your mother." Then he embraced me and retreated into his room.

The next morning, I was ready to slip out of the house at dawn. I thought it best. Surprisingly, Macro had recovered and was gone. I wondered if I would ever see him again. Six years is an eternity to a boy. Gwin was still in the same position we had left him in last night and still snoring loudly. I doubted much work of any kind would get done that day. I had dressed in my room, ready for the long walk down to Mediolanum. I had Macro's *sagum* and wore my military belt with the Medusa buckle and my razor-sharp pugio hanging in its scabbard. I hoped the real soldiers I was about to meet didn't think the rig too pretentious for a *tiro*, a raw recruit.

Mama had packed a *marsupium* for me the day before and had left it near the door in the atrium. I picked it up and threw it over my shoulder. I was just about to unlatch our door when I felt a hand on my shoulder. I turned around. It was Mama.

"Don't you dare leave without saying goodbye," she said, embracing me and burrowing her head into my chest.

I put my arms around her, held her there. I heard her voice, surprisingly tiny, surprisingly vulnerable: "I think a Roman mother is supposed to send her son off to the army with the admonition to be brave, never bring shame on the gods, the nation, or his family . . . and this is where I fail as a Roman mother. I just want you to come home to me, my child. Come home safe."

Suddenly, Mama stood up straight, breaking our embrace.

"Go now," she commanded. "Do not shame me by seeing me cry."

Mama pushed me out the door and shut it in front of me. I stood there for a few heartbeats, staring at the closed door. Then, I turned and walked down the road toward Mediolanum.

I walked four winter hours in the cold to get to the city. Despite Macro's *sagum*, my Gallic *bracae* and heavy boots, I was stiff with the cold when I arrived at the west gate. I noticed Galenus collecting tolls at the center gates. He nodded at me as I passed through.

Macro had told me that the army recruiting office was across the forum from the baths and from *Gallus Viridis*, Grifud's place, where we had bought our wine. It was near a *caupona* marked with the sign of the *Nympha Enebria*, or Drunken Fairy. I was amazed at how Macro's world was structured around a network of taverns, *lupinaria,* and bathhouses. When I got to the recruiting station, Macro said I should ask for Dalmatius.

I crossed the forum from the main street leading up from the west gate. It was winter; there was no market, and the courts had moved indoors. I shared the forum with a couple of mangy dogs looking for a meal and a few passersby, walking quickly, heads down, wrapped in heavy cloaks with the hood pulled tightly up over their heads.

When I arrived at the east side of the forum, I immediately smelled the greasy smoke of *caupona* food wafting up one of the side streets. When I found the place, it was marked with the sign of a Hunter and Dogs. I went in anyway, just to get out of the cold for a few moments. It took a few heartbeats for my eyes to adjust to the dim, smoky light in the place. There were a few customers hunched over steaming bowls of a lumpy, brown stew.

"Does anyone here know where the army recruiting station is?" I asked in Latin. "I'm looking for a guy named Dalmatius."

When no one responded, I repeated the question in Gallic.

The landlord came around the counter, "Did you say Dalmatius, boy?" he asked me in Gallic.

"Shuh," I answered him, "yes . . . the army recruiting agent."

"That Roman gob-shite doesn't hang out here with us natives," the landlord spat. "Unless he needs credit. Then I'm his long-lost brother. Gods help us if his mother dropped more like him. Look for that Roman shit at the Drunken Nymph. That's where the Romans hang out. Ya' know where that's at, *me bouchal?*"

The landlord gave me directions. The *caupona* was only two streets over. I no sooner saw the drunken nymph painted on a tenement wall than across the street I saw an eagle painted on the wall in red next to a closed door. Assuming it to be the recruiting station, I knocked.

"Whatta you want?" I heard a man's voice respond in Latin.

I opened the door and stuck my head in. "I'm looking for Dalmatius," I said.

"Well, you found him," the voice responded from the depths of the dark room. "Get your ass in here, and close the door behind you. It's damned cold out there!"

I entered and shut the door tightly behind me. When my eyes finally adjusted, I spotted a man sitting behind a table covered with slates and papers. For a brief second, I thought I was back in the *magister's cubiculum*. The man I took to be Dalmatius was dressed in a short tunic with long sleeves. He was trying to huddle as close to a brazier as he could. Typical Roman, he was barelegged in the winter.

"Like I said before," he challenged, "whatta you want?"

"Macro sent me," I started. "I'm here to—"

"Macro! That degenerate!" Dalmatius interrupted. "You must be that boy he told me about. Where is it?" Dalmatius dug around in his papers. "Yeah . . . here it is . . . Marius . . . Gaius Marius Insubrecus. That's some name you got there, boy. Whose gonna walk in here next? Lucius Cornelius Sulla Infelix. . . or Gnaeus Pompeius Minutus?"

"I came to join—" I tried.

"Yeah . . . got it here. Macro says you're for the Tenth. *Io! Sevso!*" he yelled over his shoulder.

"*Audio, Capu*?" I heard from a back room I hadn't noticed before. "Yeah, Boss?"

"Pull the requisitions from the Tenth," Dalmatius instructed. "They're dug in up in Aquileia, I think. What's the head price they're offering?"

Dalmatius turned to me. "Go ahead and drop your stuff over in that corner. Take a seat by my table here. You got some papers for me, I hope."

I hung my *sagum* on a peg in the wall and brought my *marsupium* with me over to the table. I was digging around in it for my letters of recommendation when I heard Sevso yell from the back room, "Got it here, *Capu*!"

"Well, bring it out to me, you worthless *fellator*!" Dalmatius shouted back.

Sevso, a small, bowlegged man, suitably dressed for the weather in a grey, long-sleeved winter tunic, a pair of baggy, blue, woolen *bracae*, and thick winter boots, came out and dropped a tablet on Dalmatius' table.

"You don't have to shout," he complained. "I ain't deaf, ya know."

"Deaf and stupid . . . two different things," Dalmatius shot back.

"Ain't that, either," Sevso sniffed and retreated back into his den.

Dalmatius ignored him. "Let's see what we got here," he said to no one in particular while opening the tablet. "The Tenth Legion—"

I noticed Dalmatius stuck the tip of his tongue out the left side of his mouth as he read, his right index finger tracing the text.

"*Bene*," he said, finally. "The Tenth is recruiting. Offering three *denarii* for a Type One recruit . . . a veteran with at least six years. That ain't you, but you could qualify as a Type Two . . . able-bodied citizen . . . clean record. The bounty's a *denarius* . . . so . . . let's see what we got here. Got to ask you a series of questions, and you gotta tell me the truth. *Compre'endis tu*? You understand?"

"*Compre'endo, senior*," I responded. "Yes, sir!"

Dalmatius opened a tablet and asked, "*Bene* . . . You a free man?"

"Yes, sir!"

He made a mark. "You a citizen?"

"Yes, sir!"

Another mark. "You married?"

I briefly thought of Cynthia, Athvoowin, daughter of Gwili, and decided that didn't count anymore. "No, sir," I answered.

"You wanted for any crimes?" Dalmatius continued.

Other than cutting up the son of the Roman Consul? "No, sir!"

"How old are you?"

"Sixteen, sir!"

Dalmatius sucked in his breath. "*Cacat*! That's a bit young. Might make you Type Three. Let's keep going. Can you read and write?"

"Yes, sir!"

"Read and write *Latin*?" he emphasized.

"Yes, sir," I insisted, "and Greek!"

"Greek, is it?" Dalmatius muttered to himself. "It's a bloody philosopher we got here . . . a bloody Greekling. Do you have any recommendations?"

"Yes, sir!" I handed him my two letters.

Dalmatius reviewed them. "*Bene* . . . a strong recommendation from an ex-officer. That'll go a long way. This other one . . . who's this guy to you . . . the Equestrian?"

"He's my maternal grandfather, sir," I answered.

"Your father Equestrian, too?" he asked.

"No, sir, we have a small farm west of—"

"Not important," Dalmatius interrupted. "Do you have a diploma of citizenship?"

I handed the document over to him.

Dalmatius placed the diploma on a growing pile of my paperwork, then said, "Take off your clothes . . . even your skivvies . . . and stand over by that wall."

When I gave Dalmatius a strange look, he snapped, "What? You think I get off looking at naked boys? It's part of the *probatio*, your recruitment screening."

I stripped and stood against the wall.

Dalmatius looked at some marks in the wall behind me.

"*Bene* . . . you make the height requirement. Now turn around!"

I complied.

"Look fit . . . in shape . . . no tattoos . . . definitely male. Where'd you get that scar on your shin?" he asked.

"Fell when I was a kid . . . running . . . cut myself up on some jagged stones."

Dalmatius made a note of that on his tablet. Then, he said, "Stand there!" He walked across the room.

"I'm going to hold up my fingers," he told me. "You tell me how many."

"Thumb count?" I asked.

"No . . . the thumb doesn't count, Philosopher!" he said. "*Quot*? How many?"

"*Tres*!" I answered. "Three!"

"*Denu*! *Quot*?" he said, holding up his hand. "Again! How many?"

"*Unus*," I said, "one."

"Good enough, Philosopher," he said. "Put your clothes back on before I have to marry you!"

I got dressed and went back over to Dalmatius' table. He seemed to be checking whatever he had notated on the tablet.

Finally, he looked up and said, "*Bene*, you qualify for the army. The Tenth has openings and will take you as a Type Two recruit . . . able-bodied citizen with no former military experience, conditional on your successfully completing your basic combat training. *Compre'endis tu?*"

"*Compre'endo, senior*" I responded. "Yes, sir!"

"*Bene*," he said. "Now, listen well. It gets serious from here. You can walk out that door right now if you want . . . no harm, no foul . . . but once you raise your hand to the *Sacramentum*, the oath of enlistment, your ass belongs to the Tenth Legion for the next six years. There's no backing out. You got that?"

"Yes, I understand," I agreed.

"You ready to do this?" he asked again.

"Yeah . . . let's go ahead," I said.

"*Bene*," Dalmatius said. "Sevso! Oath of Enlistment!" he yelled over his shoulder.

Sevso came out of the back room with a document. "All drawn up and ready to go, Capu'," he said. "I already filled the lad's name in at the top."

Dalmatius glanced at the document, then stood. "Stand up, Gaius Marius Insubrecus!"

When I did, Dalmatius said, "Raise your right palm to the heavens, and repeat after me: I, state your full name."

I raised my right palm and said, "I, Gaius Marius Insubrecus Tertius do solemnly swear, by Father Iove, greatest and all-powerful, whose eagle I now follow, and by all the gods, that I will defend and serve the Roman nation. I will obey the will of the senate, the people of Rome, and the officers empowered by the senate over me, and my general, Gaius Iulius Caesar, *Imperator*. I swear that I am a free man, able to take this oath, and obligated by bond or debt to no Roman. I will remain faithful to the Roman people, to the senate, to the officers empowered over me, to the army of Rome until legally discharged by my time of service, by the will of the senate and People of Rome, by the will of my general, Gaius Iulius Caesar, *Imperator*, or by my death. I offer my life as the surety of my oath."

I lowered my hand. Dalmatius turned the paper on his desk around to me, handed me a *calamus*, a reed pen dipped in ink, and said, "Sign here!"

After I did, both Dalmatius and Sevso also signed the document. Dalmatius sprinkled some sand on the signatures, then blew it off. Then, he placed it on the stack.

"You are now a soldier in the army of Rome," Dalmatius instructed. "I will act as your commanding officer until I transfer you for transportation to your unit. You are scheduled to depart in two days. That is, *Dies Martis* . . . the day of Mars . . . the eighth day before the Calends of *Februarius*. I have an *optio* coming off leave and returning to his unit over in Aquileia. He'll escort you to the Tenth. You depart at the second hour of the day. The march shouldn't take more than four days . . . five at the most. While you're here, I can give you a voucher for the inn across the street . . . the *Nympha Enebria*. It's fairly clean . . . quiets down after the sixth hour of the night. Vitilus, the landlord, is a mate . . . Seventh Legion in Spain. He'll give you the military rate. Comes out of your pay, of course . . . or you can bunk here in the back room . . . nothing fancy . . . a cot and a blanket . . . but it's free. You're on your own for chow. You got any pocket money? If not, I can advance you a *sestertius* or two . . . against your pay, of course."

"I'm good," I said, remembering Papa had given me three *sestertii* to tide me over, and Macro had given me two more. "Where's my bunk, sir? I'd like to stow my stuff."

"The door right behind you," Dalmatius indicated with his head. "No lock, so keep an eye on your shit. I'm usually here until the tenth hour. Then, you can find me over at the *Nympha Enebria*. Just ask Vitilus. Sevso sleeps in his office."

Dalmatius was good to his word about the accommodations. Three cots tossed in a room, a thin blanket on each. I picked one and checked the mattress and blanket for bugs—no use reporting for duty with my head and crotch crawling with lice and bedbugs. The bed seemed clean. I noticed there was no brazier in the room. I was thankful for Macro's heavy, woolen *sagum*; it would serve better than Dalmatius' thin blanket to keep me warm. What is it that Macro would say? "You get what you pay for!" This flop was free, and worth every bronze *as* that I was paying for it. I folded my cloak up as a pillow and propped it against the wall, placing my *marsupium* underneath it, just in case.

I lay down. It was hard for me to imagine that less than three weeks ago my only worries were how long the Trojans could hold out against the Argive hordes on the windy plains and getting the principle parts of Greek verbs straight in my head. My future as Macro's partner in the wine trade, however, and our friendship, seemed assured. Now, I was a Roman-army *tiro,* skulking in the shabby back room of the recruiting station in Mediolanum and wondering if at that very moment the consul's lictors were hunting for me to drag me off to Rome. I was working on spending more time dwelling on the irony of my predicament, but I fell asleep.

I awoke in the dark, not knowing where I was. Despite my heavy boots and woolen socks, my feet felt like blocks of ice. I lay there in the dark for a few seconds until my mind became fully conscious and informed me I was in Dalmatius' back room. I could see a slight glow coming from under the door. I sat up, and when my legs seemed able to bear my weight and I had some feeling back in my feet, I got up, crossed the room, barked my shin on one of the other cots, and opened the door.

The room where I had surrendered the next six years of my life to the Roman army was empty. I could see it was night. Dalmatius was long gone. There was flickering light coming from Sevso's office. I was about to cross over to it when I remembered I had left my *marsupium* on my cot. I managed to bark my other shin in the dark as I went back to retrieve it and my cloak. I then crossed over to Sevso's room and knocked on the lintel.

"*Mercule! Qu'est?*" I heard his startled voice. "Crap! Who's there?"

"It's me," I answered, "Gaius Marius. Remember? I'm the guy—"

"*Cacat!* Shit! You startled me," he said, coming to the door. "I forgot you were in the back room. Dalmatius's over at the Drunken Nymph, drinking up his bounty for you, I imagine."

"I don't need to see him," I answered, realizing that I was famished. "*Quot'arum?* What time is it?"

Sevso shrugged. "Still early, I guess . . . definitely first watch . . . second hour, maybe."

I wasn't sure what he meant by "first watch," but I asked, "Is it alright if I slip out to get something to eat? Can I get back in later?"

"You don't have to ask permission," Sevso answered. "Just go. I doubt the Nymph has anything hot this time of night. You might try the native place two streets over . . . the sign of the *Venator*, the Hunter. These Gauls like heavy meals at night, so they'll still have something on the fire. They might spit in your stew. Don't like Romans too much over there. I'm going to lock up soon. Just bang on the door when you get back. I sleep light. Try not to be too late."

With that, Sevso went back into his room, closing his door this time.

I managed to navigate my way across the office without doing any further damage to my shins and soon found myself out on the dark street. Across the road, I could see the light and hear the noise from the Drunken Nymph, but I had no desire to join in. I threw the strap of my *marsupium* across my shoulder and put my cloak on over it. I looked up and down the street to get my bearings. The forum was just down to my right. That meant the Hunter should be to the left and up a street or two. I strode off in that direction, removing the strap from my *pugio* just in case I encountered any thieves along the way—or official thugs from Rome.

I found the Hunter exactly where I thought it should be. It was open, but hardly as boisterous as the Nymph. I went in. There were a few customers huddled over bowls of beer, mostly keeping to themselves. I went over to the counter and was pleased to see a great pot of the steaming brown stew I had noticed before. I started to call for the landlord in Latin, but remembering where I was and not relishing the thought of spit in my food, quickly switched to Gallic.

The landlord was the same who had greeted me earlier in the day. "'Tis you again, is it, *me bouchal*?" he said. "*Crehso ee fuh n'afarn*! Welcome to my place!"

"*Bendeet'eeon uh doowee'ow ee bawb un uh shley hoon*! Blessings of the gods on everyone here," I answered, completing the ritual of entry.

"What'll be then?" he asked.

"A bowl of that lovely looking stew and a bowl of beer," I requested.

"Right," he said. "Find yerself a place to roost, and I'll be bringing it over to ya."

I found a table back in the shadows where I could keep an eye on the door, but I doubted any Romans would come through it.

Soon, the landlord brought me my food, a pitcher of beer, and two bowls. "Ya mind if I sit with ya a bit?" he asked.

"No . . . please," I said.

He sat down opposite me and poured us both a beer. "Go ahead and dig into that while it's hot," he invited.

I needed no second prompting; I was famished.

The landlord took a long draft from his bowl and asked, "So, did you find your Roman? Dalmatius, warn't it?"

"Shuh," I answered as soon as I could swallow. "Yes! He was right where you said he'd be. Thanks!"

"Math's the name, by the way," he said, extending a hand.

I dropped my spoon, swallowed, and shook it. Math was well named. Any bear would think twice before tangling with him.

"They call me Arth," I answered, using my Gallic name. No use antagonizing a man as big as Math.

"So, why'd ya do it?" Math asked.

"Do what?" I asked through a chunk of grisly meat.

"Don't be cute with me, lad," Math accused. "There's only one reason to seek out Dalmatius. It's to join their fookin' Roman army, ain't it? So why'd ya do it?"

I decided there was no point being *cute* in a place like this. "I pretty much had to," I answered. "They had my balls in a vice."

"The fookin' Romans have all 'r balls in a vice," he dismissed my excuse. "So, what's yer story?"

I shrugged and told Math the whole tale: Gabinius' estate, Gabi up in the hills, the thugs along the road, the consul's son, the pending arrest warrant.

When I was done, Math poured us both another bowl of beer and asked, "And ya didn't even get to shag 'er?" Then, he roared out laughing.

The rest of the place was staring in our direction. Math laughing was that much of a rarity. Now that he had an audience, Math raised his bowl of beer and stated, "Here's to me new pal, Arth, who put the mark on the gob-shite brat of a Roman consul!" He drew his thumb across the side of his face and drank.

Everybody in the place joined in. I heard a couple say, "Good job, lad!" and "Way to stick it to the bastard!"

Math could see I was a little nervous at that. "Don't worry, lad," he said. "They're all regulars and have no love fer our fookin' overlords. Besides, any of us could smell a fookin' Roman comin' for miles. Drink!"

"So, yer hidin' from the Romans in their own fookin' army," he chuckled. "I love it . . . really love it!"

Then, a serious look came over Math's face, "Yer know, this may not be a good time fer a Gah'el to be joinin' the Roman army."

"Why's that?" I asked.

"It's that new Roman gob-shite guv'nor they're sending up here to rule over us," he answered. "What's 'is name . . . Caisahr? That's it . . . Caisahr. Robbin' us blind is enough for most of 'em, but this one's building himself a great fookin' army. Who'd ya thinks gotta pay fer that? Us, that's who. The fookin' Roman tax snatchers'll be waitin' for us on the banks of the Styx to get 'r burial coins, they will. And whatta they need this great fookin' army for, I'm thinkin' . . . to go across the Rhenus where it'll do some good . . . climb up in the mountains and clear out those bandits blockin' the passes? I don't think so. This Roman bastard's goin' into Gallia, I'm thinkin'. Not enough gold for 'im to steal down here . . . he's got to go up there to rob and pillage . . . and them's our people up there.

This Caisahr's gonna do for them what them Roman bastards did for us when me gran'da was a pup—kill 'em and rob 'em fookin' blind."

I felt no need to defend Caesar or the Roman army at that moment, so I just nodded and drank some of my beer.

Math was on a roll. "I'll tell ya somethin' else. Couple o' the boys been tellin' me this Caisahr's recruitin' a lot of our folk up in the hills. Now why the fook would he be doin' somethin' like that I'm askin' meself. Them Romans're pretty particular about who they'll let in their fookin' army. Only citizens, it is . . . but not this time. Only one reason for that, I'm thinkin'. Gonna be a lot a fightin' in the North soon. I'm thinkin' this Caisahr's goin' to try to snap up all Gallia for 'imself . . . all the way to *Oceanus* and the *Rhenus*. Only way to explain what he's doin'.'"

With that, Math turned and spit on the floor. I was glad his aim was well wide of my food.

"The gods bless yer appetite, lad," Math said when he heard my spoon scrape the bottom of the bowl. "Would ya like a bit more of that stew?"

When I nodded, he called out, "Rhun! Rhun! Come over here, lad."

A dark-haired boy of no more than eight or nine years appeared from behind the counter. Math handed him my bowl and said, "Here, lad, fill this up with stew fer the gentleman here."

When the boy ran off to fulfill his mission, I asked, "*Eich mab*, your son?"

"*Fuh mab?*" Math answered. "Me son? No! Rhun lost both his folks and his two little sisters when that coughin' sickness came through here two winters back. It took me wife and baby girl, too. Laid me up fer most a month, but I beat it somehow and took the lad in. Must a been a reason why the gods just left the two of us and took everyone else."

Rhun returned with my stew. I thanked him.

"Who're yer people?" Math asked suddenly.

"My people?" I started, realizing Math and Mama would never see eye to eye. "Well . . . my da's got a small place a few miles west of here. He and my older brother run it. My da goes by the name Secundus. I don't know if you know him. He doesn't come to town much. He was my granda's second son. My uncle died as a boy . . . coughing sickness too I think. My gran'pa was called Cunorud . . . Cunorud mab Cunomaro."

"Cunorud mab Cunomaro, is it?" Math interrupted. Then he called over, "Teilo! Teilo! Get yer scrawny ass over here! I need yer to meet someone."

I saw some stirring in the shadows across the room as a figure detached itself from a group of men dinking in the corner. The shape came slowly in our direction and soon resolved itself into a grey-haired man. His blue eyes were washed out, rheumy with age; the cheeks of his long, thin face were garlanded with the red blooms of years of drinking. He dropped his empty bowl on our table and rasped, "I'll not be travellin' all the way over here fer nothin', Math. 'Tis a dry journey, 'tis!"

Math filled his cup from our pitcher and said, "You'll never guess who this is, Teilo! Remember a character who used to come in here years ago . . . when me da had the place . . . named Cunorud? Lived in a round-house farm west o' here? He came back from the Kraut wars and married the miller's girl. What was her name? Ceri . . . sure . . . that's it. . . Ceri."

Math looked over to me for confirmation. I nodded. It had been years since I had heard Grandma's name spoken: Ceri, *love* in our language.

Teilo seemed to be nodding, but it could have just been tremors from age— or from the drink.

"Well," Math continued, "this here lad's his *wuhr*, his grandson, Arth."

Teilo had already downed his beer and was pushing his bowl toward Math for a refill.

"Ah . . . Cunorud," Teilo began, "had a Roman name, as I remember. Used to tell all them tall tales about them nobs he knew down in Rome. What'd he call himself?" Teilo took a drink of his beer to help him remember. "Caius . . . Cai . . . some Roman thing like that. Haven't seen him in years. So . . . you're his grandson, are ya? You look to be a big, strappin' lad. What'ya doin' here?"

"Lad's went 'n joined the fookin' Roman army," Math interrupted. "Goin' up North with the new guv'nor, he is."

"Soldierin', is it? Well . . . 'tis a noble callin'," Teilo announced again, presenting his cup to be filled. I imagine he'd characterize prostitution as a noble callin' if it got his cup filled. And, Math might esteem an honest whore over a Roman soldier any day.

When his cup was filled, Teilo got up. He squeezed my shoulder and said, "You take care o' yerself up there, boy. Them fookin' Belgians and Krauts over them mountains are a fierce lot, I hear." Then he shuffled back across the room, over to his mates.

"He's some character!" Math was saying. "Had a place just north o' here. Lost it when the fookin' Romans took it to give it to one of their own. Ran it into the ground in less than two seasons. Don't know who's got it now." Math spit again. "The fookers just take whatever they fookin' please. We all pitch in best we can . . . make sure th'old man gets fed . . . has a place to sleep. Where they got you stayin'?" Math asked suddenly.

"Me?" I answered. "I'm camped out in Dalmatius' back room . . . colder than a money-lender's heart, but it'll do. I'm supposed to leave in two days."

"Bah!" Math spit. "You'll freeze yer balls off in that place . . . fookin' Dalmatius' too fookin' cheap to light a brazier. I got some space up over the bar you can use—stays pretty warm 'cause o' the cooking fire. Stay up there 'till ya go. I'll send the boy around 'n let 'em know yer here. Don't worry about the cost. Yer fookin' money's no good here . . . and if there are any fookin' Romans lookin' for ya, they won't come lookin' here."

Math didn't get that one quite right.

I spent that night in relative comfort. Math's place was in one of the old wattle-and-daub buildings left over from when the town was a Gallic backwater in the Roman world called Medhlán. Over the years, someone had built a second story on the building, and Math was using the upper floor for storage. But, as he promised, it was warm. I even got to take my boots off for the night.

I descended the next morning around the third hour, my head a bit foggy from the three pitchers of beer Math and I had drunk the night before. I saw Rhun cleaning up, and he told me that Math had gone out to the market to pick up the day's supplies. He served me some bread and watered-down beer, which took the edge off of the remnants of the night before. I decided to walk over to the recruiting station just to let Dalmatius know where I was.

When I got there, Dalmatius was gone, but Sevso was in his office. When I appeared, he seemed surprised to see me. I asked after Dalmatius, but Sevso said he rarely made an appearance before the fourth hour.

"Where'd you spend the night?" Sevso inquired.

"The Hunter," I answered. "Didn't Rhun . . . uh . . . the Gallic boy with the dark hair come by and tell you?"

"Uhhh . . . yes . . . yes, he did. I had forgotten," Sevso seemed to stammer. "Are you planning to stay there again tonight?"

"Yeah . . . unless there's a problem—" I started.

"No! No! No problem!" Sevso interrupted again. "Just like to have an idea where our recruits are. Uh . . . remember . . . you're going North tomorrow. You got to be here by the second hour."

"*Bene*," I confirmed. "Tomorrow . . . second hour . . . anything else I should know?"

"What?" Sevso answered. He seemed surprised by my question, almost panicked. "Uh . . . no . . . nothing! Why'd you ask?"

"No specific reason," I assured him, "just asking, that's all."

"No . . . nothing . . . just make sure you're here tomorrow . . . second hour. That's all," Sevso concluded.

I left the office. Sevso's behavior confused me. Was he always that nervous? Maybe it was just his way. I didn't know the guy at all, so I dismissed my concerns.

That almost cost me my life.

I wandered over to the *thermae*, the baths Macro and I had visited, but the attendant told me they were open only to women until the sixth hour. So, I spent most of my morning wandering about Mediolanum. The weather wasn't too bad—sunny, no wind, a bit balmy for midwinter. I walked down to the west gate, but Galenus wasn't on duty. I even gave some thought to visiting Rufia's place, perhaps renewing my acquaintance with my "wife," Cynthia, but the thought of going there without Macro was a bit intimidating—frightening, actually—so I passed.

In wandering about the place, I found a *biblioteca*, a bookseller in the forum. I browsed the scrolls on display in the shop. I was not impressed with the selection. No Greek, a couple of minor histories, a couple of plays, a few speeches—none by Cicero, though. The shopkeeper was no more impressed with me than I was with his selection. He informed me that I was in a shop that *sold* books, not a *reading* library. I should buy or get out.

On a side street off the forum, I found a *cultrum molaris*, a knife-grinder. He put a razor edge on my *pugio*, and for a Minerva, a bronze *triens*, he sold me a small, rectangular piece of *cos*, a portable whetstone, to keep my knife sharp. He advised me that the whetstone worked best if I put a thin layer of olive oil on it.

I finally wandered back toward the Hunter around the seventh hour. My belly was rumbling, and I couldn't get my mind off a bowl of Math's pork stew. After a good meal, I thought I'd go back to the *thermae* and soak in the hot water. It was a warm day, and I had money in my purse, so the prospect of a good meal and a hot bath, in spite of all that had happened to me over the last few weeks, was beginning to seem serene, peaceful, almost normal.

Rhun intercepted me about a block from the Hunter.

"Thank the gods I found ya!" he said breathlessly in Gallic. "You can't go back to Math's place . . . not now, anyway!"

"Why not?" I quizzed him. "What's wrong?"

"There's a couple of Romans there lookin' for ya," he told me, "big fookin' brutes. They's carrying swords."

Gabinius lied! He didn't wait the three weeks he had promised. He had sent his lictors up after me. They'd call out the militia to help them round me up.

"Were they wearing red tunics?" I shot.

"What?" Rhun said, sounding a bit confused. "Red tunics? No . . . these gob-shites is Roman street trash. Smell like a sewer, they do."

"*Cacat*! How'd they know where to find me?" I wondered out loud.

"That dwarf of a Roman who works for that fookin' Dalmatius told 'em," Rhun answered. "I heard 'em talkin' between 'em selves. They don't imagine I understands their fookin' Latin, bein' a native brat 'n all. They says they gives that fookin' little dwarf a whole *quadriga* to tells 'em, 'n if they don't finds ya, they gonna take it outta his scrawny fookin' hide, they said."

A *quadriga*! A silver *denarius*! This was serious. Whatever was going on, there was some money behind it. It wasn't Gabinius. He didn't need to hire thugs to do his dirty work. The state provided him with those. That left Iunior, the younger Gabinius. *Cacat!* Shit! Would that stinking *mentula* never let up?

I had an idea. "Rhun, do you know where Rufia's place is?" I asked him.

The boy looked at me like I was daft. "Ya means the redheaded Roman whore? Everybody knows where that is," he dismissed my question.

"Good," I said, not wanting to dwell on why a ten-year-old would know where a *lupinarium* was located. "Let your da know . . . I mean Math . . . you found me, and that's where I'll be."

Rhun nodded and ran back toward the Hunter.

I should have worried more about *my* knowing where Rufia's place was. I got turned around in some of the backstreets, and it took almost half of an hour before I found the blue Venus door and the overly excited Priapus. I knocked, and Wulfgar, the massive German enforcer, came to the door. He looked down at me as if a *blatta*, a cockroach, had just appeared before him.

"No open!" he grunted. "*Abi tu!* You go away!"

"I'm not here to . . . uh . . . I'm not here for . . . for business," I stammered back. "I need to talk to your . . . uh . . . mistress."

Wulfgar took a second to decide whether it was better to step on a cockroach or to reason with it. Luckily, he chose the latter. "You go away!" he said and started closing the door on me.

Then I heard Rufia's voice from inside, "Who is that, Wolfie?"

Before the German could respond, I yelled past him, "It's me, Rufia! Gaius Marius! Macro's friend!"

Rufia suddenly appeared next to Wolfie, like a redheaded poppet next to a blond colossus. "Ah! Gai! What's wrong? Is something wrong with Macro?" she asked urgently.

"No, mam!" I answered. "Macro's fine. Can I talk to you? I need your help."

Rufia looked relieved when I told her Macro was alright. "Yes. Come in! Come in," she urged. "And don't call me *mam*. I'm Rufia to my friends."

The German stepped back, and I entered, following Rufia down into what served as her *vestibulum*. I could still detect that strange, earthy smell lurking behind her perfume.

"Sit!" she told me over her shoulder. "I'll get you some wine. You look like you need it."

While Rufia arranged for the wine, I heard her front door close, and immediately Wulfgar appeared. He gave me another cockroach look and retired to his post, a small cubicle behind a curtain under the stairs.

Rufia returned, followed by a girl carrying a tray with a pitcher, two cups, and a plate of bread and cheese. The girl placed the tray down on a table. I thought I recognized her as the girl who had witnessed my "marriage" to Cynthia. Rufia was dressed modestly in a plain, green, long-sleeved, woolen tunic down to her ankles. She wore no makeup and had her dark red hair tied back in a ponytail that reached halfway down her back.

"Please, excuse the way I look, Gai," she was saying as she poured our wine. "It's a bit early in the day for me. We usually don't get going until the eighth hour at the earliest. Now . . . drink some wine. It's a warmed *mulsum* with honey . . . and have a bit to eat. Then tell me what's going on."

Rufia sat down opposite me while I dug in. I had forgotten how hungry I was, and the warm *mulsum* was delicious on a winter day. It almost restored my sense of well-being. Finally, I put down my cup and told Rufia the whole story and my reason for being there.

Rufia looked at me for about five heartbeats and asked, "If you believe that someone in Rome is paying a lot of money to have you killed, what makes you think you can trust me?"

I hadn't considered that angle, but after a moment's thought, I said, "Macro . . . you're a friend of Macro. If he can trust you, so can I."

Rufia nodded. "Good answer," she agreed. "So, do you just want to hide out here for the night? Those *percussores*, Roman hitters, will probably be waiting for you when you try to report to Dalmatius tomorrow."

"I don't know what else to do," I admitted.

Rufia thought about it for a moment. "I may have an idea," she said finally. "The day I can't lure two men to my place is the day I go out of business. You wait here, *carissime*. Relax. I'll have Meriope bring you some more of the *mulsum*. Wolfie, *carissime* . . . we need to talk . . . in the back!"

The German appeared from behind his curtain, grunting in disgust as he passed me. I was beginning to believe that he treated all Romans like cockroaches. He followed Rufia into the back, where the girls' *cubicula* were. A few moments later, Meriope appeared with another pitcher of the warm, honey-sweetened wine. The combination of the warm, sweet wine, the warmth of Rufia's *vestibulum,* and a sense of being safe were lulling me into a stupor. I must have fallen asleep because Rufia seemed to appear abruptly before me, wearing that benevolent grin of a mother looking at her baby just waking up from a nap.

"Welcome back, Sleepyhead!" she greeted me. "We've come up with a plan. It's a bit risky, but it should work out. It'll require a bit of playacting on your part. How well do you trust those people at the Hunter?"

"Well enough," I answered. "I know they have no love for Romans."

"Good enough," Rufia answered. "You're going to be the bait to lure those two Roman gangsters here. I'll send that boy from the Hunter . . . Rhun? I'll send him around to tell them you're here. If that stylus-pushing wimp, Sevso, could hang them up for a silver *quadriga* for information, Rhun should be able to make more than a few bronze *asses* from selling you out. Once we have them here, we'll make them tell us what this is all about. Won't we, Wolfie?"

The giant grunted something that sounded like "Ya."

"He so likes an opportunity to hurt Romans. In memory of something that happened to him in his childhood, I should think," Rufia observed. "Once we find out what we need to know, we'll dispose of them. You *do* have the stomach for this, Gai?"

Dispose of them? I wasn't so sure. But, I didn't have many other choices. So, I just nodded.

"*Euge,*" Rufia finished. "I imagine these two *stulti*, these idiots, are carrying around with them the money they got to off you, so I propose an even split. That work for you, *carissime?*"

Again, I nodded.

"*Bene,*" Rufia concluded. "We are agreed. Nothing left except to get this cart rolling. Wolfie, *carissime*! You know what needs to be done."

Again, the grunting "Ya" and Wulfgar went up the stairs and out into the street.

Rufia then led me into the back, past the *cubicula* for her girls, past the kitchens, then up a flight of steps into a dark, narrow corridor lined with doors on one side.

"We're on the first floor of the *insula*, the tenement," she told me. "I've owned it for some years. These rooms are walled-off from the other apartments. This is where I entertain my special guests . . . people who don't want to be found and don't want to be seen."

Rufia gave me a broad wink as she unlocked one of the doors. Inside, after she finally managed to light a small oil lamp, I could see a bed and an end table.

"Not very luxurious, I know," she apologized with a slight bite of sarcasm, "but quite secure. The *latrina*, if you need it, is through the kitchens in the back. I'll send one of the girls up with some more *mulsum* and maybe a little *cenula*, a snack . . . some olives . . . radishes. Relax. You're quite safe here. I'll send someone up to tell you when our guests have arrived." Again, the wink.

Rufia's confidence lulled me into a sense of security. I made a quick trip out the back, and when I returned to the room, I found another jug of her excellent *mulsum* and a bowl of olives. I hadn't finished my first cup of the warm, honeyed wine in the dimly lit room when I fell asleep. Suddenly, I felt someone shaking my shoulder. When my mind finally had climbed up out of the deep, black pit into which it had fallen, I saw a young boy, a slave, maybe eight or nine years old.

"Master," he whispered, "my lady says to tell you the Romans are here." Then, he quickly departed.

Rufia hadn't provided many details about this part of the plan. I had assumed that I would hide until she had Wulfgar "dispose of" my pursuers. That was why I was rather shocked when I heard a loud commotion coming up the stairs from the *lupinarium*. First, the heavy tread of a couple of pairs of feet, then Rufia's voice saying, "Yes! Yes! Right up the stairs! He's in the first room!"

I was fumbling for my *pugio* when the door burst open and a pair of strong hands grappled me and stood me up. Then, a blow to the side of my head that added yellow sparkles to the darkness of the room.

"Siglis! Watch out!" I heard a guttural voice from beyond the black sparkles. "The little shit was reaching for somethin'!"

As I fumbled blindly, my world was suddenly filled with the smell of garlic breath and body odor.

"I got it, Muco!" another voice answered. I felt a tug where my knife was hung. "The little *cunnus* was going for this. Got a bit of a sting, does ya?" Then, my head exploded again.

I vaguely heard Rufia's voice saying, "Not here, you idiots! Bring him this way!"

So, once a *lupa* always a *lupa*! Rufia had decided to make her profits on me, not with me. "*Cunna*," I managed to spit out at her as they dragged me down the stairs.

"Teach that little shit some manners, Wolfie," Rufia snarled. My head exploded again. Darkness.

When I began to crawl out of yet another dark hole, I realized I was on the ground. The air felt cold, damp, like I was in some sort of cellar. Rufia's voice was saying, "The access grates to the sewer are just down around the bend. You can work on him all you want down here. No one will hear a thing." I suddenly lost all interest in consciousness and let myself slip back down the black slide.

The next thing I knew, I was in a sitting position. Someone was urgently patting my cheeks. I heard Rufia's voice calling my name. I opened my eyes. Rufia's face! She took a step back. "*Gratias Bonae Fortunae*!" she said. "I was afraid Wolfie had hit you too hard. Poor lamb doesn't know his own strength— especially when it comes to hitting Romans. You just sit there until your head clears, *carissime*!"

She took a couple of steps to her right, down what seemed to be a tunnel. I heard her say to someone, "Where were we now? Oh, yes . . . I was asking you who paid you."

I heard a spitting sound in response.

"What frightful manners," Rufia said calmly. "Wolfie! The next finger!"

I heard a snap and a scream.

Then I was puking.

I heard Rufia say, "Boys, I think Gai can walk now. Take him up to the kitchens. Some bread to settle his stomach first. Blows to the head can be tricky. Then some wine to calm him down."

Two strong pairs of hands helped me to my feet and led me down the tunnel to my left. From behind me, I again heard Rufia, "Please, accept my apologies for the interruption. You were just about to tell me who paid you."

I had been in the kitchens for what seemed like the better part of an hour when Rufia finally joined me. Although I worked out that she had just come from torturing two Roman skells in some musty tunnels leading to the city sewers, she looked flawless—dress, hair, cosmetics—and her only concern seemed to be for my well-being.

"Oh, dear," she was saying while examining my face. "I'm afraid there's going to be some bruising . . . though the eye might not turn black. Are you feeling dizzy at all?"

"Couldn't you have given me some warning?" I interrupted. "When those two killers burst into my room, I thought you had set me up!"

"And that's exactly what I wanted you to think, *carissime*!" she answered quite calmly. "If you were convinced, they'd be convinced. And, except for a couple of bumps and bruises, it worked like a charm."

I didn't know how to respond to that, so Rufia continued, "Perhaps you'd like to know what they told me?"

I just nodded.

"*Bene*," she said. Then she turned and said, "Wolfie! *Carissime*! Would you ask one of the kitchen girls to bring me a bit of wine? I am parched. Where was I? Oh, yes . . . the two ex-gangsters from *Mater Roma*."

"*Ex*-gangsters?" I questioned.

"Oh, yes," she answered without the least hint of guile or regret. "We couldn't just leave them hanging about down there, now could we? Oh . . . thank you, *cara*," she said when one of the kitchen girls served her a cup of wine.

"Interrogation is such thirsty work!" she declared putting down her wine cup. "Are you at all familiar with a Titus Annius Milo Papianus?"

That was a new name to me. I shook my head, no.

"Well," Rufia continued, "This Titus Annius Milo Papianus is quite a celebrity down in Rome. The best way I could put it is that he's a political agitator for Pompeius Magnus. Without that august connection, he'd just be a common street goon."

Rufia took another drink from her wine cup, then dabbed her lips with a cloth serviette.

"It seems that the two boys, with whom you have had such a fleeting relationship, worked for him. So, what could you have possibly done to cause Milo, or perhaps even Pompey himself, to send two of his third-rate thugs all the way up here to cut your throat?"

"I don't have a clue," I admitted, a bit stunned at the company I seemed to be keeping down in Rome. "Unless it was Aulus Gabinius Iunior again. He'd have the money for it."

"That is a possibility," Rufia said. "But, our two friends didn't know . . . a shame, really. Could have saved themselves a lot of pain had they convinced me sooner. They took the contract and the money from one of Milo's underbosses."

I sighed. "Will this be over now, you think?" I asked her.

"Possibly," Rufia said, "with you going North with the army, there wouldn't be much of a point sending any more goons up here. Of course . . . I'll have to send the money back. No point in offending someone as powerful as Milo. He'll understand. This is not his territory, and he did not have my permission. I'll keep a bit of his money . . . as a *damnum*, a fine."

I was beginning to wonder just who *I* was dealing with in Rufia. "I guess I'll be off, back to the Hunter," I said. "I can't thank you enough for your help."

"You're right," Rufia answered. "You can't. But, you're a friend of *m'amicus*, Macro, and even more importantly, I like you. I wouldn't hear of you going back to that dirty, little Gallic *caupona*. This is your last night before you go North, and you'll stay here as my guest."

Rufia signaled the boy I had seen earlier and whispered into his ear. He nodded and ran off down the hallway where the girls worked. In almost no time, he arrived with one of the girls in tow. It took me a few heartbeats, but I recognized the one called Cynthia from my last visit.

"*Qui' vis tu, Domina?*" she said to Rufia without raising her eyes. "What do you wish, my Lady?"

"Cynthia, I'm giving you the rest of the night off," Rufia said. "I want you to take this young Roman soldier up to the private apartments for the night."

"*Obsequor t'i, Domina,*" she said. "Yes, my Lady."

Without looking up, Cynthia extended her hand to me. When I took it, our eyes finally met. At first, Cynthia didn't recognize me, but after a few heartbeats, she said to me in Gallic, "*Fuh n'goor a gullwuth*! My lost husband! Where have you been all this time? I was becoming jealous!" Then, she laughed.

As I got up to follow Cynthia, Rufia said, "Just one more thing!"

I stopped and asked, "Yes?"

"Wolfie, *carissime*," Rufia called gently.

The German stepped up to us, opened his giant fist, and let five silver coins fall onto the table, five newly minted Roman *denarii*. Like a five-headed Ianus, the god of beginnings and endings, five sharp, unworn profiles of Gaius Iulius Caesar—with crowns of oak leaves, receding hairlines, strong jawlines—looked off in different directions as if toward all different, yet possible, outcomes.

"What's this?" I asked Rufia.

"Your share," she answered. "Milo has to understand the high price of screwing up."

Rufia's boy woke me up early the next morning. I had to be at Dalmatius' office by the second hour to journey North to the legion. Cynthia still lay sleeping next to me in the bed. I had never truly *slept* with a woman before. I don't know whether it was the warmth of her body on a cold winter night or the sense of security she gave me after the events of the previous day or my need to cling to some last fleeting vestige of my youth or her simply being a woman, but our bodies hadn't parted the entire night.

I dressed quietly, not wanting to disturb her. As I slowly opened the door to leave, I reached into my *marsupium* and removed three of the silver denarii that Rufia had given me the night before. I hid them in the folds of Cynthia's discarded chiton lying on the floor. I bent over and lightly kissed her cheek and was rewarded with a sleepy, inarticulate murmur, which I allowed myself to believe meant *bona fortuna*, good luck.

IX.

De Itinere Frigido
A COLD JOURNEY

ontrary to Dalmatius' almost delusionary sense of geography, the march to the legionary camps around the Roman *municipium* of Aquileia took us twenty-one days. The entire journey was along well-maintained Roman military roads, and the ambition of our officer, Cossus Lollius, a veteran *optio* returning to the Eighth Legion from leave, was to cover the almost two-hundred-seventy miles between Mediolanum and our destination in a sequence of smart, regimented military marches of twenty miles a day. We were snowed in for two days just short of Verona, and some of our party of five *tirones*, military recruits, and two *veterani*, experienced soldiers who had reenlisted in the legions, weren't up to such a daily pace.

Before we left Mediolanum, Dalmatius issued us travel funds, the equivalent of three months' pay: fifty-six *denarii* and one *sestertius* each. We didn't see any of the coin, of course. That was given to our *optio*, Lollius. We each signed a receipt for the funds and transferred it over to the care of our officer. Dalmatius told us that Lollius would negotiate our room and board during the trip and pay the landlords as we went. When we reported to our legions, he would turn the remaining funds over to the *Aquilifer*, the standardbearer of our legion, who would deposit them in our names in the legionary treasury, after standard deductions for things such as equipment, food, retirement, and the burial club.

At Dalmatius' suggestion, we also deposited any money we were carrying with Lollius. He warned us that Roman inns were dangerous places, full of thieves and cut-purses. Just in case, I held back a few of my *mercurii*, as the *sestertius* coins displaying the head of the messenger god were called back then. Before we departed, Dalmatius gave each of us a carrying case for our paperwork, which we were to turn in to an officer called a *tesserarius* when we finally arrived.

Finally, he issued each of us what looked like a small, lead amulet. One side was stamped with the letters, SPQR, for *Senatus Populusque Romanus*, the symbol of the Roman state, to whom we now belonged. The other side was engraved with our names. At Lollius' suggestion, I hung mine on the same leather strap as my *Bona Fortuna*.

We were then on the road to Aquileia. I discovered that because of the squinty cast of his eyes, Lollius was called "Strabo" by his mates in the Eighth Legion. He tolerated this informality from the two *veterani* in our detail, but we *tirones* learned very quickly to address him respectfully as "*Optio*, sir."

Since we had, at least by army standards, a late start on that first day, Strabo only marched us fifteen-thousand paces. He didn't do a pace count, but instead relied on the mileposts along the road. Since our route went straight down the Padus Valley and the terrain was relatively flat, we marched to a standard military pace, not the abbreviated pace used in hilly and rough terrain. We marched north, out of Mediolanum, and crossed the Ticenum River on a well-constructed stone bridge, reaching the town of Como on our second night. The next day, we marched in an easterly direction with the high mountains on our left, re-crossed the Ticenum, and reached Bergomum by the third hour of the fifth day.

Strabo and the *veterani* had no problem with our pace. My legs ached a bit, but by the fifth day, I was well used to the pace. A couple of the other *tirones* weren't as accommodating, and soon Strabo was hearing complaints about the tempo of the march and demands for rest stops along the way. Strabo promised these grumblers that after a week with the legions, they would consider this pace, without armor, equipment, and *impedimenta*, quite leisurely, and after a day with the legions, they would understand that *tirones* were not at all authorized to bitch about anything. Complaining to an officer about the pace of a march was begging for a beating.

Despite this, one *tiro*, a lanky, blondish boy named Tertius Melonius, whose accent definitely identified him as a Padus Valley *paganus*, continued to complain about the pace and how much his feet hurt. We had just arrived at an inn halfway between the towns of Leuceris and Brixia when Strabo had finally had enough. He told the kid to sit on the edge of his bunk and take off his boots and stockings. Strabo examined his right foot for no more than five heartbeats, then whistled. "*Mercule*, Melonius, these dogs of yours are flatter than piss in a plate! How did you sneak these by the recruiter?"

"Never looked at me feet, *Optio*," Melonius replied, "just me balls. And then he said I was fit for service."

"*Irrumptores* . . . recruiters! Just interested in the bounty," Stabo snorted. "When we get up to Aquileia, you let the *medicus* take a look at these. They could be your ticket outta the army. You can't bloody well march on these."

"But I don't wanna get out!" Melonius complained. "Ain't nothin' for me back at home!"

Strabo shook his head. "What did you do in civilian life?"

"Me pa's a *faber*, the blacksmith in our village," Melonius answered. "I helped out around his smithy . . . shoeing horses, repairing plows and equipment, that sort of shit. But, I'm the third son. After me brothers get theirs, there's nothin' left over for me."

Strabo shook his head again. "I don't know if you can march on these. See what the doc says. If they want to muster you out, the army can always use someone who can work with metal. Maybe you can get hired on as a civilian. Meanwhile, try to keep up best you can."

Melonius' feet slowed us down to a mere fifteen miles a day, which did not improve Strabo's attitude about his charges. Despite knowing that Melonius was not a slacker, Strabo started calling him *Mollis*, Softy—not the sort of sobriquet that would serve him well once we joined the legion at Aquileia.

In the evening of the tenth day of our march, we crossed the River Clevis and limped into a small hostel a few miles east of Verona. Most of the *tirones* were dragging, and even our *veterani* were beginning to show a bit of fatigue. All day, dark, grey clouds had lowered over us and a cold, biting wind, smelling of snow, blew down off the mountains in the North. As we settled down into our cots in the common dormitory, after our *cena*, the main meal of the day, Strabo announced that if we got an early start the next morning, we might be able to make up some of the time that Mollis' flat feet had lost us. None of us were excited by the prospect, especially not Mollis.

When we awoke the next morning, we discovered that the world had been swallowed by an opaque white cloud of swirling snow and freezing winds. Even Strabo, despite his extensive army training and august rank, could neither see through this mess nor order it to cease. Even he had to surrender to the gods of winds and weather and call a halt to our advance. *Sic dicta Aeolo!* Thus decreed Aeolus, the god of storms and now the protector of road-weary soldiers! We had a day of rest.

After *ientaculum*, a light morning meal of watered wine, flat wheat bread, and salt, we returned to the dormitory and mostly napped throughout the day. One of the *veterani* in our group announced that the one thing a *pedes*, a leg, a Roman infantryman, had to learn was to sleep wherever and whenever the opportunity presented itself. Strabo stirred long enough to snort in assent and then started snoring again.

Around the fifth hour, I realized that I wasn't yet a good infantryman; I couldn't sleep anymore. I went over to the common room of the inn and opened the door wide enough to confirm the weather hadn't changed. I wouldn't put it past Strabo to try to get a couple of miles down the road if the storm broke. I sat down at one of the trestle tables comfortably close to the fire.

The landlord came over and asked, "What can I get yas, soldier?"

I was going to say nothing. Only Strabo was authorized to make purchases. Then I remembered I had a few coins of my own in my *marsupium*.

While I was figuring this out, the landlord offered, "I got some *posca* . . . fresh. Just cooked it up. It's cooling outside. Could I interest yas in a pitcher?"

"*Posca?*" I heard a voice say. "Bring it on!"

One of our *veterani* had also decided that he had had enough of being a good Roman *pedes* and sleeping the day away. He joined me at the table and dropped a few bronze coins down. "That should cover it!"

He looked at me and winked. "I can afford to be generous now that Rome is paying my bills again. Whatta you called again?"

"Gaius Marius," I answered and offered a hand. "Please, just call me Gai."

He took it. "Bantus . . . Lucius Bantus," he offered. "Recently a landed gentleman and the leading drunk of Acerrae on the right bank of the beautiful, pristine river Adda! Now, a humble Roman *mulus*, a poor Roman grunt and member of the august and celebrated Tenth Legion." He inclined his head toward me.

"What made you get back in?" I started to ask when the landlord arrived with our pitcher and a couple of clay cups.

"You might want to bring a couple more cups," Bantus said. "I'm sure some of the other lads will be along in just a bit."

The landlord swept up one of Bantus' coins and nodded.

Bantus poured the *posca* into our cups and, without waiting, took a deep draft of his. He actually grimaced, then smacked his lips, saying, "Ah! That's *posca*! The much-loved drink of the legions! Drink up, boy!" he urged me.

I did and immediately regretted it! It tasted like vinegar with an aftertaste of honey. The back of my throat began to burn; my eyes bulged as my jaw locked, which was the only thing that prevented me from gagging.

Bantus laughed, "Nothing like your first swig of *posca*! Now you're a Roman soldier!" He took another swig from his cup.

"Something wrong with my *posca*?" the landlord asked as he placed a couple more clay cups on our table.

"Nah!" Bantus said. "It's the boy's first shot at it." They both laughed.

Bantus wiped his mouth with the back of his hand as the landlord retreated; then he asked, "So, what brings you to the army?"

I didn't think I should confide in Bantus that I was one step ahead of the consul's lictors. "I'm a younger son. I need to do something with my life. Army's as good a choice as any," I offered. "What about you? Why'd you get back in?"

Bantus shrugged. "When I got out last time, they gave me some land. Not cut out to be a farmer. Couldn't make rocks grow. Sold the place, then drank the proceeds. Money ran out, and here I am!"

He poured himself more *posca*. Then, he noticed I hadn't touched my cup since almost poisoning myself with my first drink. "Drink up, Gai!" he urged. "It gets better with every swallow. Grows on you in a way." He chuckled.

Strabo wandered out of the dormitory, stretching and yawning. First he spotted us, then the pitcher. "That what I think it is?" he asked, rubbing his hands together and taking a seat.

"*Posca*!" Bantus confirmed and filled another cup. "Mother's milk of the Roman soldier. Get enough sleep, Strabo?"

"*Cacat*! There's never *enough* sleep!" Strabo countered, emptying half of the cup and belching. "It's not like you can store it up and carry it around in your pack for when you need it."

Both *veterani* nodded together and chuckled. Then, Strabo noticed me. "What's a matter? Don't like your drink, *Tiro*?" he asked.

I was just about to attempt some manly, soldierly sounding answer to that when Bantus said, "Hey! Buyer's rules. I paid. Let's just be three guys having a drink. You're scaring the shit outta the kid."

Strabo nodded, but regardless of Bantus' "buyer's rules," I decided to keep my mouth shut unless spoken to.

"So . . . you headed back to the Eighth?" he asked Strabo.

Strabo nodded. "Supposed to be on leave until the Calends of *Martis*, but the new governor's really stirring up the shit. They say the tribes are moving again north of the *Provincia*. Even heard the Krauts are over the Rhenus in Gallia again. I'm hoping my unit's still in Aquileia, but they may have already moved north before the passes closed in November. I may get stuck with you guys in the Tenth. Ninth's supposed to be in camp with them too."

"*Cacat*!" Bantus exclaimed. "That's a lot of manpower in one place. Who'd they leave to keep a lid on things over in Hispania?"

Strabo shrugged. "Shit like that's way beyond my pay grade! Governor's assembling an army; that's for sure. Must expect some real shit up in Gallia."

I noticed the pitcher was empty. I reached into my *marsupium*, laid a couple of bronze *minervae* on the table, and signaled the landlord. I figured as long as I had money on the table, I was covered under buyer's rules.

Bantus was nodding, "Yeah . . . I heard that too. We haven't seen anything like this in what . . . forty years? Way back when Crassus was a corporal? Makin' some people nervous. Guess the governor wants to stop it before it really gets going."

Strabo agreed, "Army's offering top price for recruits. Even this skinny specimen here's worth a silver *quadrata* or two. That's what *iste irrumptor*, that bloody wanker, Dalmatius, got for you?"

"Hey! The kid just bought you a drink," he cautioned Strabo. "Some respect for a man who stands his round, eh?" He winked at me and held up his cup in a toast. I took another sip of the *posca*. Bantus was right; it did seem to be tasting better.

"I'm pretty sure that lazy *podex* got three for me," Bantus continued. "And, I heard him telling that creepy, little dwarf that works for him that they're authorized to recruit noncitizens for some new legions the governor's raising in Aquileia. Never heard of the army doing anything like that. This new governor—what's his name? Caesar? This new governor must think he's Gaius Bleedin' Marius himself, back from the underworld. *Istae verpae*, those pricks in the senate're gonna have a fit when they hear he's recruiting long-haired Gauls into the legions."

"Rome's a long way from here," Strabo said. "And, the day those *viles landicae*, those worthless pussies, down in Rome have a clue about what the army needs to get a job done up here is the day I start carrying the mule instead of the mule carrying me."

Bantus nodded at that. "If only they were *landicae*, we'd know where to stick—" he started, but then we were joined by the other *veterani* in our group.

"Thought I smelled a pot of *posca*," he announced, grabbing the pitcher and pouring himself a cup.

"Thank our *tiro* . . . Gai . . . here," Bantus told him. "He sprung for it."

"Thanks, kid!" he said raising his cup to me. "*Tullius Norbanus*. Just call me Tulli."

I returned his salute and took another drink. "Gaius Marius—" I started, when Strabo interrupted.

"Are the other *tirones* stirring back there?" he asked Tulli.

"Nah," he answered, "they'll sleep for a week if you let them."

Strabo grimaced. "I wanna get back on the road. Playing nursemaid to a bunch of wet-behind-the-ears recruits is not why I came back from leave."

"Quit ya bitchin', Strabo," Bantus told him. "There are worse details. Besides, what's your skim on this job? A bronze *as* on every *quadrata* you're carryin'?"

Strabo was just about to say something when Bantus asked Tulli, "What was your last posting?"

"I was with the Third in Asia—" he started.

I interrupted, "The Third! You know an *optio* named Macro?"

All three men stared at me blankly. I had just pushed the limit of the buyer's rules. The *posca* must have been getting to me. All of a sudden, it didn't taste so bad.

Tulli didn't seem to mind. "Macro . . . no . . . never met the guy. Heard of 'im, though. First battle-line man . . . the "bleeding edge". . . Had a good rep with the squaddies . . . good man."

Bantus pitched in, "So, what brings you back to the eagles?"

"Bored, I guess," Tulli started, "broke, for sure. This new nob coming up from Rome sounds like he's gonna stir things up. Could make some money out of this."

"There is that," Bantus agreed.

"Yeah," Tulli continued, "living with civilians was driving me crazy. Their shit's so petty: potholes in the street, the furnace in the bath getting clogged. It's a major, world-endin' crisis for them. Wonder what they'd do if they saw a phalanx of Greek hoplites or a mob of screaming Krauts charging down on them?"

"Shit their pants," Strabo interrupted.

"Shit their pants and run," Bantus added.

All three clunked their cups together. I didn't think I was expected to participate, so wisely, I did not.

We drank through most of my *minervae*. Around the seventh hour, Strabo got up, stretched, and said something about taking a nap before we ate dinner. The rest of us got up to follow. I was about to snatch up the last remnant of my money, two bronze *asses*, when Bantus stopped me.

"Leave it for the landlord," he said. "You never want to piss off someone who could spit in your stew." Then, he winked.

We arrived at the legionary camps at Aquileia the day before the Ides of *Februarius*. We walked into a beehive of activity around the town. Three veteran legions camped side-by-side. I saw, too, their *vici*, the temporary villages of camp followers who served the needs of the soldiers—from laundry and grooming to a warm body to sleep next to on long winter nights; merchants from throughout the region, who were selling anything the soldiers needed, from winter cloaks and woolen Gallic *bracae* to pieces of military equipment and weapons; and the townspeople, who seemed, for the most part, to be gawking at the carnival.

Strabo quickly got directions to the camp of the Tenth Legion and led his details to its *Porta Praetoria*, the Headquarters Gate. Since Strabo didn't know the day's password, the sentries kept us outside the gate while the sergeant of the guard, the *tesserarius*, was fetched. The gate itself was part of the camp's *vallum*, a log-reinforced wall constructed from soil excavated from the *fossa*, the ditch which surrounded the entire camp. The gate was constructed by overlapping the *vallum* to create a passageway between two walls, where an attacking force could be trapped. On each side of the gate, the legionaries had constructed two low towers on which were situated large weapons, which looked to me to be giant bows.

Tulli noticed me staring up at them and said, "*Ballistae* . . . you don't want to get on the wrong side of those."

It was then that the *tesserarius* arrived at the gate, "You Cossus Lollius?" he asked Strabo.

"That's Cossus Lollius, *optio* of the Eighth Legion, *Tesserarius*," Strabo corrected the soldier.

"We've been expecting you. Follow me, *Optio*," the soldier replied and executed an about-face into the fold of the gateway.

Strabo spit on the ground, muttering something about the stuck-up *cunni* in the Tenth, then followed the *tesserarius* around the gate.

When we got through, we were on a straight, well-worn pathway, a street really, about five paces wide. On each side of the street were tents reinforced with log walls.

"Squad tents for the frontline cohorts," Tulli said to me. "The fact you don't see any squaddies hangin' about's a good sign. They keep the boys busy in this legion, even in winter quarters—boredom's the worst thing for discipline."

We finally arrived at an intersection of roads. Ahead of us to our right was a large tent, in front of which two legionaries stood guard. Our escort said, "Wait here, *Optio*!" and entered the tent.

"The *Praetorium*," Tulli told me, "the legion's headquarters. It always sits here in the center of the *castrum*."

Before I could reply, the *tesserarius* reappeared and said, "*Optio*! You and your detail may enter and report to the *Praefectus Castrorum*."

We entered the tent.

Post Scriptum

When I entered that *castrum*, that legionary camp, my youth ended.

Quam simplex me! How naïve I was!

I believed that by joining the legions, I left the attempts on my life by Gabinius and his murderous brood lying dead in the sewers of Mediolanum.

Erratum! I was wrong!

I believed that my hitch in the army would be a mere six years of polishing armor, sharpening swords, and marching about. I reasoned I would get no farther from home than *Provincia, Hispania,* or perhaps *Graecia.*

Erratum!

I believed that my family's claim of *patrocinium*, the patronage of the *gens Iulia* and the new proconsul of *Galliae* and *Illyricum*, Gaius Iulius Caesar, was a family myth, that I would never as much as see the man.

Erratum!

I believed that when I was discharged, I would rejoin Macro, who would have our grapes thriving and would have ships, filled with *amphorae* of our brew, sailing to all the corners of the *imperium*.

Quam erratum!

I soon discovered, as did Macro, that a rich and powerful man never shares his good fortune, especially with those he considers his inferiors, those powerless to oppose him. That would not be *Romanitas*, civilization as we Romans have established it throughout the world with sword and fire.

I also discovered that *patrocinium* to a powerful man is like wearing golden chains in the great man's triumph: they glitter beautifully and many desire them, but they are chains none the less. One must constantly anticipate the inevitable descent into the pit for the entertainment of the mob.

But, all that lay in the future as I entered the *Praetorium* tent of Caesar's army those many years ago and left my youth—and my *simplicitas*—behind.

A GLOSSARY OF LATIN TERMS
USED IN THE STORY

-A-

Abire—to go away

    Abi– Get outta here!

    Abeas—You may go.

Ad manum—literally, at hand, available; figuratively, personal assistant

Agere—to do, act

    Age—Do it!

    Bene actum—Well done!

Ala (pl. alae)—literally, a bird's wing; militarily, a Roman cavalry unit of twenty to thirty troopers

Amens (pl. amentes)—mad, crazy, stupid

Amicus (pl. amici)—friend, pal, chum

    Amica (pl. amicae)—girl friend

    Io, Amice—Hey, buddy!

    M'amice—My friend!

Anima (pl. animae)—soul, life-force

Aqua vitae—the water of life; whiskey

Aquilifer—a minor Roman officer who carries a legion's eagle, *aquila*.

Arduor—Harder!

Ars (pl. artes)—a skill

As (pl. asses)—small bronze coin, a Roman penny

Atrium (pl. atria)—a space in the front of the house where guests and clients
were greeted

Auctoritas—reputation, a primary Roman virtue; prestige, clout, influence

Audire—to hear

M'audite—Listen up!

Avaritas—greed, a vice opposed—at least in theory—by *pietas*

-B-

Baiulus (pl. baiuli)—porter

Ballista (pl. ballistae)—a piece of Roman artillery that launched a large,
arrowlike bolt over great distances

Balnea (pl. balneae)—bathhouse

Balneator—manager of a bathhouse

Basium (pl. basia)—a kiss

Basiare—to kiss

Bas' me' culum—Kiss my ass!

Bas'me—Kiss me!

Bella—beautiful

Quam bella—How beautiful!

Bene—Good! Great! Yeah! Sure! (literally, well)

Bene gestum! Well Done!

Beneventum (pl. beneventi)—Welcome!

Biblioteca (pl. bibliotecae)—bookstore

Blatta (pl. blattae—cockroach; anyone who's live in an NYC apartment knows
there's never only *one* of these!

Bracae (sing. braca)—trousers

Bulla Praetexta—a hollow charm of gold or leather, which parents placed about
the necks of infant children to ward off evil spirits

-C-

Cacare—to defecate

    Cacat—Shit!

Calamus (pl. calami)—an ink pen

Caldarium—room containing a hot-water pool in a bathhouse

Calendae—the first day of each month

Campus Martis—The Field of Mars; a section of Rome (At the time of the novel, it was outside the walls and the official city limits along the Tiber, just north of town.)

Capsarius (pl. capsarii)—literally, a slave who carried a school boy's book case, *capsa*; military, a field medic.

Capu'—boss, chief, from Latin caput, "head"; Modern Italian, *capo* (Military jargon coined by the author.)

Carus (f. cara)—dear

    Carissime—dearest one, sweetie!

Castrum (pl. castra)—a legionary marching camp constructed at the end of each daily march

Caupona (pl. cauponae)—cheap bar and grill

    Cauponius—the innkeeper, landlord

Celebratio (pl. celebrationes)—a party, dude!

Cella (pl. cellae)—a small room

Cena—dinner

    Cenula—snack

Centuria (pl. centuriae)—an element of a Roman legion consisting of ten *contubernia*, eighty legionaries, commanded by a *centurio*

Centurio (pl. centuriones)—a centurion, a Roman officer; basically, one who commands a *centuria* of eighty men

    Centurio Primus Pilus—"The First Spear," senior centurion of a legion; commands the First Centuria of the First Cohors and also commands the First Cohors; in the absence of the *Legatus Legionis* and the *Tribunus Laticlavius*, the "Broad Stripe" Tribune," commands the legion.

Cerasum (pl. cerasa)—cherry, the fruit, not the virgin

Certe—Yes! Certainly! I agree!

Cinctus—a belt

Civis—citizen

Clientela—the relationship between the *patronus* and his *clientes* (sing. *cliens*), clients; the relationship was hierarchical but obligations were mutual; the *patronus* had *patrocinium*, protector, sponsor, and benefactor of the client

Cognoscere—to know, recognize

Coleo (pl. coleones)—figuratively, scrotum; literally, a sack.

Comprehendere—to understand

    Compre'endis tu?—Do you understand?

    Compre'endo—Yes, I understand!

Constare—literally, to stand together; figuratively, to agree.

    Constat—Yes!

Contemplatio—thinking deeply, contemplation

Contubernium (pl. contubernia)—a squad, a grouping of eight legionaries who shared a tent in the field or a squad room in a permanent camp

Contubernales—members of a common *contubernium*, "mates," "squaddies"

Cornucellus—the "little horn"; a hand gesture used to ward off the evil eye

Corona Civica—Civic Crown, the second highest Roman military decoration, after the "grass crown"; reserved for a Roman citizen who saved the lives of fellow citizens by killing an enemy on a spot not again held by the enemy that same day; the citizens saved must bear witness to the act—no one else could be a witness; any recipient of the Civic Crown was entitled membership in the Roman Senate.

Cos—whetstone

Credere—to believe

Cubiculum (pl. cubicula)—small rooms in a Roman house used for bedrooms

Cucullus—hood

Culina—the kitchen of a Roman house

Cultrum molaris—a knife shop

Culum—ass, buttocks, or anus, in a coarse sense

Cunnus—a vulgar term for female genitalia; used as an insult for both men and women

Cura—trouble, worry, distress, cares, a major pain in the ass, but not quite *dolor*

Cursus Honorum—the "track of honors"; the standard career plan of a noble, therefore ambitious, Roman; a series of civil offices to occupy, culminating in the consular chair

-D-

Damnus—condemned

Debitum—debt

Decet—It's proper.

Denarius (pl. denearii)—a Roman silver coin

Denu'—Again! One more time! From *denuo*

Deus (pl. di)—god

Dea (pl. deae)—goddess.

Di inferni—gods of the underworld

Deversorium (pl. deversoria)—an inn, lodging

Dexter—right as opposed to left

Dies (pl. dies)—a day

Divitiae—fortune, wealth

Divus (pl. divi)—divine, deified

Dominus—Lord; how a slave addressed a free man if he didn't want to be hoisted up on a cross. *Domina* is the feminine version: Ladyship

Domus (pl. domus)—a house, household; a "stable" of slaves

Donatum (pl. donata)—gift, bonus

Dulcis—sweet

Dulce—Sweet! Nice!

Durus—hard, solid, firm, tough

-E-

Enarratio (pl. enarrationes)—academic lecture . . . Take good notes!

Enibrius—drunk

Equites—knights, a class of citzen in Rome

Erratum—wrong, incorrect

Quam erratum—How wrong!

Etiam—Yes!

Euge—Great! a mild exclamation of appreciation

Expeditus (pl. expediti)—unburdened, lightly armed, ready for combat

-F-

Familia—a Roman household, including in-laws, slaves, the house, the property; anything owned by the *pater familias* and anyone who was mooching off his table

Fastus—a day on which it was propitious, therefore legal, to conduct business; opposite of *nefas*

Februarius—February

Fellator (pl. fellatores)—figuratively, an insult roughly equivalent to calling someone a bastard in English; literally, one who plays the "female" role in non-vaginal sex

Festinare—to hurry

Festina–Hurry up!

Fibula—a broach, pin

Ficus (pl. ficus or fici)—fig

Fidelitas—loyalty, a major Roman virtue

Fidelis—faithful, loyal

Filius (pl. filii)—son

Filia (pl. filiae)—daughter

Foetor—smell, stink

Fortis—strong, brave

Fortissime—bravest one

Fortuna—fortune, chance

Bona Fortuna—goddess of good fortune

Fossa—a ditch; part of the standard fortifications of a *castrum*

Frigidarium—room containing a cold-water pool in a bathhouse

Fututrix (masculine form, fututor)—figuratively, to be someone's sex toy, bitch; from *futuere*—to have sexual intercourse.

-G-

Galea (pl. galeae)—a soldiers helmet

Gallia—the land of the Gauls

    Gallia Cisalpina—Gaul on the near side of the Alps; northern Italy

    Gallia Transalpina—Gaul on the far side of the Alps

    Gallia Comata—Long-haired Gaul

Gallus (pl. Galli)—a Gaul; the Celtic inhabitants of northern Italy and most of modern France

Garum –a fermented fish sauce used as a condiment in Rome

Geminus (pl. gemini)—a twin

Gens (pl. gentes)—a people, nation, or a family clan, such as gens Iulia of Gaius Iulius Caesar; gens Gabinia of Aulus Gabinius; or gens Maria of Gaius Marius Insubrecus

Gladius (pl. gladii)—basic Roman infantry short stabbing sword

Gloriosus—one who boasts

Grassator (pl. grassatores)—gangster

Gratias—Thanks! *Multas gratias*, thanks a lot; from the phrase, *Tibi ago gratias.* I give you thanks.

Gratulationes—congratulations.

-H-

Hercule—Holy Crap! (literally, By Hercules!)

Hypocaustum—furnace

-I-

Ianitor—doorkeeper

Ianuarius—January

Ientaculum—the morning meal

Ilex (pl. ileces)—holly oak

Immunis (pl. immunes)—a military status in which a soldier was excused from fatigue details and got extra pay

Impedimentum (pl. impedimenta)—equipment, baggage, military kit

    Impetitus—burdened; military, marching under full pack

Imperator—a Roman title given to a victorious general by acclamation of the troops; General

Imperium—Roman power, authority, and jurisdiction

Impluvium—basically a drain pool; a shallow, rectangular, sunken portion of the atrium used to gather rainwater, which drained into an underground cistern

Inare—to enter

    Intres—please come in

Inique—unfairly

Insubria—Roman name for what is today the Po Valley of northern Italy; probably from the native people the Romans discovered there when they finally got around to conquering the area: the Gallic tribe, Insubreces

Insula (pl. insulae)—literally, an island; figuratively, a tenement building

Intellegere—to know, understand

Io—Hey! (Remember: Rocky Balboa was Italian.)

Ioudaia—Judea

Ironia—irony

Irrumtor (pl. irrumptores)—figuratively, bastard; literally, one who plays the "male" role in oral sex

Item—next, in a list; Item . . . item . . . item

Iterum—Again! Another time!

Iugerum (pl. iugera)—a Roman measurement of land area, approximately 240 x 120 feet

-L-

Laconicus—steam bath

Laena—woolen cloak

Landica (pl. landicae)—an insult roughly equivalent to calling someone a pussy in English; literally, a clitoris

Latifundium (pl. latifundia)—wide farm, large estates, factory farms

Latrina—privy; water closet

Laxa—Relax! Stand at ease!

Lemur (pl. lemures)—malevolent ghosts; the spirits of the restless dead—to be avoided at all costs!

Liberalia—a festival celebrated on 17 March, the festival of Liber Pater and his consort, Libera; the traditional time when young men assumed their *toga virilis*

Libertas—candor, a primary Roman virtue bound to get the speaker in trouble with his superiors

Libra (pl. librea)—Roman measurement of weight, about $11^{1/2}$ ounces

Ligula (pl. ligulae)—a Roman measure of liquid volume of about 12 ml

Lorica—Roman upper-body armor

Lupa (pl. lupae)—literally, a wolf bitch; figuratively, a whore

    Lupinarium (pl. lupinaria)—whorehouse

-M-

Magister (pl. magistri)—teacher, master

Maior Domus—head butler

Male—No good!

Malus—bad, evil

Manes or di manes (sing, manis)—underworld spirits thought to be or represent the souls of deceased loved ones

Manicae—gloves

Manus (pl. manus)—hand

Marsupium (pl. marsupia)—a purse; a carry bag

Martis—*Mensis Martis*, the month of Mars; the beginning of the campaign season; March

Matrona—woman of the house, a married woman, Mrs.

Medicus (pl. medici)—doctor

Mensa (pl. mensae)—office, table, counter

Mentula—(pl. mentulae)—figuratively, prick; literally, prick.

Mercule—a mild expression of surprise. Oh, wow!

Mercurius (pl. mercurii)—a Roman god; military slang invented by the author for a *sestertius* coin

Merda—shit; not necessarily what you call someone, but the stuff you step in—although it can be used to describe an unpleasant situation; *immerda*, "in the shit"

Meridies—middle of the day, noon

Minerva—a Roman goddess; soldiers' slang for a bronze *triens* coin

Mos Maiorum—the custom of the elders, Roman tradition

Mulieres castrorum—literally, women of the camps; camp followers

Mulsum—a heated, spiced wine drink

Mulus (pl. muli)—literally, a mule; military, an infantryman, legionary, a "grunt"

Munera (sing. munus)—gladiatorial games; originally games held in honor of the manes, the spirits of the dead

Municipium—a type of Roman town

Murus (pl. muri)—a wall; in the military jargon of the author, it describes a close-order defensive formation, a *murus scutorum*, a shield-wall

-N-

Nefas—inauspicious, wrong, horrible

Nil—nada, nothing

Nos—we

Nympha (pl. nymphaea)—a fairy

-O-

Obsequor—I comply; I yield

Obsessio (pl. obsessiones)—an obsession

Occupatum—occupied, busy

Officium—duty, a major Roman virtue

Optime—The best! Great!

Optio (pl. optiones)—"chosen" one; a junior army officer; second in command of a *centuria* under the centurion

-P-

Padus—The River Po

Paganus (pl. Pagani)—a country boy, hick, bumpkin

    Io, Pagane—Hey, Hick!

Palla (pl. pallae)—a stole worn over a *stola* by Roman women

Palus (pl. pali)—pole used to practice sword drill

Parare—to prepare

    Paratus—ready

Passus (pl. passus)—a complete stride from when the left foot went down until it came down again; about five and a half feet on flat ground

Patronus (pl. patroni)—patron

    Patrocinium—protection; the relationship of a *patronus* to his clients

Pedicor (pl. pedicores)—figuratively, an insult equivalent to the raised middle finger; literally, one who performs anal sex.

Pediceatur—Screw him! Literally, May he (she or it) be sodomized!

Penates—household gods who guarded the household's food, wine, oil, and other supplies; they became a symbol of the continuing life and welfare of the family.

Percussus—literally, a blow, strike, punch; in this book, it's used to describe a soldier's use of dagger, sword, and offensive shield techniques; also, it means hit man, someone who strikes his victim with a dagger.

Peristylium—a small garden often within the house and surrounded by a columned passage

Pes (pl. pedes)—foot; army slang invented by the author for an infantryman

Phantasma—illusions

Pietas—piety, an essential Roman virtue; the ability to put gods, family, and country—in that order—before self-interest

Pilum (pl. pila)—a Roman throwing spear

Piscina (pl. piscinae)—a fishpond—decorative or functional, depending on how much one liked fresh fish; a necessary element in finer Roman homes

Pius—pious; one who possesses *pietas*

Pomerium—the sacred boundry of Rome

Podex (pl. podices)—figuratively, an arse; literally, one who farts

Populares—a political grouping of Roman senators in the late republic; "liberals"; the party of the people

Porta (pl. portae)—a gate, portal; a Roman marching camp, *castrum*, had four standard *portae*

    Porta Praetoria—the main gate

    Porta Decumana—the "Gate of the Tenth Cohort," the back gate

    Porta Principalis Dextra—right side gate

    Porta Principalis Sinistra—left side gate

Posca—a drink made from vinegar and herbs; mother's milk for a Roman soldier

Posse—to be able

Praeceptor (pl. praeceptores)—teacher, mentor

Praefectus—a Roman officer, often of the centurion or tribune status, in command of a *vexillum* or an auxiliary unit

    Praefectus Castrorum—senior centurion of the army

Praetorium—a headquarters

    Preatoriani—headquarters of security troops

Principium—literally, beginning, origin; military, field headquarters.

Primus—literally, first; Military jargon coined by the author for Top Soldier, Number One; in direct address, "*Prime!*" pronounced PREEM-eh!

Princeps—top guy; leader of the pack; one of the titles assumed by Augustus

Pro qua?—Why? from *Pro qua causa*? For what reason?

Probatio—approval

Provincia (pl. provinciae)—a province; a conquered territory; the Roman-occupied are of southern Gaul, modern Provence

Puer (pl, pueri)—boy

Pugio (pl. pugiones)—a Roman knife usually carried by soldiers; a noble weapon carried by real manly men and true Romans

Pulcher (fem. pulchra)—pretty

Putere—to stink

    Putor—stench

    Quae putet—literally, she who stinks; figuratively, a whore

-Q-

Qu'accidit—What's up?

Quadrita (pl. quadritae)—literally, a four horse rig in a chariot race; street talk coined by the author for a denarius, a roman coin. (yes, a pun)

Qu'est—Who's there? From *Quis est?* Who is it?

Quiris (pl. quirites)—a Roman citizen; a Roman citizen would state, "*Quiris sum,*" to announce the franchise

Qui'vis m'agere?—What do you want me to do?

Qui vult dicere quis?—What does that mean?

Quintilius—Month of July.

Quomo'?—How? from *In quo modo?* In what manner?

Quomo' vales—literally, In what manner are you going? from *Quo modo vales?* figuratively, How's it going?

Quot—How many?

Quot'arum—What time is it? from *Quot horarum?*

-R-

Recte—Correct!

    Quod est rectum! That's right!

Res publica—public affairs, the Republic; description of the Roman state

Rhenus—Rhine River

Rhodanus—Rhone River

Rogare—to ask

Romanitas—Roman culture, hence, civilization

Rostra (sing. rostrum)—literally, the prows of warships; the ancient Romans hung what was left of the Carthaginian navy in their forum, from which spot their politicians and other demagogues periodically harangued them

Rudis (pl. rudes)—literally, a stick; military, a weighted training sword or dagger.

Rusticus (pl. rustici)—a rustic, bumpkin

-S-

Sacramentum—the military oath taken by soldiers

Sacrilegium—sacrilege; a violation of a law ordained by the gods… really bad juju

Sagum (pl. saga)—a military cloak, woolen and treated to be waterproof

Sapientia—wisdom; knowing the reason for things

Salve (pl. salvete)—a formal Roman greeting

Saturnalia—a Roman holiday celebrated in late December; major party time
  probably equivalent to the mardi gras.

Saxum (pl. saxa)—a stone; also a unit of weight

Scriba (pl. scribae)—clerk; one who writes

Scire—to know

Scortillum—a little whore, a wench

Scutum (pl. scuta)—Roman infantry shield

Senior—Figuratively, Sir! Literally, older. Military jargon coined by the author.

Servus (m. pl. servi; fem. sing., serva; pl. servae)—servant, slave

Sestertius (pl. sestertii)—a Roman coin, worth two-and-a-half *asses*, or two
  loaves of bread

Sextilis—the month of August

Si'—Yes! literally, so, thus; shortened form of *sic*

Sica (pl. sicae)—a knife, dagger; the tool of assassins, thieves, easterners, non-
  Romans, and other lowlifes

  Sicarius—assassin; one who uses a *sica*

Simplex—simple, naïve

  Simplicitas—naiveté

Sinister—left as opposed to right

Spatha (pl. spathae)—a long sword, used mostly in the cavalry because a *gladius*
  doesn't reach well when one is sitting on a horse

Spiritus (pl. spiritus)—breath, spirit

Stabulum (pl. stabula)—a stable; a slave barrack

Stat'—from *statim*, immediately, same as in the doctor shows

Stipes (s. stips)—literally, a donation, contribution; functionally, a donation or
  gift one offered to a politician or government functionary to get him to put
  your request on the top of the pile or just to do his job—some things never
  change!

Stola (pl. stolae)—an outer garment worn by married Roman women

Stultus (pl. Stulti)—Idiot!

Stylus—an implement used to write in wax tablets

Subura—a section of Rome; the slums.

-T-

Tabula (pl. tabulae)—a wax tablet used for notes and nonpermanent documents

    Tabularium—the place where *tabulae* were stored; an office; the hall of records

Tacere—to be silent

Tesserarius (pl. tesserarii)—a Roman officer, usually third in rank in a *centuria*; named after a tesserae, a clay token on which was written the daily password

Thermae—baths

Tiro (pl. tirones)—rookie; in the army, a trainee

Toga—a Roman outer garment worn over the tunic; favorite party garment of John Belushi

    Toga virilis—the "toga of manhood" assumed by Romans boys in their late teens

    Toga alba—white toga, basic getup worn by young men as their toga virilis

Totus—all, everybody

Trepidarium—the hot room, sauna, in a bathhouse

Tres—three... *unus, duo, tres*... one, two, three

Tribunus Militum—tribune of the soldiers; a Roman military officer

Triens—a Roman coin of less value than the *denarius*

Triumphus (pl. triumphi)—a celebration including a parade and a citywide drunken brawl given in honor of a victorious general

Io Triumphe! An acclamation of a *vir triumphalis*

Vir Triumphalis—the guest of honor for a *triumphus*; the victorious general

Tunica—male outer garment

-U-

Unus –one, the lonliest number

Uxor (pl. uxores)—a wife

-V-

Vagina—Scabbard for a sword. No! Really!

Vallum—a rampart, palisade

Vanator (pl. venatores)—a huntor

Venire—to come

Verpa (pl. verpae)—an erect penis

Vestibulum—the entrance hall of the Roman house

Veteranus (pl. veterani)—veteran, an experienced soldier, an old man

Via (pl. viae)—a road, way

Vilicus—bailiff; supervisor of a villa or an estate; overseer

Vilis (pl. viles)—cheap, worthless, mean, common.

Viridis—green, fresh, young

Virtus (pl. virtutes)—manly strength; being a "stand-up guy," both physically and morally

Vitis (pl. vites)—literally, a grape vine; military, the cudgel carried by a centurion

Voluptas—physical pleasure and luxury

Vulgus—the rabble, mob

CPSIA information can be obtained at www.ICGtesting.com
Printed in the USA
LVOW06s1222270915

455904LV00006B/858/P